William Platt

Angelo Lyons

A novel. Part 3

William Platt

Angelo Lyons
A novel. Part 3

ISBN/EAN: 9783337046019

Printed in Europe, USA, Canada, Australia, Japan

Cover: Foto ©Andreas Hilbeck / pixelio.de

More available books at **www.hansebooks.com**

BY

WILLIAM PLATT,

AUTHOR OF 'BETTY WESTMINSTER,' 'YORKE HOUSE,' 'GRACE OF
GLENHOLME,' 'ALICE HYTHE,' &c., &c.

IN THREE VOLUMES.
VOL. III.

LONDON:

SAUNDERS, OTLEY & CO., 66, BROOK STREET, W.

1866.

[The right of translation reserved.]

CONTENTS TO VOL. III.

ANGELO LYONS.

CHAPTER I.

SHEWS WHAT GOOD REASON PERCY THORNHILL HAD
TO PLACE HIS TRUST IN HIS SISTER CLARA; AND
HOW TRUE IT SEEMED THAT 'WHATEVER ANGELO
LYONS TOUCHED, TURNED TO GOLD.'

PERCY THORNHILL was in barracks with his regiment at Windsor, and "hoped to be able to run
down and have a ·blaze in the coverts and turnips
before shooting was over." When he told his sister
Clara, with two dashes under it, he meant to "come
to the scratch with Rachel, and, if old Crassus," as
he called her father, "would do the right thing,
polish that little matter off nicely :"—

"Meanwhile, I leave everything to you, my pet
of pets," wrote Percy, "in whom my confidence is
as unbounded as my love. Your inimitable sketches
of my beautiful *fiancée* supply me with inexhaustible
pictures of what a devilish lucky fellow I ought to

think myself, with my *penchant* for *blondes* with blue
eyes, and the pressing necessity there seems at Buck
for some tin before long. I suppose it's all right
with old Crassus? Buck must be mine, mind that!
If there's any haggling about it, shew him who's
who. Just ask him in the civilest way imaginable
whether it's nothing to have been one of the first
and foremost on the roll of Battle Abbey? Lady
Rachel! It must tinkle sweetly in his ears. Of
course he won't let you see it does. He's as deep
as old Nick. The Governor's getting short again, I
suppose, by his last? Else, a trifle, *per next*, wouldn't
give offence. I tell you what it is, Clarie——a fellow
can't live, as a Sub in a crack regiment anyhow, on
less than I have. Harry Chilvers spends double.
It's wonderful how I do it! And I shouldn't, but
for my mother being such a brick as she is. It's all
very fine at home telling us officers and *gentlemen*
to *screw in*. Do you know what a 'screw' gets?
The *dead cut*. Have you the smallest conception
what that is? Cashiering's comfortable to it. Please
just to put this mildly to the Governor, but firmly,
next time he talks of 'screwing in'—papa dearest,
what's the meaning of 'officers and *gentlemen*?'
Something's due, isn't there, papa, to the 'traditions
of the service,' as a fine writer terms it, as well as to
the 'letter of regulations?' Won't that settle it?

"About that muff of a chap, Alan Lambert, so he's
booked and provided for? Not that I think Rachel

Lyons behaved quite the thing in pumping him up
as she did till he didn't know himself. Not a bad
move of old Crassus's, though, sending him out
there; for he was just the sort of mealy-mouthed
fellow to wheedle himself into the good graces of a
silent, shut-up girl like Rachel. But I'll soon break
her of that sort of nonsense when she's mine, you'll
see. It never does, Clarie, to give in too much to
those quiet girls. It's not shyness with her, she's as
deep, if she chooses, and determined as her father.
But that may be, mayn't it, from living with him?
Hang me! Clarie, if he's not the awfullest man I
ever came across. There, then, I'd rather close doors
with a bear; for you might make Bruin dance and
grin for a cake, but when did you ever see the ghost
of a smile worth a gingerbread-nut on old Crassus's
bloodless phiz. It puts me into a cold-shiver to
think of it. But there's plenty of tin, eh? Bless
you, Clarie! what matters it now a days who or what
your father-in-law is, so that he stumps up like a
gentleman? It isn't as it used to be. In a hundred
years there won't be a drop of pure blue-blood, they
say, in anybody. Look at Carlton Ormslee, heir to
the Earldom, who married Tom Tubbs's, the Russian
tallow-merchant's, daughter! Well, you don't call
him a fool, do you? He borrowed the tin to get
spliced with; and now how's his blue-blood, with not
at all a bad-looking wife, all his own, in his 'four-in-

hand,' and five-thousand a year, down, just to help
to keep the pot boiling till old Tubb's death, when
they'll roll in tallow? Exceedingly jolly! And
what do you think—there's some blue-blood in the
Tubbs's, too. They never knew of it till they hunted
out their arms the other day, and found they were
lineally related to at least two Earls, and three
Baronets, and several Knights, and Heaven knows
how many M.P.'s, and Aldermen. We must rout
out these Lyons's. There's a decidedly aristocratic
cut about Rachel—tip-top—when she's dressed well.
I say, Clarie, you must keep her up to that; I mean,
make her tog-out like other girls, you know. By
Jove! she should see the women in Hyde Park on
Sundays. Can't you get her photo for me? I want
to shew it to some fellows here. Tell the Governor,
mind, to keep old Crassus up to standing for the
Borough. Angelo Lyons, Esq., M.P., eh? Not a
bad idea at all of my mother's. Bye, bye; and
with implicit brotherly trust in my pet of pets,

" Your's for ever and ever—P. T."

Clarie rather liked having trust placed in her. It
was so contrary to the daily dunnings at home from
one quarter or another, that it was quite elevating and
refreshing to find somebody who had unlimited
confidence in her. Any one could see in a minute
when Clarie had received a letter from her brother
Percy. Up went her head and out went her chest,
and her step was as firm, yet springy, as if there were

not a farthing's mortgage to pay off before she could shew old Crassus, as Percy called him, "who was who" at Buck Park and Greystone House, as she longed to do.

The Squire sometimes called himself 'an old fox,' when he wanted to impress them at home with a due sense of how quick of comprehension he was, when they thought to hood-wink or outwit him. He could tell by Clarie's dignified air and dilated nostrils when she had heard from Percy ; and, if he could get away anyhow, was off across country as far out of reach as possible, till her stately fit had calmed down; unless he happened to be flush of money, when he stood fire manfully, and stumped-up like a fine old English gentleman "must do," Clarie told him, "who had a son in the Guards."

The truth is—Clarie found it by no means an easy task to always fulfil the duties imposed on her by those 'implicit trusts' of her spendthrift brother. For as he never owned to all his debts, when, to save him, his mother put him into her lawyer's hands, in the fond belief that "now he was free to face all men "—there was no end to the duns. And it was indeed a bright day which brought a letter from Percy, in which 'want of money makes us sad' was not the burden of the song, and tradesmen were called by the names to which their extraordinary simplicity and meek forbearance in so many cases entitled them, notwithstanding the young Sub's philippics.

In short, it was a plain statement of the facts of the case when Mr. Lyons said to Faith, in his brief, dry way—"Something must be done with those debts of Percy Thornhill's. His father can't pay them." The knowledge of which might well call for more than Reynard cunning in that fine old English gentleman, Sir Compton Thornhill, Bart., to know how to agree with Clarie's " it must be done, papa," without an available guinea towards it till *Flower-of-the-Flock* won the *Derby*. No fine old English gentleman's will in the matter could be clearer than Sir Compton's. When she got hold of him, Clarie had only to ask and to have—what he could give her, after being told what he "must do," out of respect for the "traditions of the service," as Percy injoined her to put it to him, " mildly but firmly;" which amounting to 0 in the present instance, Mr. Lyons's opinion was verified, and poor Clarie was put to her wits-end to know how to act.

Lady Thornhill was powerless. Of what avail would be the trifle she could ill spare Percy, her first-born, out of her purse, towards stemming the torrent ? It would beggar her without benefitting him. There would be little wisdom in that just then, when every shilling was wanted so much at home. For now Sir Compton was so deep in with his

racers, that he must carry it through, though the
draughts on him were ruinous. But " if *Flower-of-
the-Flock* had ' fair play,' it would be all right
enough, if he could only raise the ready to tide them
safe over next May."

Clarie carried herself coldly and consequentially
towards her friends and acquaintances in general,
but loved her home, and fought its fights with a
warmth and staunchness that would have been heroic
in a better cause. Perhaps she did not go so far as
to wonder what would become of the world if the
Thornhills of Buck were no more ; but it was evident
she deemed them of no little consequence to the com-
monwealth, by the increased zeal and industry with
which she espoused and vindicated them in propor-
tion to the suicidal attempts at self-humiliation one
or the other of them was always making, as if they
were so high that nothing could pull them down low
enough to affect them. Clarie's great pride was in
her family. So that nothing materially jeopardized
them at Buck Park, she took things as they came,
and had no particular fault to find with the world,
though she read the essayists and moralists who were
always marking mankind's sins and miseries, and
doing their best to put her out of conceit with herself. Clarie liked the world very well as it stood, so
long as nothing more troubled them at Buck than
common. She knew that none were exempt from

that inevitable quantum of 'dirt' which all had to
swallow, first or last, in this life, from the Queen
down to the shoe-black. So whenever her turn
came, she made a wry-face, gulped it down, and re-
membering she was, in all and through all, a Thornhill—thanked her stars that it was so! And by
comparing her actual with her possible state, Clarie
behaved, on the whole, with astonishing com-
placency, considering what a deal of the 'dirt' still
stared her in the face, and which must be got through
somehow, to keep them up anyhow at Buck Park
with good grace.

At the anxious epoch under notice, rendered still
more so by her brother Percy's pressing pecuniary
wants, Clarie had three Fifty pound bank-notes in
her desk, and some few pounds more in gold. It was
a nice little sum of her own, in case of need, and as
long as Clarie could go up to it, and look at it, and
count it, and put it back again, undiminished, she
felt a strength within her which, though utterly in-
commensurate with the hundred and one ways she
had for its use, was gigantic to what it would have
been had Percy owed double what he did, and his
'pet of pets,' in whom he placed such trust, had had
nothing 'towards it.' How Clarie reckoned was
her own affair. At all events, be the sum-total sent
her of Percy's little accounts what it might, she had
a hundred and fifty pounds up-stairs of her own, to

do as she pleased with. There was immense comfort
in it. And, so, Clarie sat down, with pen in hand,
to think how best her three Fifties could presently
suffice for the Fifteen Hundred Percy wanted, and
leave something for "anything that might happen
at home to plague them." For after quite agreeing
with her as to what a father "ought to do for his son
in the Guards (if he could) who had proper respect
for 'the traditions of the service,' let alone 'an
officer and a gentleman,'" the Squire had produced
his cheque-book, and shewn her, "as surely as he
had a head on his shoulders, that, if Angelo Lyons,
his banker, hadn't been a devilish good fellow, it
had been all up with him months ago."

There was no help for it, therefore, but for Clarie
to make known to Percy the then state of the
family finances, as feelingly as possible; knowing as
she did how it disgusted him to hear they were
short of cash, "just when it always happened he
could have done so much with a few hundreds,
judiciously used."

But Percy was of a buoyant disposition, and if
easily cast down, was quickly up and hopeful again
as ever, though with only a straw to catch at.
Clarie's letter was a clever compound. It depressed
him rather till she began to cross it, and then from
that moment to the end of it every line teemed
with fresh hopes, so delightfully depicted, that he

forgot all about the first part; and feeling himself
master of a Fifty pound bank-note—which, to tell the
truth, was more than double what he looked for—
away he went, like his father, whistling to the winds
"any such disgusting nonsense as a Thornhill of
Buck being beaten for the want of a few paltry hundreds, when by that day twelvemonths there was no
knowing the wealth they might have."

How, with £50 in hand, as a stop-gap, the young
Squire of Buck "made it all right," as he expressed
it, with his tradesmen, is of no consequence to the
story. His grateful letter of thanks to Clarie left it
clear that he could now "tide it over," he hoped,
"till the Governor got that awfuly old Crassus to
come down with some more; which of course he
would be only too happy to do, now it was as as
good as an understood thing that the next heir
to the baronetcy would make pretty Rachel *my
Lady*."

Old Crassus, or, to speak more respectfully, Mr.
Lyons, the great shipowner, merchant, banker, &c.,
&c., of Greystone House, had every wish to aid his
noble friends at Buck Park to the best of his power.
And, as a proof of it, he sent for Mr. Salisbury, his
solicitor, immediately Sir Compton made it known to
him that he wanted "a couple of thousand or so more,
to make it all right enough by next May."

What were Two Thousand Pounds, sterling, to

Angelo Lyons, of The Broadway ? No more than a
pailful of water, as you might say, out of the river
in which floated his ships within view of his house.
But however rich they may be, people don't 'come
down,' as Percy Thornhill expressed it, with their
loans, large or little, without security; and it was
only an act of proper prudence, on Mr. Lyons's part,
to wish to consult his lawyer before he made over to
himself a fine estate like Buck, which he feared
"must be the attendant consequence of a further
advance."

Mr. Salisbury was no less well-affected towards
the Buck Park family than his wealthy client Mr.
Lyons was ; but Jonathan Salisbury was a just man
by all accounts, and took as much care of the
superfluities of the rich, which he had to invest for
them, as of the smallest savings for which he had to
get five per cent. interest, and as much more as he
could. Mr. Salisbury's clients felt safe in his
hands; and although he had a peculiar short, dry,
rather testy, snappish way of dealing with those he
had no more time or patience for, and his tone and
manner, even in his best key, could scarcely be called
genial, his probity was unimpeached. So Mr.
Lyons sent for him again, in Sir Compton's behalf,
without a doubt but that the result would be
mutually satisfactory, even though it were found
that if he, Angelo Lyons, had done himself strict

justice, he would have resolved that the last loan should have been the last.

Mr. Jonathan Salisbury heard all his opulent client had to say of his " earnest desire to advance double two thousand, or ten times two, to his friend Sir Compton, provided there were anything like fair security for it."

But Mr. Salisbury said nothing. And this tacit mode of dealing with the question of *security* never betokened that amount of satisfaction, in Mr. Salisbury's mind, which might conscientiously justify him in handing the needful needed to the impatient borrower as quickly as he wished. In the present instance Mr. Salisbury had a large margin given him, in favour of the Squire of Buck, and was free to stretch a point, nay, to proceed in a way for which there was no regular official precedent. But, all the same, Jonathan Salisbury had a duty to perform in this case as well as in every other professionally intrusted to him ; and, so, he sat grave and silent, when it would have rejoiced Mr. Lyons so much if he could have met the Squire's wishes off-hand. Especially as he had reason to know that some 'ready' must be raised somehow, even to permit of the continuance of his, Angelo Lyons's accustomed visits at The Priory, the charming mistress of which had drained her purse almost dry to help her sister Adelaide, and, naturally enough, was not in the best spirits about it — which deeply hurt him.

"What's to be done?" asked Mr. Lyons, with a glance up from the floor at his lawyer.

"Buck will bear no more," said Mr. Salisbury, clearing his throat of the dryness always in it when he communicated anything grating to his own feelings as well as his hearer's.

"Otherwise," observed Mr. Lyons, "I believe they are a good deal pressed."

"Buck won't bear any more," repeated Mr. Salisbury in a clearer key.

"Hem!" mused Mr. Lyons, with a perplexed look, as he bent his fingers tight down on to his palms and counted the nail marks left by it.

"Not a shilling!" added Mr. Salisbury.

"They must get some money somehow," rejoined Mr. Lyons, visibly moved by his friendship for them.

"You know best," said Mr. Salisbury, again clearing his throat.

"Hem! If I took his I. O. U.—how then?"

"We could add it to the others."

"Hem!"

"Or he could give you power of sale over what is in the house and about. Though it's awkward."

"He must have some money."

"There is nothing else."

"Hem! No settlement, or anything of that sort?"

"Not available."

"Hem! And Lady Ada Chilvers can do nothing?"

"More than she has done—how?"

"A wonder she don't marry again?"

Mr. Salisbury smiled.

"A charming woman!"

"Exceedingly so!"

And again, while what little blood there was in his face left it ashy pale, Mr. Lyons dug his nails into the palm of the hand he had his eyes on, till he almost made the blood come.

"Hollo!" said Mr. Salisbury to himself, as he noted his client's pursed brow; "smitten with the charming widow, is he? Ah, then, the money must be found somehow; and the only question is how—if the wind's in that quarter?"

"Those horses in training—how about them?" asked Mr. Lyons, as if struck by a sudden thought.

"Not a bad horse *Flower-of-the-Flock*."

"Any chance, do you think, of his doing well at the *Derby*?"

"Who's to say? See how the knowing ones were sold last time. He looks a likely beast. I shouldn't wish to be in for much against him. A good deal depends on the jockey. You might take an I. O. U., if you liked, for the money. Of course it would be

an act of friendship, and be so considered. I pity
Lady Ada most. She's a good creature. Very! Not
a better in the county. A perfect lady—lady by
name and lady by nature. It *is* strange she don't
marry again. Clearly, she might, if she would, fast
enough."

" Hem—eh— ah—might she ?"

" Barleymow, the great brewer, worth Two Hundred Thousand, wants her ; and so does Mr. Basil
Horne, of Barbadoes, who knew her when she was sweet
Ada Belmore, and has got hale and hearty again,
they say, and wants a wife, and is coming over on
purpose, and will ' let her ride in a coach of gold,' he
says, if she'll have him."

It amused Mr. Lyons, as well it might, the idea
of Basil Horne, of Barbadoes, his senior by twenty
years or more, talking of marrying, when the doctors
had said " good bye to his liver before he was
forty : "—

" Oh—eh—let her ride in a gold coach," he
laughed. " With himself at her side ? She needn't
go begging, then ? What will they say to it at Buck
Park ? Bravo, Basil ! So he can have no thoughts of
his hearse yet ? We West Indian boys never say
die. Well, I suppose I must take the I. O. U. for
the money, and get what I can. I mustn't let
Basil, of Barbadoes, outshine me, must I ? A coach
of gold ! How come up to that anyhow. if I

should want to go courting there?" and mightily tickled by it, Mr. Lyons chuckled again.

"You have just done it nicely," laughed Jonathan Salisbury, in chorus. "There is a little personal condition, if I understand Mr. Basil Horne right, annexed to the gold-coach, viz., the necessary possession of himself with it; but it does not appear that you lay any such stipulation on the friendly advance of the £2000, in lawful British money, which will have great weight, I imagine, with a noble nature like Lady Ada's, when she appreciates it as she certainly must."

"For what it is worth and no more?" smiled Mr. Lyons, with sparkling eyes; and evidently put in excellent humour by it, notwithstanding his ambiguous little shakes of the head, he wrung his solicitor's hand so warmly, that, encouraged by it :—

"A gold-coach is a gold-coach," ventured Mr. Salisbury, with the door-knob in his grasp; "and who's to know in this life what may happen to any woman, with a coach of gold, all her own, at the door? It's a dashing world we live in. There's myself, for instance. Mr. Gribble, my opponent, has just put another roan to his four-wheels. Well, *ipso facto*, it won't ruin me. No! But can I permit Mr. Gribble to give Mr. Salisbury the go by? My advice to my clients who have marriage settlements to make, is—make them. Or, rather,

let Jonathan Salisbury do it for you with all convenient speed, when, come who may in their gold-
coaches—the deed's done, eh—done—which—you
know what—is pretty conclusive proof that it is?
Good morning. I will run up to Buck bye and bye,
and see Sir Compton. A power of sale will be
ample, with the I. O. U. It will relieve their
minds. Lady Ada's especially. I may as well
drop in and tell her?"

" As you please;" and, to judge by the look that
accompanied it, it was as well just then that Faith
Lincoln could not take that peep into the book of
fate which she sometimes longed to do. For, as it
was, if much were hidden from her that she sighed
to know, nothing was revealed to crush those hopes
but for which how would she have patiently and
perseveringly gone on with her appointed task that
had for its fulfilment His mighty will, " Who often,
though we know it not, make sour deepest griefs
and lamentations the one sole security for our eternal
joy?" was Faith's unshaken creed.

Altogether, Mr. Lyons was well pleased with his
lawyer's visit. It was satisfactory to him in several
ways. Though the security he should have for his
money was insufficient, it would give him increased
power at Buck Park; and Lady Ada could not but
be gratified, as Mr. Salisbury foresaw, at so evident
a wish on his part to forego his own interests to

befriend them.   Sir Compton, too, would be drawn
closer to him than he had yet been, by reason of his
pride ; and Lady Thornhill would be humbled ; and
Clara taken down ; and the young Squire taught a
wholesome lesson.   So, if the aim and end of the
game he was playing were the marriage of his
daughter to the next heir to the Buck Baronetcy, and
of Lady Ada to himself, Angelo Lyons had reason
to congratulate himself on his success so far, and on
the truth, seemingly, of what the folks said of him,
that " whatever he touched—it turned to gold."

CHAPTER II.

MR. SALISBURY kept his promise, and ran up to
Buck Park in the evening. It was a delicate mission
he was charged with; but "money must be got
somehow," as Mr. Lyons said, and it nerved him
for his interview with the choleric Baronet, who, if
he had been stripped of everything but his dressing-
gown and slippers, was a *Buck* Thornhill, and "let
any man affront him who dared."

Mr. Salisbury knew something of human nature,
as well as all that was needful of official routine.
He studied the various idiosyncrasies of his clients;
which perhaps was the reason they liked him so
much more than his rival, Mr. Gribble, who, though
he studied his own interests less than Mr. Salisbury,
had an unfortunate mode of making it appear that

2—2

he studied them more, when and where, in fact, he was sometimes going out of his way to do very liberal things, for which Jonathan Salisbury called him an ass. But this by the way.

It really was necessary to know how to handle Sir Compton Thornhill, when what you had to say to him, or do for or against him, was not most complimentary either to him or yourself. It was ticklish ground up at Buck Park, if you went there for anything that had the shadow of a chance of lessening a Thornhill in his or her estimation. Then mind what you were about. The Squire's friends called him "the soul of truth and honour, though much to blame for spending double his income." But have the audacity to be candid with him, so as to offend a drop of that lion-rampant blood in his veins, and see what you would get for it pretty quick.

Mr. Salisbury knew what. He and the Squire of Buck had had too many money-matter meetings together, to leave either of them in any doubt as to the temper and tactics of the other. And it does much towards simplifying and dispatching business where such is the case. Mr. Salisbury was perfectly sure that the great art in proving a proud man to be penniless, was to do it without wounding his pride; and it was no less clear to Sir Compton, that if he *must* pledge his last hold-fast, he *must;* but he'd be hanged if he'd do it, to save him from starvation, for any mortal man who didn't know what was due to a gentleman, let alone Compton Thornhill of Buck."

I say the Squire said he'd be "hanged," if, &c., which was not the word he used. It was a much stronger word than "hanged;" and so demonstrative of what Mr. Salisbury might expect from the testy Baronet (when compelled to ask favours) if he said or did aught to wound him, that it was well he studied human nature a little before he went to Buck Park, with proposals in his pocket enough to stagger any conscientious man to think of, who laboured under the amiable impression that there was any earthly way to deal with those who *must* have money, but one.

"He must have the money," Mr. Lyons said to his lawyer; and, so, with the matter duly digested, Mr. Salisbury crossed the fields to Buck Park, and being informed by a servant that Sir Compton was "somewhere about the grounds," sure enough, after a stroll through the shrubs, he found him playing at hide and seek with old Noble among the ferns.

In good health, and when free from mental pressure, the Squire of Buck, though turned fifty, was "as big a boy as ever," Lady Thornhill told her friends. And now that the weight he had had on his spirits all day was removed by a pencil-line sent him by Mr. Lyons from The Priory, where he was dining, just one line and no more, to say—*you can have the money*—to have seen Compton Thornhill sniffing the breeze, without his hat, and his long, fine, silky white hair as white as snow already, the sport of the winds, and old Noble leaping and barking with joyful impatience at his side, till the proud moment came when he was bade begone to find and bring back the old broad-brim from out the bushes—shew us the picture of a happier big-baby anywhere under the face of the sun, when at play, than Sir Compton.

"Hallo!" cried the Squire, catching sight of Jonathan Salisbury watching the sport with great glee at a little distance—"talk of the—gentleman in the handsome black suit there in the ferns—by no means *old*—and there he is! Hang me!" with a grasp of the fist, "if you haven't been running in my head all day. There's a dog!" taking the 'wide-awake' from his mouth. "What will you bet he wcn't nose it out of the bush there when we get to the house, if I hide it?"

"Without his seeing where you put it?" demurred Jonathan, with a dubious chuckle, to render the feat, if achieved, more triumphant.

"There!" cried the Squire, tossing Salisbury his canary-coloured silk pocket-handkerchief with the snow-spots on it. "Blindfold him, while I do it. Take him behind the trees there. Only don't hurt his nose any, whatever you do. Look sharp, or he'll get away. Can you hold him?"

"It seemed doubtful, at first; but Jonathan
Salisbury had studied dogs as well as men, and
loved the one, if he did not always love the other.
Understanding which, no doubt, Noble suffered himself to be blindfolded, perhaps because he was proud
of the pocket-handkerchief; while, thoroughly entering into the fun of it, Jonathan made the welkin
ring again with laughter, possibly at the thought of
what a comic prologue it was to the rather tragic
drama coming after it.

Was the Squire's heart in what he was doing with
the old broad-brim in the bushes?

Yes, every bit of it, thoroughly taken up with it,
wherever else Jonathan Salisbury's might be. It
was just the difference between the two men. Jonathan Salisbury had a thousand other things to think
of besides the business or pleasure on hand; the
Squire had none. In the saddle, after the hounds,
or with old Noble, in the shrubberies, playing at
"hide and seek," Sir Compton fully realized the
present; and if it were the sort of *present* he liked,
the past and future, if not wholly to be ignored and
shut out, melted away into such a hazy indistinctness
as to be no more visible, or worth thinking of, than
the ugly leaps and stiff fences well over or easy
enough, when, full-cry, in at the death he would be,
though it brought him safe enough to his own.

"Now, then, Salisbury, hold hard!"

And there was need for it—pulling as the old dog was to get away.

"Come along!" and having cleared the ground between them and the house, a distance of about half-a-mile—

"Hist!" hallooed the Squire, with a shrill whistle that brought Noble leaping round him again—"away!—find it!"—and in the library, and the door shut—"Sit down," said Sir Compton, with as much dignity as he would have shewn to a prince; and taking the chair facing the man of law, he did his best to shew Mr. Jonathan Salisbury that though the lord and master of Buck loved a bit of sport with horse or hound as he loved his life, he perfectly well knew what was demanded of him as a man of business, if it were in that capacity Mr. Salisbury desired to engage his attention that evening.

Mr. Salisbury gave a smiling glance round him, and so did Sir Compton. It was a spacious, handsome room, solidly and superbly furnished and fitted up as a gentleman's library should be; and very likely it occurred to them simultaneously what a charming room it was, and how proud and happy he ought to be who could look round such a noble domain as Buck Park, and say—this is my own.

But the experienced eye of the practical man had noted the twitch of the lips and the palpable departure of the rosy-hue from the Squire's cheeks, as he dived his hand into his breast-pocket for the little packet of papers tied together with red-tape, with which to open the business he had come on; so without further preliminary :—

"It was Two Thousand Pounds you wished advanced, I think, Sir Compton," began Mr. Salisbury, after clearing his throat, and picking out the paper he wanted. "It so stated, I believe, in your note?"

The Squire nodded "yes."

"You know, Sir Compton, these things are matters of business. If you will be kind enough to run your eye down that paper"—handing it him—"you will see what we propose, and which will meet, I think, all that can be fairly required on both sides. Of course the question in these cases is, simply, of *security*. It is not the softest or sweetest word, but it's a safe one for all parties. It brings us into sad broils, sometimes, nevertheless. At first, on referring to memorandums, I was afraid there might be a little difficulty in this instance. But you will see how I thought it might be got over, as between friends, better than by any further charges on Buck, if it would bear it. In this way you can have the money at once; any other would take time, and might not succeed after all. Security, security! But you wouldn't lend your money without it, eh? I know I wouldn't, even to my own brother. You will see I have clubbed the whole together, in case you wanted a little more than the Two Thousand Pounds. With security, Twenty Thousand would be as easy as Two."

During the pleasant delivery of which, the Squire read—as well as the mist that came over his eyes permitted him to do—to the end of the paper. Nothing could be simpler or more intelligible than its contents were. It merely proposed that—"In consideration of a given sum to be immediately paid to Sir Compton Thornhill, Bart., &c., &c., by way of loan, he, Sir Compton, should give Angelo Lyons, Esquire, of Greystone House, &c., &c., for security, power, by sale, over the Furniture and Effects of Buck Hall, in the parish of Buck, &c., &c., in the event of the non-return of the said sum or sums borrowed within the time specified, together with such lawful interest of five per cent. as might be owing thereon. And, further, it went on to require, that should the Furniture and Effects, as they then stood, be insufficient, as security, to cover the proposed advance, then, and in that case, that *Flower-of-the-Flock*, and all other Race-Horses of which Sir Compton was possessed, either at Buck or elsewhere, should be included in the deed, subject to such conditions as might be mutually agreed on. In consideration of which, it was to be optional with Sir Compton whether he would increase the loan to Three Thousand Pounds or leave it at Two."

Nothing, on the face of it, could be fairer or more liberal; ample time was granted for the repayment of the money; no objection could be made to the interest; in many respects the security given would be such as none but a friend would take for cash down; the proposition clearly came from a friendly desire to oblige,—and, yet, for a minute or more, the Squire, after seeing the Three Thousand Pounds as good as in his pocket, felt as if some rascal-arm had knocked him on the head, and dizzied him, and taken away his breath, so that he was obliged to clutch the arm of the chair he was sitting on for support, till the dizzy feeling went off, and he was himself again.

Then opening his eyes wide on poor Jonathan, who really felt anxious to serve him as far as he conscientiously could :—

"Ho !" he cried, as the blood crimsoned his face with the difficulty he had to suppress the wrath he was bursting with—"come to this, has it, that I must pawn the bed under me ?"

"Nay, nay, not so bad as that !" returned Mr. Salisbury, in rather a hurt tone. "If you can suggest any other feasible mode of getting the money, I am sure I shall be only too glad, Sir Compton, to assist you as far as I can. Buck is already overcharged. I thought you might be pressed. And with the unquestionable certainty, as you said in your note of Thursday, of ample means in hand between this and next year, for all purposes—pardon me, if I made sure of seeing the beds, and saucepans, and frying-pans, and gridirons, &c., in *statu quo*, without spot or blemish, and in hospitable use as ever when I came up to enjoy a mutton chop with you, with that little *Release* in my pocket; unless I had had which, for a surety, in my mind's eye, should I have dared to have taken the liberty I presumed to do, with those sacred articles above and below, as the lesser of two evils, as it seemed to me, in case the money *must* be got somehow, whether we could get it or not."

It drew a deep breath from Sir Compton; for it was a long-winded speech to make to a man who, though seemingly about to pawn his bed and kitchen utensils, &c., &c., was a gentleman, and knew what was due to himself as such. The Squire of Buck owed it to himself to calmly listen to Mr. Jonathan Salisbury till he had finished what he had to say; when—

"I am exceedingly obliged to you, Mr. Salisbury," he said, rising, as if unwilling to prolong an interview that must be distressing to them both; "very much obliged indeed for your kind intentions; but"—and the Squire paused a moment to breathe again,—"but, pray understand—my bed, and the beds my children and people lie on, and my kettles and saucepans, are one thing—my horses and hounds another. We rate them perhaps differently. That's no fault of yours. The horses and hounds will fetch most at market. That's the chief point. Take them—in pawn, I mean. You can judge how *Flower-of-the-Flock* stands at Tattersall's, against the Favourite. Come next May, and we shall see. Till when, if you please, I think I had rather not part with the beds, and frying-pans, and gridirons. They're not worth much to anyone but myself, after the years they've been in use. Somehow one gets fond, you know, of even one's own old pots and kettles. I'm as big an old fool, that way, as ever lived. Yes, I am! You wouldn't have thought it? Not of a fox-hunter, eh?"

Mr. Salisbury was visibly moved.

"Well, then, I won't pawn *them*," went on the Squire, when he had gulped down what was sticking in his throat. "I sha'n't do that just yet. What I may be obliged to do, if I go to the dogs, there's no knowing. But I'll stick as long as I can to *home*. Put a fair price on the horses and hounds, if you like, and I'll try and make it do. *Flower-of-the-Flock*—eh—how much do you think he'll be worth if he come in first? What would you give me for him *then*?" Which making the 'old boy' blink and wink :—

"Good bye!" said Jonathan Salisbury, shaking

fists. "I shall see Mr. Lyons about it to-morrow.
We are in excellent hands there. The idea was
entirely my own. I know he wishes to do it; and
will, if he can. You shall hear in a day or two.
Farewell!"—and who should greet his departure
with a grace all his own—as became a staunch and
faithful ally of the noble house in which he had
grown as grey as he had—but gallant old Noble himself, on the door-mat, with the hidden ' broad-brim,'
brought to light, under his great paw, and seemingly quite ready and willing to go for his beloved
master to the world's end if he wished it.

And next day there was a cabinet consultation at
Greystone House between the opulent head of that
palatial residence and his solicitor, Mr. Jonathan
Salisbury, touching the warm-hearted Squire's
pathetic determination to stoutly stick to his beds
and old pots and kettles and frying-pans and gridirons, though everything else he possessed took unto
itself wings and flew away, never more to return.

"Hem!" said Mr. Lyons, who seemed deeply
interested in Mr. Salisbury's account; "stout and
determined as that, is he? Just what I expected."

Mr. Salisbury stared.

"Ask Lady Ada. We talked it over there after
dinner. I thought it best."

"So it was," agreed Mr. Salisbury, a little

confusedly, as if he hardly understood, yet, the drift of it.

" And I may have *Flower-of-the-Flock*, eh, and the other Blood-Horses, and the Hounds, and"—

" Nothing else."

" Oh, not his old roadster, Sir Roderick, that he wouldn't take any money for ? Hem ! He ought to be worth a good bit."

" Who'd have the heart to propose it ?"

" True ! And I suppose old Noble's not to go in with the Hounds ?"

" It wasn't mentioned. Did he ever tell you the story of the fox-hunting friend who wanted to buy him, for bringing his hat out of the river where the wind had taken it, as they rode to cover."

" No."

" What will you give me for him ?" asked the Squire.

" What you like."

" Fifty shouldn't buy him."

" I'll give you sixty."

" Seventy shouldn't buy him."

" I'll give you eighty."

" Ninety sha'n't buy him."

" There's a hundred, then."

" Wait a minute, and we'll hear what he says to it himself."

So when they got off their hacks—

"Ask him," laughed the Squire.

"Will you be mine, for a hundred, eh, old boy?" coaxed the General.

"What does he say?" roared Sir Compton at the ugly face he made, and the whine he gave.

"*Yes*—can't you hear?"

"What he means by it? Plain enough. He'll leave his old master, he says, and go with you—if I can't find it in my heart, as an old friend, to send a bullet through his head first! How then?"

Mr. Lyons smiled, and gazed on his nails.

"What's to be done?" asked Mr. Salisbury, as he tied up the bundle of parchments and papers he had taken out of the blue bag at his feet.

But his client was wrapped in thought.

"Will you say One Thousand."

"No."

Mr. Salisbury squared his jaws :—

"Less than which would scarcely suffice, I fancy, heavily pressed as he is."

"Nothing would suffice for long, though I beggared myself for him."

"His father made ducks and drakes of his money; so does he; and so will the next heir, if he have it to spend. You must tie it down tight for my Lady Rachel, if so she's to be. You can do that. But they must have something now—must!"

"I suppose so."

"What will you do?"

"All, or none."

"*Flower-of-the-Flock* stands well at Tattersall's.

"So I see."

"Anyhow, you couldn't lose much, with *him* and the others?"

"That's true."

"You can think of it?"

"Yes."

And Sir Compton found the following note on his breakfast table next morning, not a little to the surprise of them all;—

"Greystone House, &c., &c.

"My Dear Sir Compton.

"Your handsome offer of *Flower-of-the-Flock*, in trust, at the moment when you have reason by all accounts to be so proud of him, convinces me of your friendship and regard. Let me also convince you of mine by the inclosed draft for the Three Thousand Pounds which Mr. Salisbury says will meet your present purposes, and for which your note of hand will be sufficient. I am glad to hear of Percy's intended run-down next month for a holiday. Remember me to him when you write; and, with best wishes

"Believe me, my dear Sir Compton,

"Ever yours very faithfully,

"Angelo Lyons."

Generosity in any shape found instant way to
Sir Compton's heart; and, as may be imagined,
they were all very happy at Buck Park over such a
proof of the high estimation in which the Squire was
held by his wealthy friend of Greystone House, as
" spoke for itself" that morning.

Lady Thornhill was never loud in her praises of
anyone, least of all of Mr. Angelo Lyons. From the
first she treated him with perfect breeding, but with
a distance that rather fretted Sir Compton, after he
had opened an account at his Bank. She relaxed a
little when she heard how munificently liberal he
had been to the Squire on two or three occasions;
but somehow her Ladyship and Mr. Lyons always
seemed to eye each other with, if not positive mis-
trust, anything but that confidence and cordiality
which Sir Compton was continually expounding the
Christian expediency of, "especially among those
who were, or would be, as you might say, of one
family."

But the Squire had got her Ladyship ' on the
hip' now, with Three Thousand Pounds in his pocket
—and "from whom?—and how tendered?—and
giving evidence of what?—would my Lady answer
him that?"

" It was unanswerable; it spoke for itself," as
Clara quite agreed with her father; "nothing could
be more conclusive of the high esteem in which the

Thornhills, of Buck, were held wherever they were known."

It brought some colour back to Lady Thornhill's cheeks; for, truth to speak, she had been very pale and pulled of late, what with one worry or another. It was so cheering, too, to see her eyes brighten again, and something like the old smile in her face, that the Squire absolutely left his bit of fun with old Noble's head between his knees—waiting till he was told to toss the shilling off his nose and catch it—to sidle up to her, and, before she was aware of it, make a snatch with his lips "at the rose," he said, " on each cheek," it looked so " tempting."

Altogether, Angelo Lyons's little Three Thousand Pounds' speculation on the Squire's breakfast table that bright early autumn morning, promised to yield him good fruits. Clearly it was a judicious investment, if he hoped by it to conciliate Lady Thornhill, who no doubt had this much weight with Lady Ada Chilvers, her sister—that Lady Ada would scarcely marry again without her sanction. As sisters they loved each other, though materially differing in opinion on many points; and it was well known how Ada ran to Adelaide, and how Adelaide ran to Ada, when neither, with all her pride of independence, could in moments of perplexity do without the other.

Clara was immensely up about it—up in a way

she never was so *up*, as when, with head erect, and chest out, and those handsome nostrils of hers telling of the blood she came from, and her pride in it, her father had it in his power to trot off on Sir Roderick, with a face it really was inspiring to contemplate, when, flush of money, his only wish at heart was to see every one as happy as himself.

But, talking of happiness, it is time we thought again of Alan Lambert, and of what he was doing, while they were all so happy at Buck and Ship-hampton, towards the attainment of that most difficult of all earthly acquisitions for himself.

CHAPTER III.

AT the time they were all so happy at Buck Park over the proceeds of Mr. Lyons's draft on *The Old Bank*, for the Three Thousand Pounds of which special mention was made in the foregoing chapter, Mr. Alan Lambert was spending the day in the mango-grove, where lay—IN THE BOSOM OF HER SAVIOUR, as it was engraved on her tomb—Angelina Lyons, the mother of Rachel.

According to promise, Mr. Lambert had written to Mr. Lyons on his arrival at Trinidad, to set them at rest as to his personal safety; reserving what he would have to communicate, when he was in a condition to do so, till a future day, by when he would have made himself master of the subject. He had also sent Lady Ada and Miss Lyons an amusing sketch of his journey out, and its thrilling adventures:—How they 'encountered a tremendous gale

of wind before they cleared the Channel, which
made him very sick and sad, notwithstanding the
'morphine globule;' but how, 'when some time
after they fell in with the trade-wind, they went on
fast and pleasantly.' Then how 'there was another
violent storm all night that tore some of the sails to
pieces, during which how he thought of *home, sweet
home*, and *The Priory, and Greystone House*, in
particular, who knew but himself?' Then how 'it
was a succession, in certain latitudes, of alternate
heavy gales and dead calms, during which, though
all of them, the ship included, seemed to be doing
so much, they made little way.' But 'how pleased
he was when the captain called him to see a Flying
Fish, and they caught some Dolphins, though it
gave him a turn to see the sailors spear them.'
How, 'after entering the tropics, it rained incessantly,
but not so as to still the wind and stop them.' Then
'how delicious the weather got, how smoothly and
steadily they moved on, how brilliant the sun
was, how cloudless the sky, how calm the sea, how
like,' as he had read somewhere in some book,
' one extended sheet of blue glass,' and 'the nights
how heavenly!' And then 'how nothing happened worth relating till they came in sight of
Trinidad, when they were becalmed,' and, while
the ship seemed gone to sleep, how they had
'nothing to do but to amuse themselves with the

Porpoises, tossing and tumbling about under their
noses, and spouting the water up in the sunbeams
in the most ornamental manner.' And when at last
he set foot within half-an-hour's ride of her ' dear
old home,' as Miss Rachel called it, how all that she
had said to him about it, how ' every, even the
minutest picture she had ever drawn for his instruction and delight, recurred to his memory with a
vivid distinctness and reality that for a little while
agitated yet depressed him so—that, instead of filling
him with joy, it made him feel quite wretched.'"

And this was all he could then tell them, to be
in time to inclose it in the packet for Mr. Lyons.
But he hoped to write again soon ; and then, as he
meant to adopt Miss Lyons's suggestion and keep
a *diary* of his doings in the West, he would endeavour to omit nothing in his next which he
thought they would read with interest :—coming
as it would from the ' dear old wooden house,' nay,
' from the very chamber, with the Venetian blinds
to it, and the sweet flowers round its windows,
which Mr. Mungo said was Rachel's own, because it
faced the ' old mill ' at the bottom of the garden,
and the mango-grove where her mother was buried."

Mr. Lambert might well feel greatly pleased with
his reception at Trinidad by Mr. Mungo and those
with him, who came, *en cavalcade,* in their best holi-
day-clothes to bid him welcome to Old Mill

House, so called from the crumbling ruin of the
first sugar mill ever erected on the estate, and still
standing at the foot of the mango-grove. It was
a strangely novel scene that awaited Mr. Alan on
alighting from the carriage that conveyed him from
the place of debarkation to his new home. If it
had been 'Massa Lyons' himself come to listen to
their grievances and redress their wrongs, the
rapturous shouts, and gesticulations, and dancings,
and skippings, and tumblings, and rollings over each
other, to see which should do him most honour,
could scarcely have been more abundant. It was,
simply, an every day picture of the negro-heart full
to overflowing of slave-attachment, coupled with its
necessary conditions—kind Massa's heart and hand
in unison, and plenty of time for fun and frolic, and
fine clothes, and rum and sugar.

It agreeably surprised Alan Lambert. He had
fancied, from Mr. Mungo's report, that the slaves
were in a state of such insubordination that he could
do nothing with them; whereas, was it possible to
conceive a state of greater apparent negro-happiness
than met his gratified gaze at every turn? There
was not a dull or downcast face ; genuine unaffected
joy revelled in every countenance; universal plenty
and content smiled on him at every turn. And the
negro-habitations how picturesque and pretty most
of them were! each surrounded with its own pro-

ductive garden, and bearing ample evidences, inside and out, of an amount of comfort, nay, in many instances, costliness, seldom to be found in English villages, even where work and wages are most plentiful. The air, too, loaded with sweet-smelling plants and woods and flowers, how delicious it was! and when the north winds came, how cool and refreshing! "How call those poor creatures for pity and commiseration, who, instead of seeming to be in need of anything, rolled, apparently, in ease and profusion?"

"It would indeed seem so," assented Mr. Mungo, as Mr. Alan stopped to admire some of the negro houses constructed of wattles and rafters of sweetwood, and though only plastered and whitewashed inside, presenting an air of cleanliness and rural prettiness, that, with their gardens round them filled with shaddocks, and oranges, and cocoa-nuts, and peppers of every description, and, here and there, natural bowers of the Abba, or palm-trees, with their pine-cones of scarlet seeds as bright as coral, contrasted strongly with the British labourers' dwellings, where, as Mr. Lewis pleasantly says in his 'Journal,' what's to be seen but 'a few cabbages and carrots, just peeping up, and grovelling on the earth, between hedges, in square, narrow beds, and where the tallest tree is a gooseberry-bush.'

"Aye, aye!" laughed Mr. Mungo at his young novice's innocent quotation; "but if the English cottager didn't have his cabbages and carrots and gooseberry-bushes in the bit of ground round him, he must buy or go without them. Not so with us. We are great dons in our wattle-homes, and must have our pleasure-grounds. But we can't live without food. So, bye and bye I will show you the kitchen-gardens where they grow their vegetables. We call them provision grounds; and woe to those who are lazy on them; I mean when they go up for the week's stores; for often they have nothing else to live on but the fruits of their own labour."

Which bringing to mind "the many times he had been told it before by Rachel Lyons, during their Priory rambles, Mr. Alan heaved a silent sigh, as he gave ear to Mr. Mungo's fruits of long experience, evidently now tendered him on the supposition that, as he was to be the overseer ere long, he could hardly be too soon made familiar with his duties.

Why Alan Lambert sighed he could scarcely have told you. He was where he was with his own free will; nay, had embraced with ardour the offer made him by Mr. Lyons to do as he had done. He came to Trinidad a free agent, and could there remain or return to Shiphampton as it pleased him. And was he not there under bright auspices? and, as Lady Ada said to him, on bidding farewell, "with the making of his fortune in his own hands, if he acted to the satisfaction of a munificent patron like Mr.

Lyons would be to him if he served him faithfully?"
And was it not with Rachel's entire approval, too,
that he had undertaken the trust reposed in him by
her father? Yes, and did not every object that met
his gaze sweetly remind him whose 'dear old home,'
at heart, it was, though the sea rolled between them?
and, in comparison with the humble 'old wooden
house' she prized so much, how her then dwelling
was a sumptuous palace which was soon, they
said, to make her a titled lady? Was there no
comfort in that? Was Rachel to be made a
princess against her will? Had she not vowed
she would never be Lady Thornhill? But nevertheless, sigh Alan did, though not another face
round him but was beaming with mirth.

Ah, who shall truly tell us why the heart involuntarily sighs sometimes, or why it is sad? when,
for any reason it could give for it, it should perhaps have smiled when it sighed, and sighed when
it smiled, had it known what was best for its peace.

Certainly sad looks just then would have been very
ill-timed; so, brisking up, Mr. Alan surrendered
himself with the best grace he might to the full-tide
of revelry and merry-making running to its height,
and seeing no help for it, was fairly carried away by
the stream.

Of course it was a general holiday; which meant
at Trinidad all that unlimited freedom implies. And

when Mr. Alan told them that "the festivities were
to last till the week's end, with no stint of slaughtered
cows, and salt meats, and rum and sugar—then
describe what followed who can.   It may be easier
conceived than depicted.   Some things defy delinea-
tion, and this is one of them.   In a moment the
works were deserted—who would work in the West
Indies when the Massa himself blew the loud trum-
pets for play ?   Any one would have imagined, to
have seen them rush from their labours to put on
their best clothes, and then to vie with each other
which should laugh, and shout, and sing, and dance
the loudest, that they had been bound hand and
foot, with the cart-whip over them, ever since Massa
Lyons left.   Whereas for the last six months they
had done little else, by all accounts, than eat, drink,
and sleep, and dress, and make-holiday, and give the
overseer to plainly understand what would be the
certain consequence of any unpalatable measures on
his part to prevent it.

"Well," smiled Alan, while curiously watching the
sports, "if negro-slavery in Trinidad is not happiness, either I am in a dream, Mr. Mungo, or you
are inimitable actors.   Which is it ?"

"We can act our parts marvellously well," replied
the overseer, "when we please. We are clever adepts
at that. It's a pretty play, isn't it ? The announce-
ment of your coming was the prologue to it, and, be

sure, they'll act it out *con amore*. And then—we shall see. Anyhow, you have made a rare hit. That letting old Rosa and Judy kiss you, and those parental pokes of your fingers through the woolly-hair of their ' little lily negers ' they held up to you, to caress, was a master-stroke. You went straight home to their hearts there."

And so it seemed, by the exuberant fruits it produced. For though, when bed-time came at last, Mr. Alan was not quite eaten up alive, he had not earned his triumphant popularity for nothing—to judge by the deafening din and clatter kept up till early morning under his windows, to amuse him, with their frantic songs and outlandish dances, to the piercing tones of the *shaky-shekies*, and *gambies*, and *kitty-katties ;* till with day-light, and no more rum left, at length poor Alan was left to his slumbers.

" Oh !" he sadly murmured to himself, as sleep at last stole over him, " how happy I ought to be ! Will she think any the less of her ' old home,' for my being here to tell her all about it—to place the fresh flowers daily on her mother's grave—and—and —oh, what proud, what promising tidings I shall have to send them—how delighted she will be ! Rachel—Rachel—Lady Rachel?—Oh, no, no !— what said her lips to me when she pressed them to mine, at parting ?"—which bringing a smile into his face, he sank to 'rest ; and if he dreamt, his dreams should have been happy—as happy as the sinless dreams of those ought to be, over whom angels are said to keep special watch and ward that no harm may come to them.

There is a time for all things. Play-time was over. And now it seriously behoved Mr. Lambert to make lovely Rosa and Judy and the rest of his ardent admirers perfectly understand, if possible, why he was then and there among them—viz., "to temporarily represent their lawful master, Mr. Lyons, with the view of reporting to him what state the works were in; how his negroes were behaving themselves; and which of them would merit reward, and which punishment, when he came to Trinidad to judge for himself, which he meant to do as soon as possible."

It had a salutary effect. Rosa and Judy wept for joy! at the thought of what "kind Massa would be sure to do for *them*, if for nobody else, when he came." Which rousing the spirit of emulation among the rest—well reckoned on by Mr. Alan in his touching address to them—some sort of order was restored; the works went on again with fresh vigour; and really there seemed a hope of a tolerably favourable next report for Greystone House, if only the present very promising aspect of affairs would last.

Mr. Mungo "hoped it might;" but he shook his

head when he said it, as though he preferred waiting a little while before he spoke too confidently.

There was every wisdom, however, in making his young charge, Mr. Lambert, who might soon fill his place on the estate, acquainted with his whereabouts, and what he would have to do, as overseer, to rule the unruly spirits under him, who, though they could occasionally be grateful, were intensely selfish and perverse, though excessively indignant towards any-body and everybody who failed in their duty towards "good kind Massa"—but themselves. So, as soon as the revelries were at an end, Mr. Mungo took Mr. Alan over the estate, to give him a clear notion of it, as well as to shew him what a fine property it was; but how shamefully it was neglected, in spite o all his efforts, and what must be done before it coul be restored to its former richness and fertility. For it had sadly fallen off of late, since the infamous *Obeah-ists* had come among them, and turned the silly heads of the negroes so, by practising on their superstitions, that—

"Now I can do nothing with them," said Mr. Mungo, gravely. "Whip or no whip, it's all one, while that reprobate rascal Samson is at large. If we could put him down, there might be a chance; though when once those villanous Obeah-men get hold of the negroes, it's all up with them till you can root them out, and hang the ringleaders. We must do for Samson, or he'll do for us before long, as sure as that's a cotton-tree."

"And, yet," said Mr. Alan, "you were prospering so, were you not, when Mr. Lyons left you?"

"We were? And why? Shew me another master of negro-slaves on this side the water who could rule them like Angelo Lyons."

Alan listened.

"It was the most perfect thing of the kind I ever saw in my life," went on Mr. Mungo, kindling at the thought of it—"and I have been at the work, off and on, for nearly forty years. I don't know whether you will understand me, but he ruled them, so to say, with a silk thread and a thong of iron in one."

"With kindness and firmness, you mean?"

"Well, call it so. I mean with sympathy and severity combined. It's the great secret. His clemencies were kingly, but his vengeance was sure and terrible. 'Mungo,' he used often to say to me, 'there's but one way to rule the negro. If he have no more fear of you than he has love, you will never do it. Don't lash him, if you can lead him. He must obey you, Mr. Mungo, or tremble.' And Mr. Lyons was right. What education may do for them we shall know when it's tried. Perhaps make some better, and some w se; but it won't alter their African blood much, I expect? Any more than it will alter the colour of their skins, except by a mixed breed; and how then? Why, then, there's the *mulatto*—and the *sambo*—and the *quadroon*—and the *mustee*—and the *mustee-fino*, sometimes the worst turn-out of them all. Anyhow, while they are as they are, if they have no more fear for their 'good kind Massa' than they have love, it will be pretty much as you see me now, with all my 'leadings' and leanings—for I haven't used the whip once since Mr. Lyons left—a nice state to be in, with about as much power over them, come a revolt, as you would have if they didn't fear what you could *tell* of them, though you let all the old hags on the island hug your breath out of you, for what they could get by it."

It was not the most pleasing picture of the fate in store for him, if he were congratulating himself on his bright prospects in Trinidad, and, naturally enough, Alan Lambert's face grew rather grave.

"All the same," added Mr. Mungo, in a livelier tone, "you have made a wonderful hit.   "For I see that scoundrel Samson has crept back again, and is sawing and hammering away over there loud enough to be heard."

"I shall try the 'leading' system," said Mr. Alan, with glowing eyes, as Samson's hammerings rang cheerily in the breeze.

"By all means!" smiled the old overseer.   "It's

by far the best plan. Only, if you have a tender heart, look at me—"

Which Alan Lambert did with all his eyes and heart and soul, till the tears almost came.

"Good! But you are not an Angelo Lyons—no, no, nothing of that sort. I was going to say, if you have a tender heart don't let their hypocritical kisses, and cryings, and 'God-a'mities,' and blarney and pilaver, quite melt it into oil and butter, or they'll have a nice feast. Still, if you can draw them any-how away from that reprobate Samson, it will be a God-send. Else, spite of his busy tricks over there in the sheds, to make believe there's no harm in him, as sure as my name's Humphrey Mungo we shall be all burnt out some night, or stabbed, or poisoned, *Obeah*-fashion, in one of his drunken fits when he goes about raving like a maniac."

"They do shocking things sometimes, those Obeah men, don't they?" asked Mr. Alan, calling to mind what Miss Lyons and Faith Lincoln had told him about them; "and cause much mischief? What sort of gentlemen are they?"

"Very idle, very cunning, very wilful, and very wicked. They lie, they thieve, they murder, which comprises enough to make one look sharp round when they shew their hateful faces. Besides which, they are rank magicians, and carry about bags-full of incantation-charms—thunder-stones, cats' ears' feet of animals, human hair, fish-bones, alligators' teeth, &c., &c."

" So I have read."

" Yes, it's their stock-in-trade, and, while it lasts, a thriving one it is, to work on the ignorant credulity of the blacks—who believe they have power over life and death—and, so, buy of them their *slave-medicines*, as they call them, to ' make massa good to them,' to charm him into compliance with their wishes, and if not, to ' deliver them from their enemies' off hand."

" And is this fellow Samson one of them ?"

" We suspect him. He was traced to an Obeah-man's hut just before you came, where they found the divers-sized and shaped and coloured string of beads the rascals use in what the negroes call the Myall-dance. That looks like it."

" The Myall-dance? Yes, yes, I recollect. Performed to prove the Obeah-man's supernatural powers ?"

" Yes, by the pretended killing, in the course of it, of some one present, to do away with any doubts they might, otherwise, have about it. But I need not tell you if you know."

" I know only what I have gleaned from hearsay, and Mr. Lewis's ' journal.' "

" Which describes it well ! Yes, it's the Myall-dance does the mischief. The Obeah-man fixes on his chosen victim, sprinkles him with powders, blows on him, and dances round him, makes him drink something ready prepared, then seizes him and whirls him round and round till the poor wretch is dizzy and falls down, as if dead. Then comes the miracle. The chief Myall-man—for there are more than one of them—shrieks, rushes about half-frantic, and flies to a neighbouring wood, from which he returns in an hour or two with a bunch of herbs. Now, then, he will raise the *dead* to life. So he squeezes the juice of some of the herbs into the mouth of the *corpse*, and with others anoints his eyes and the tips of his fingers, during which he does all sorts of wild things, and howls, and chants, while his helpers, hand in hand, dance round in a circle, and stamp the ground as loudly as they can with their feet, to keep time."

"And the dead-man comes to life again?" smiled Mr. Alan; for solemn as the old overseer looked, there was something exceedingly ludicrous as well as horrible in it all, and he could not help it.

"At last? Yes. But not for a considerable time. There's no hurry. That would spoil it. We never hurry here. Yes, the *corpse* sits up in due time, sometimes jumps up, as well as ever, grins, cuts a caper for joy, and there's an end of the fun."

"But not of its consequences?"

"No, no! The Myall man has not danced to

them for nothing. He means to be paid. So, after giving such proof of his power—which of his auditory is there that won't have some of the same wonderful powder in hand, who want to be revenged on their enemies, and—to send them to sleep?"

"Not to wake again too soon, eh?" added Alan, changing colour. "There's nothing said about the antidote, then?"

"No; nor whether the little purchase is, simply, a strong narcotic only, or what it is. They take what's given them, and unscrupulously use it, too, I can tell you. We must keep an eye on that Samson. He's a black villain, every inch of him. Mind what water you drink, which he can get at, if you offend him. Best not quarrel with him, if you can help it. When he's drunk he would cut down his own father with his hatchet for more rum. He is penitent now; and, while it lasts, there's not a cleverer workman of his craft on the island; but he is so thick in with the Obeah-men, you may as well trust to Satan. The worst feature in the negro character, and the most dangerous and difficult to deal with, is their gross superstition, as you will find very soon."

"Chiefly arising from their ignorance and prejudices? and, in most instances, I suppose, from their want of religion and the knowledge of a future state?"

"Perhaps so. Though great pains are often taken

with them to no effect. Physically, they are lazy
and luxurious; morally, incapable, the major part of
them, of further exercise of reason than is absolutely
necessary for self-indulgence. And they are so in-
tolerably vain as well as selfish, that you may talk
the wisdom of Solomon himself to them, and when
you have talked yourself hoarse, what do you get for
it? Pretty much the same as they said to 'good,
kind, Massa,' of Cornwall House, when he asked
them 'if they would be sure to come to prayers next
Sunday?'—'Aye, aye, we'll do *anything* to oblige
Massa.'"

"May be," said Mr. Alan, rather from what he
had been told than what he could tell himself, "there
has often been more zeal than discretion shewn by
those who have tried to enlighten them. With them,
as with us, the spirit must be reached through the
flesh; and, perhaps, the missionaries who worked
hardest did the least, because they thought more of
the good seeds they had to sow, than of preparing
the ground for it; began at the wrong end; had to
work back, which, seemingly, is 'labour in vain,' as
the picture books call it, 'or, his reverence confounded.' Still, they must be taught and enlightened;
and nothing proves more that they can learn and
be instructed, if they will, than how quick they
are to take wrong impressions, and how tenaciously
they retain them, and resolutely act up to them,

which shews capacity of mind enough, if not good quality. That can only come through instruction, I imagine, the instruction that convinces. If men are adepts in evil, they can be adepts in good. Clearly, there is the capability?"

" For lying, and thieving, and murdering at Trinidad, as well as elsewhere? Oh, yes! Hark at that penitent *hammer* there in the carpenter's shed. Adept? Aye, at anything in his own way. Who has had more pains taken with him by the missionaries than Samson? But perhaps, as you say, they ' began at the wrong end' with him. You can try the other. I sha'n't. Only mind, if you offend him, what jar you drink your water out of. You know about the Cassava, don't you?"

" A little."

" Its juice, carefully expressed from its root, produces, during fermentation a small worm, any portion of which is a deadly poison, if received into the stomach. It is the deadliest of all our poisons. And those who use it, for hate or revenge, are very cunning about it. They conceal a little bit of the worm under one of their thumb-nails, allowed to grow long for the purpose. The ' journal' gives a good account of it. And then when their victim is eating or drinking with them, or they are handing him a dish or cup, they contrive to drop the worm into it, which, if swallowed, is certain death. The

Arsenic-bean is another sure means of destruction.
It grows in their gardens, though neither useful nor
ornamental ; and if you ask them why they cultivate
it, they grin, but don't know, which is the way they
account for everything incomprehensible. But I
need not tell you. You will find it all out fast
enough. Any how, we must keep a sharp eye on
Samson, in the shed there, now he's so good."

But though life in Trinidad had its dangers as
well as its delights, Mr. Alan saw enough of it,
before he had been there many days, to understand
in what its joys consisted for a mind like Rachel
Lyons's, and what must have been her wretchedness
when her father first took her to see Greystone
House, and told her it was to be her home.

A West Indian alone can realise the true charms
of West Indian life. It is scarcely too much to
assert that a native planter, at the special epoch
under notice, could live, happily, no where else.
Nothing elsewhere was like it to his eye—no country
so beautiful, no scenery so picturesque, no air so
delicious, no living so luxurious, no earthly possessions so much a man's own, no earth so green,
no sky so blue, no sea so calm and clear, no food
so rich and varied, no drink so exquisite, no flowers
so sweet, no fruits so luscious, no men so brotherly,
no women so sisterly, no pretty girls so lovely and
loving. In short, no homes, inside and out, so like

what happy homes should be, for those who, having tasted the joys of undisputed dominion, knew what real sovereignty was in perfection, as it was no where else to be found in the world.

But Rachel's love for her "old home" sprang from other thoughts than these. She loved it with the love that has its root in earliest cherished memories, memories in which a beloved mother's first tender kisses greeted her, and which witnessed her dying smiles. Trinidad was her birth-place. Till after her mother's death she knew no other home; it was inseparably interwoven with her happiest associations; and all that had happened since she left it had rather strengthened than lessened their force. On her father's accession to the Balfour property, it pleased him to make Shiphampton his home; and Rachel, of course, with child like eagerness to see the beautiful sights "no where else to be seen but in England," people told her, left the land of her birth with less regret, because of the promise her father made her, after her last visit to her mother's grave, to re-visit it as soon as he could. A promise that was never absent from her mind—a promise, the thought of the bare possibility of his not being able to keep which bathed her pillow with the first bitter tears she had ever shed, when, hand in hand, he had taken her to see the blood-stained spot on which he was " going

to build them," he said, "a new house, to wash
away the *stains*," which "never could be washed
away," her shuddering heart told her, "till the
day of judgment."

And did not Alan Lambert know it all as well as
Rachel did? Had she not often talked with him,
during their rambles, of that wretched first night of
their arrival at Shiphampton? "all through which
she could see only poor Aunt Joyce and Ann
Balfour walking round her bed with ghastly faces
full of woe. But, no, no! not with any anger in
them towards her, who had done them no harm;
but, rather, with grief and pity; which was what
made her feel as though her heart would break if
she had to live in The Broadway, and those
anguished looks were ever on her, turn which way
she would."

Oh, yes, he knew it all! And how, though a
princely palace stood in the place of the blood-dyed
old business house that was swept away to dry her
tears and bring back the native colour to her cheeks,
those "anguished looks," as she called them, were
never absent from her sight; but seemed to grow
more piteous, and piercing, and persistent, the
richer her father got, and the more he affectionately
strove to surround her with delights. Rolling in
riches as she was, where was her heart? And why
was it there? All Shiphampton was ringing with

the talked of grand alliance between the Lyons's and Thornhill's—but what were her own last words to him at parting?

"They may force you to be his, I said to her," ejaculated Alan, as he often called to mind those blissful last few minutes at The Priory which had sealed the precious bond for ever: "Force me!" she answered with a thrilling calmness, how like her father's, "to break my plighted word to *you?* It is well you blush!"

Oh, what mighty powers of quenchless hope and endless trust and joy unspeakable were in those two priceless words *to you!* And with the new wreath of *immortelles* in his hand, as the best of all accompaniments to them, away went Alan to the mango-grove, to tenderly deposit it, with all due reverence, on Angelina Lyons's marble tomb, as he had said he would.

CHAPTER IV.

TIME flies fast when there is plenty to do.

On his first inspection of the Old Mill House estate, Alan Lambert felt almost drowsy during some of Mr. Mungo's rather lugubrious details. To use his own words in one of his letters to The Priory, " There seemed such a lazy look over everybody and everything, as if, though labour they must, they did it with as much ease to themselves as possible, and for two farthings would desist and go to sleep and do no more." Mr. Alan was conscious of the contrary, by the number of hands at work on all sides ; but he could see there was an obvious lack of that right good will in it which gives to industry its best spirit and pulse and animation.

The works went on; but the main motive principle was wanting to keep them going; and so was produced on Mr. Lambert, perhaps, that "dead-alive" feeling, in the midst of it, experienced by those who, though in a trance, are doing such great deeds, and, though so mightily busy, may at any moment come to a dead-stop, by reason of that tiresome "screw-loose somewhere" which alike baffles empires and individuals at times.

It was obvious to Mr. Alan that there was "a screw-loose somewhere" on the Old Mill House estate, the fine property of his princely patron; and he was determined to do his best to discover where the "loose screw" was, as the best means of putting that other "screw" on with which "good kind Massa" had provided him, in case of necessity. But negroes are artful, and Mr. Alan was young, and inexperienced, and simple-natured, and kind-hearted; and seeing such evidences on all sides of penitence and amendment, he had well nigh fallen asleep himself once or twice when he ought to have been wide-awake.

Mr. Mungo smiled. Humphrey Mungo was an old stager, and had been a plantation agent and overseer for nearly forty years. So he knew a little more of negro life and their manners and habits than Mr. Lambert did; though Humphrey could not but grant that his young successor's unwearied

energy among them had done a " deal of good," and
that his letters home about it—or, rather, such passages
from them as Mr. Alan read to him—were " very
true!" Humphrey Mungo had " learned a thing
or two" in his day. In Trinidad alone he had
wielded the overseer's sceptre for more than twenty
years ; so Mr. Humphrey had seen all those years'
harvests growing under his nose, and got in. He
had seen the more than twenty years' laborious
hole-diggings on the Old Mill House estate for the
plantings ; he had watched the canes from their
first growth to the mill ; helped with his own hands
to crush and collect the juices from them ; then to
convey away the *trash* for fuel ; then, when the
juices had gone through their several processes till
they were formed into sugar, Humphrey Mungo had
not deemed it beneath him, by way of example, to
help carry it into the *curing-house*, and put it into
hogsheads ; nay, to have a hand, too, in the molasses,
and the "low-wine," as they call it ; till out came
such *rum* from the next distillation, as might well
make their eyes dance and their mouths water, when
they got a bottle of it in old England, "if they
wanted a nosegay when they uncorked it, or had a
pain in their stomachs."

It proved Mr. Mungo to be a practical, pains-
taking person, and one who "had no right to be a
master, unless he knew how to do with his own

hands what it devolved on him, as such, to order to be done for him." And this was exactly the view that Alan Lambert took of it, with regard to himself, and the necessity there was for him to obtain the influence over the negroes which he imagined would follow his setting them those good examples, without which his precepts and preachings would have fallen with about as much effect as so many snow flakes on a pond.

And to work he went in good earnest.

It satisfied him how fast time flew, when not an hour but was fully employed. It also disabused him of the funny notion that they were " half-asleep on the Old Mill House estate," because on his first glance at the slow and easy pace they did everything in, it made him yawn so rudely in Mr. Mungo's face, to hear him talk as he did of " what an active scene it was around them," and how, as Mr. Lewis said in his journal, "A plantation possessed all the movement and interest of an English farm, without its dung, and its stench, and its dirty accompaniments."

The yawns disappeared entirely when Mr. Alan heartily set about the work of personally *doing*, rather than listening to what others did. Then he found that the constitutional *nonchalance* of the negroes over their labours was no sign of positive idleness. True, they would lay down their loads

and stand laughing and chattering together, as
though, seemingly, it were optional with them whether
they ever took them up again; and, though time
pressed and the most had to be made of the fine
weather, saunter along with them at a pace which
the master in England would probably have longed
to kick them for; but at which the "good kind
massa" in Trinidad only smiled; perhaps from
feeling very much, as his slaves did, the impossibility
of keeping the blood up, under tropical suns, higher
than fever heat, without serious inconvenience therefrom.

So, what with one active operation or another,
Mr. Alan had no leisure for a moment's more
drowsiness, after once boldly throwing himself into
action, and plainly seeing, as he did, what must be
done before he could render such an account to
them at Greystone House as he flattered himself he
should be able to do before long, notwithstanding
those dubious shakes of Mr. Mungo's head, in
return for his sanguine hopes.

It was enough to bewilder any overseer's head
which had Samson, the carpenter, in it. And there
was no way of getting him out of it that Mr. Mungo
saw, now he was so diligent again, and would "never
be bad-mannered any more," he declared, "if
Mr. Lambert would say him good Samson to Massa
Lyons." In fact, the whole estate, with the excep-

tion of a few of the worst on it, were in perpetual
dread of Samson, and never so much so as when he
was on his best behaviour. For then he was the
greatest hypocrite. In his drunken fits he was for-
midable; but it was when he was setting them all
such a "nice-mannered example," as Rosa and Judy
called it, that his cold heart was plotting the mischief that his hot brain hatched. More than once
Mr. Mungo had been cajoled by Samson's "nice
manners;" but he knew him now; and so had
thought it best to put his young successor—as he
believed Mr. Lambert would be—on his guard.
Especially as Mr. Alan had made no secret of what
he should tell Mr. Lyons, "if he found any negro
of his in communication with an Obeah-man, or
having any dealings with one."

Now it so happened that one Aaron Pope, a reputed Obeah-man—who, when it was made known
at Old Mill House that Mr. Lyons, or a deputy from
him, was coming, quitted the neighbourhood—had
the audacity to shew his face again within Mr. Mungo's
lawful territory shortly after Mr. Alan Lambert's
arrival. And it was the more daring and audacious
of Aaron, as he must have heard of Mr. Lyons's
solemn address to his slaves, through Mr. Lambert,
touching the serious complaints made him of their
disobedience, and the severe penalty any and every
one of them would instantly have to pay, in person

and pocket, who were convicted of harbouring or conversing with an Obeah-man. All the same, Aaron had been seen again, lurking in the woods near Samson's house; though when questioned about it, Samson's indignation knew no bounds :—"As if him Samson would behave so ungentlemanly—as if him would be so bad-mannered—him Samson that Massa so kind to, and going to make free-neger when him come back, if Samson get a substitute— God-A'mighty! tink of Samson doing dat!"

Mr. Mungo did think of it; and so did Mr. Alan, as in duty bound. The result of which was the making known to every one on the Old Mill House estate, as I have said before, "what would be the consequence of Aaron Pope's being seen in company or communication with any of Mr. Lyons's people, whether high or low, or rich or poor, or white, or black, or brown, or tawny, or good-mannered, or bad-mannered—no matter who or what they were, Mr. Lyons's injunctions were positive and final, and would be strictly carried out."

It created quite a panic among the better-man-nered, as it was well known that Aaron, the Obeah-man, was skulking about the plantation, and had slept one night in a hut near Samson's dwelling. For though Samson was " behaving so well," under Mr. Lambert's eye, few even of his best friends cared to trust him; it nearly always happening that

their sufferings, consequent on the advent of Aaron
Pope near Samson's house, far exceeded their ex-
pectations.

On this occasion, however, of Aaron's craving for
a night's lodging in Samson's hut, nothing occurred
to wound Mr. Samson's feelings for permitting it,
beyond a sound lecture from Mr. Lambert on "the
fatal folly and mistake of his trusting to any power,
but the Great God of them all, for what he wanted,
that was good for him in this life, and the eternal
reward he would be sure to have in the next if he
loved and served Him as he ought." For Samson's
eyes were so full of contrite tears and his demeanour
was so expressive of unfeigned sorrow for the past
and intended amendment for the time to come, that
Mr. Alan was very gratified about it. And not
without reason, apparently, to judge by the good
effect that Samson's reformation had upon the other
negroes, who seeing the fruits of good behaviour
falling into his lap so plentifully at every visit of
their "young Massa," as they called him, vied with
each other which should please him most. So that
the works went on so well, and things began to
resume an appearance so promising, that even Humphrey Mungo prepared for the next cane-planting
with his pristine vigour, so hopeful was he of
Aaron Pope's permanent defeat and the substantial
fruits that would certainly spring therefrom.

And thus being incessantly occupied in making himself master of the subject he had been sent to Trinidad by Mr. Lyons to investigate and report on, the months of constant employment it necessitated succeeded each other very fast. So fast, that our "young Massa," as the negroes called him, got more than one sharp reminder from The Priory, which tingled his cheeks, for his inexcusable remissness in writing only one letter to them there by every mail, and that one so short, that Rachel "concluded" in a postscript "he was getting a mighty grand man, to afford to have so many excuses for neglecting his friends."

But Alan made up for it by the next British mail, and in a way that not a little surprised them at Grey-stone House when they heard of it.

Hercules, the old carpenter, and maternal uncle of Samson, had returned after an absence of more than twenty years battling it with the world in diverse parts, till it had so altered him, that for a while he stood among them at the ' Old Mill ' works a stranger.

"Then when he made himself known," went on the letter, " and shewed them for a fact that he was not dead, as they insisted he was, but that it was really and truly their long lost Her-cules, in the flesh, that was kissing and hugging them—oh, mercy, what a clatter ! Off they all ran

from the works, old and young, big and little, who
had legs to carry them, to where the huzzaing, and
shouting, and laughing, and dancing, and tumbling,
and rolling on the ground called them together—
just as if Massa himself had dropped from heaven
among them with all sorts of nice things, and it
was first come, first served, to judge by the frantic
haste they were in for priority.   Never was heard
such a din.   Talk of Babel let loose!   But it not
being a case that occurs every day, and as none
of them have been very 'bad-mannered' of late,
Mr. Mungo was moved to give them a day's
holiday, and I need not tell you what followed.

"For his age, and the hardships he has gone
through, Hercules is the handsomest *mulatto* I ever
saw.   He must have been à perfect Adonis among
them when young; and the women look at him
now with clasped hands and adoring eyes, though
his face is seamed with furrows and his mop of a
head is as white as snow.   He looks a mighty
fellow when he stands upright, and throws his
brawny chest out, and flourishes his long sinewy
arms, big and strong enough seemingly to knock
a bull down.   Bent and broken as he is, I shouldn't
like a blow from that fist of his.   And though,
when he smiles, 'none of the fire has left his eyes,'
they say, there's an expression in them so keen
and crafty, while he is telling you of what he has

gone through, and how meekly he has submitted
to God's will, that I should not like to be too sure
Mr. Hercules has always been the innocent, inof-
fensive, and deeply injured individual that he seems
now. He is the picture of one of two exceedingly
interesting characters, as the world goes—either of
a grey-growing saint, or sinner. Opinions differ.
But to me he looks, as you may say, the present
virtuous evidence of a vicious past. Clearly he has
the cut of a countenance not wholly unfamiliar with
loose ways, and that is rather ashamed of them.
He has done a queer thing or two since he was a
boy, or his face belies him. There is roguery in
those rolling, restless black eyes of his that the
women turn theirs up to the skies at till you can see
nothing but the whites of them; and if his sensual
mouth mean just the reverse of self indulgence, then
so does his enormously big body mean that there's no
bone and muscle in him. Though, to shew them it
was their own Hercules who was kissing and
squeezing them, he took two of the prettiest
young women near him, Miss Venus and Miss Juno,
up together in his arms, till they sat each on a
shoulder, and then snatched up old Judy and
dandled her in his hands like a baby, to keep Miss
Venus and Miss Juno company. So you may suppose how popular he is. It beats my parental feat
hollow of twisting my lily-white fingers in the ' little

lily-negers'' woolly polls as I did so beautifully. Taking old Judy to his bosom with the young ones was tip-top !

" How to credit half his story of himself is another matter. Never were such dangers and disasters heard of as Hercules has to tell of. Twice he has been shipwrecked, thrice nearly torn to pieces by wild-beasts, once all but burnt to death, then saved from the stake and sold by savages to savages, and kept for years by them in bondage, four times he was brought to death's door by hunger and thirst, and no end of times by sickness and misery. When, on obtaining his manumission from Mr. Lyons, he left Trinidad on his travels, his intention was to return to it, he says, after transacting the business for which he went to France. But man proposes, and heaven disposes—and it was not fated that Hercules should ' set his eyes on dear Old Mill House again for all those twenty years.' Why I cannot comprehend. He hardly seems to know why himself. It would puzzle a conjuror to make head or tail of his strange story. It is full of wonders. Clearly he has fought a hard fight since they saw him last; and has made some money, too; and would be very glad, he says, to settle down and do what he could to increase it on a plantation, and spend the rest of his days in peace. He is an immense favourite with them all; so it's only fit you should know it.

Sinister looking as he is—and that may partly be
because of the perilous, wild, wandering life he has
led—there's some right stuff I think in the fellow.
And I name it thus willingly, because of the liking
he has taken to me, and his nephew Samson's
whimsical jealousy about it; for he's a most sensitive gentleman is Samson, and thin-skinned to an
extent, unless he can be Grand Seigneur, which
perhaps he fancies he sha'n't be, 'now him uncle
Hercules come back to fret him.'

"I was to be sure to give Hercules's humble duty
to Massa Lyons, and to say he 'meant to go to
England soon to see him, and tell him his history,
and get him to do something for him.' His re-
appearance has been quite an event. Nothing else
is talked of. Go where I will, 'Oh, Massa Lambert, tink of him Hercules come to life again, him
Hercules dat was dead so long, dat go away free-
neger twenty years, and come back now! God-
A'mighty, tink of dat!' We are gradually subsiding
into the ordinary routine; but Samson evidently eyes
his uncle as a great dog might another great dog
come to share pot-luck with him. And what is
worse, I have greatly sunk in his esteem, they tell
me, since Hercules cast such kind eyes on me;
for Rosa and Judy heard him grumbling about it,
and saying what 'bad-manners it was of me, when
him Samson was behaving so gentleman.'"

It was indeed startling intelligence for them at Greystone House; for Mr. Lyons in particular, who had always favoured Hercules so much, and, as a mark of his regard, granted him his freedom at considerable loss to himself. Hercules was also the trusted bearer of important papers and letters from Mr. Lyons to his sister, Mrs. Ruth Lyons, when he sailed for France; and his universally believed death, in consequence of his not having been heard of for so long after he left the Pyrenees, had affected Mr. Lyons a good deal.

But we shall know more in a future chapter of the pleasure it gave them at Greystone House to hear of Hercules' 'resurrection,' as Mr. Alan termed it; so will continue the relation of how it led to such jealousy in Mr. Samson's sensitive bosom, and then to so diabolical a determination on his part to rid himself of his *enemy*, that the whole island resounded with it, as the blackest act that had ever been laid to his charge.

Mr. Samson's two chief failings were jealousy and ingratitude. He had other faults, but those were his worst. He was jealous of every one who took or threatened to take precedence of him, and, I am sorry to add, exhibited little other knowledge of the definition of thankfulness than what might be comprised in his several appreciations of benefits *to be* received, let alone what *had been*. Mr. Samson

had a provident eye for the present, but small
sympathy for the past, or care for the future. The
present ruled him. He wanted this, or he did not
want that, and what he wanted he would have if he
could, and what he did not, he would wash his
ponderous hands of, though, like his mighty pro-
totype of scriptural renown, he had, while putting
out his terrible strength, brought the house down
over his own head as well as others. In short, Mr.
Samson was as thorough a black lump of selfishness
and laziness as ever adorned a plantation, when
playtime came, and holiday clothes, and as much
rum and sugar as he could drink. Then Mr.
Samson was rather a good-looking fellow than
otherwise, and his grin, which displayed a faultless
set of white teeth, really had something almost
genial in it. He liked companionship in his mirth,
and had not the least objection to others enjoying
themselves to the full, so that it took nothing from
him. He would fraternally link arms with the
drunkard as drunk as himself, till came the next
chance of a drink, when woe-betide brother black
if he got a drop more than his share. Mr. Samson
was highly sensitive, as I said before, and deeply
sensible of what was due to himself. Seeing which,
Aaron Pope had marked him out for his man; he,
Aaron, like the subtle Master he worked for, knowing something of human nature under black skins

as well as white, and concluding perhaps that the selfish could be cruel, and the cruel cunning, and the cunning cowardly, and the cowardly brave enough to occasionally do dangerous deeds as well as dirty ones, to save themselves.

It was evidently no gladdening news for Samson when came the loud shouts and jubilations in the wind that heralded his long lost uncle's return. While he mourned "him lamented Uncle Hercules" as dead and gone, Samson was heartbroken, and could bring the tears into his eyes in a moment when Hercules' skill as a carpenter was talked of and how kind it was of Mr. Lyons to let him, Samson, fill his place. But now Hercules had come to life again, may be Samson remembered the tears he had shed for nothing; so had no more left, not even one for joy, though every one else's bounding heart on the estate was brimming over. Notwithstanding which, Samson threw himself on his uncle's neck and sobbed aloud.

"Eh, ho! see him Samsom dere!" giggled Rosa to Judy. "God-A'mighty! how him cry! Eh, ho! what Samson do, now him Hercules head man? Likely him Samson tink of that—ho! ho!"

And if Samson did, it was no more than what his old friend, Aaron Pope, in hiding somewhere till he could crawl forth again unseen by Mr. Lambert, anticipated would be the case with a highly sensitive creature like Samson was. So what did Aaron do, when he heard for certain of Hercules' return, and "what a favourite he was of Mr. Alan's," to show Samson "how silly he was to be jealous about any such rubbish?"

We shall see.

Alan Lambert had given Rachel Lyons a touching description of his first visit to the marble-tomb in the mango-grove, and of how he had placed the new wreath of *immortelles* thereon, in obedience to her instructions. To convey a clearer conception of which, and of how the tomb, and the sweet spot it hallowed, looked, now he had had both thoroughly repaired and put in order, he sent her a water coloured drawing of it, as it then stood, with the new wreath on it, and the umbrageous nook in which it was embowered, without an eyesore. How Rachel prized that drawing may be safely left to the correct conceptions of those who care for her as she is depicted in this story. She had it framed and glazed by her old friend, Isaac Nathan, of Market Street, and hung under her mother's portrait in the boudoir, "where she could see it whenever she gazed on that loved face," she told Alan in their next letters, "and gratefully think of him who drew it."

And sometimes, after his visits in the cool of the day to the mango-grove, Alan would stroll on through the bamboos, and logwoods, and prickly yellows, till he came to 'The Old Mill,' from which the estate took its name; after tarrying on his way to sketch the fantastic cotton-trees, alike picturesque to his artistic eye, whether in full leaf or with their 'bare white arms widely extended,' or with 'the wild fig and various creepers mantling their stems and branches, and their wreathing limbs streaming with numberless green withies and strings of wild flowers.' But the Old Mill was his usual halting point; for it recalled to mind another 'Old Mill,' dear to memory, a clever drawing of which, by Rachel's hand, hung in Lady Ada's drawing-room. And, furthermore, the two 'Old Mills' were in many features somewhat similar, or, at all events, fond fancy made them so; added to which, there were the sparkling little rivers to them both that set and kept them going. In the one of which, not a cross-bow shot's distance from Molly's cottage on *The Green*, how often had Alan gladly plunged of a morning for an appetite for Hester's nice hot breakfast rolls and new-laid eggs and bacon; and in the other, not five minutes walk from the Mango-Grove, how delicious it was to disport himself under the shadow of its verdant, sloping banks—when the excessive heat made its cooling waters indispensable—far from all fear of sharks or galli-wasps.

And hither had Alan Lambert come from his usual pensive leisure hour in the mango-grove, for

his customary after-swim in the sparkling waters of
'the Old Mill,' on the day specially appertaining to
what has next to be recorded of his and Hercules'
singular interest in each other. And a most eventful day it was for him, little as he imagined what it
teemed with of vital moment to himself and her,
whose welfare and happiness were no less dear to
him than his own.

It had been a sultry, suffocating day, and Alan
had returned from a long ride over a neighbouring
plantation so fatigued, that but for his desire to see
how the masons had restored the weather-damaged
sculpturings of the tomb, he would have stayed at
home and slept himself into a brisker mood than he
had been in since the morning.

The tomb was now complete, and he sat down to
contemplate it, and think—"whose beautiful blue
eyes would have glistened, if she could have seen it,
as gladly as his own did." The air was stifling,
and for the first time since he had set foot on the
island, a sense of such weariness and lassitude stole
over him that he could hardly keep his eyes open.
What ailed him?

"Am I in my right senses?" Alan said to himself,
with an effort to shake off the drowsiness which he
had been told was 'often the first symptom of the
fever prevalent thereabouts at that season of the
year.' "What makes me so sleepy? How insup-

portably hot it is. Oh, for a sniff of the bracing
heather breezes at dear old Buck!" and with heaving
chest he jumped up from the grass, as if determined
to no longer give way to such languor. " Perhaps
a dip in the mill pool will drive it off;" and no
sooner said than done—presently he was stoutly
swimming along with manifest relief, to judge by
the pleasure he seemed to find in it, and the time he
stayed in. He stayed in too long; and his head
ached so badly, on coming out, that he sat down,
from the pain in it, to dress himself under one of
the beautiful Abba, or palm-trees, that bear those
' bright cone-shaped vegetable-looking fruits towards
their tops, formed of brown and purple seeds, and
some as red as coral.'

Alan Lambert loved trees; but it was an indiscreet
act of his, sitting down at all, after leaving the
water, with such a violent head-ache as he had,
and, yet, feeling as chilly as he did from the long
time he had been in the stream. But he thought
he would sketch the Abba-tree while he was there,
and send it in his next packet to The Priory, as
Rachel was so pleased when she got any of his
drawings. He reckoned wrong that day. He ought
to have gone straightway home, with those throbbing
temples, taken some warm tea or cocoa, and got
into bed; for, before he was half-dressed, such a
dizzy, drowsy feeling came over him, that he lost

all consciousness of where he was or what he was
doing, and yielding to the stupor it produced, he
soon lay on the turf fast asleep.   His straw-hat
was beside him, the scorched-up grass pillowed his
bare head, he had not yet donned his upper garments, his shirt collar was unbuttoned, and his
naked neck and chest presented as fair a mark for
curious eyes or the coward-blow, if either had awaited
him, as he could possibly have given them.   But
what then?   He slept sound, and as safe, he thought,
from harm of any kind as if he had been in his
bed.   The bluest and most beautiful eyes in the
world, for him, might have been watching him while he
slept, without a heart-throb more, unless his dreams
had told him of it, or the assassin's hand might
have ended in a moment his hopes and fears for
ever, for any power he had to help himself, at the
mercy as he was of the fevered blood that was
burning in his veins.

Twilight was coming; but Alan still slept as
though he had imbibed some narcotic, or were in
a lethargy.   And he might have slept on all night
where he then lay on his mossy-bed, and caught
his death by it, but for the accidental evening visit
to the Old Mill—after fishing the river—of Mr.
Hercules, who having a mind for a quiet look again
at the 'old ruin,' took it on his way to the House

where he was going to leave what fish he had caught for Mr. Lambert.

His survey of the 'ruin' gratified Hercules; and with his thoughts on the past and his eyes on the ground, he walked moodily on, as if deep in his own reflections; till arrested by some strange object near him, he looked up, and seeing a straw-hat on the green-slope above him, stopped to think " what could have brought it there?" as, from the lower ground he stood on, only the hat was visible, and the trees round it. Curious to discover the meaning of so strange a waif-stray, Hercules went back to the turf-path up from the water to the slope, and presently espying the hat—there, within a yard of it, was the very much-esteemed person he was taking his fish to, stretched on the earth, either dead, or so like it, that the cold drops came out thick on Hercules's forehead, as falling on his knees beside him, with clasped hands and starting eye-balls, he must have thought he was lifeless, by the horrified look of terror and wonder with which he gazed on him.

And so Hercules continued fixedly staring at the naked neck and chest of their 'young Massa,' as they called him, as if stupefied by a sudden crushing blow he could not rally from; or as if he expected to see the blood trickle from the murderous wound that had laid him there on his back, never to trouble his enemies more; or it might have been

that he so rivetedly gazed on them, because he saw
he was not dead, but that the heart still beat, and
that there was no villain-wound, no blood, no reason
but that he would open his eyes again and be a living
witness to the flood of joy that rushed through
Hercules's breast, at the thought that perhaps Providence had led him that way to save the 'young
Massa' from what would have been no less fatal to
him than the assassin's hand, had he lain there
after the night winds had filled the air with
poisons.

"God Almighty!" ejaculated Hercules, with his
straining eyes still fixed on that defenceless neck and
chest, open to the night winds; "Almighty God!"
—awoke by which, Alan Lambert started up, stared
confusedly round him, as if he had been dreaming;
then becoming conscious of where he was and what
had brought him there :—

"Ah, is it you, Hercules?" he said, with a smile,
and shaking his offered hand. "How lucky! By
Jove! and I am not dressed. Such a sleepy-fit came
over me, when I got out of the water, that I couldn't
keep my eyes open. But I'm all right now."

To prove which, Alan was no sooner on his feet
than pressing his hand to his aching brows, Hercules required no more to see what was the matter,
and that if Mr. Alan were to be got home to his
bed, it must not be by the unassisted aid of his

legs to convey him there. For he staggered like a drunken man when he tried to walk by himself, after taking Hercules's arm down the slope; so that it became evident that Hercules must either go for a conveyance, or see what he himself could do to dispense with it, by the simple use of his strength.

It was a case of necessity.

"Yes, yes," urged Hercules, with deep anxiety, "do, sir, pray!"

"No, no, thank you, Hercules," smilingly objected Mr. Alan, on the score of his weight, though visibly touched by the kindness intended—the case in question being whether Mr. Lambert would listen to reason, and have the goodness to let Mr. Hercules carry him home on his back, or not.

"Weight!" said Hercules, with a grin of self-satisfaction. "No, no—no more than if you were a little *pickaninny* of six months old. Hold tight round my neck, and then we needn't halt once."

"I can't think of it, Hercules."

"Mr. Lambert, you must!"

"Oh, no, Hercules, no!"

Mr. Hercules dropped his head, deeply grieved.

It settled it. There was no resisting so eloquent an appeal, no misunderstanding that dejected look, those hurt glances which he cast first on his young Master's white hands, then on his own tawny twain. An instant's more hesitation would have belied a heart like Alan Lambert's. "What had colours of skin, or creeds, or classes to do with His one great universal law of love that made all alike brothers and sisters, in His own image, from the beginning of the world, as He meant they should all be to its end?" Fraternally impelled by which, Alan Lambert clung to his tawny brother; and being "no heavier much than a baby," Hercules declared, he carried him home without once stopping, as he said he would—his, Hercules's, only fear being his young Massa's ability to "hold on long enough, as weak as he was."

"God Almighty! Almighty God!" continued Hercules to mentally ejaculate, as he went slowly homeward. "Think of that! Yes, yes! Power of Heaven!" and raising his eyes and outstretched hands, as if in supplication to the Almighty Spirit he had been told 'reigned over him and all the world,' he fell on his knees, and smote his breast, and tore his grizzled hair; and, till the seeming fit of mingled grief and exultation was over, went on in so extravagant and incomprehensible a way, that any one who had seen him would have supposed he was intoxicated or out of his senses, who had not known to the contrary.

Meanwhile our 'young Massa' had drank the warm drink Mr. Mungo had made for him, and taken the composing draught given him by the doctor, and

had sunk again to sleep. But the doctor shook his
head when asked—

" Will he be well again to-morrow ?"

" No," he said, shortly.

" When will he be, do you think ?"

" Humph ! He may bless his stars if he get well
at all."

It called for all the more skill on Doctor Yorick's
part; also for all the more care and kindness on Mr.
Mungo's ; and then, " with faith and patience," as
the doctor said, " nothing was impossible to physic,
with a good constitution to work on, and nature left
to do her own work unchecked."

But pressing affairs at Shiphampton, connected
with our story, must now take us back there with all
speed, as soon as we have seen poor Alan safe out of
—not the doctor's hands, no, no !—out of a worse
peril by far than he ever was in, clothed or naked,
from the winds or the waters.

For three weeks during which Alan lay ill in bed,
with a face one hour so flushed, and the next so like
a dead man's that Hercules was well-nigh distracted,
the doctor answered the anxious questions put to
him on all sides with little more than shakes of the
head.   In truth, he need have had a good constitution, in his young patient, " to work on," or of
what avail would have been the art and skill of even
Doctor Yorick himself? more potent to deal with the

ills and ailments the poor flesh was heir to, on that
side of the ocean, than the Queen's physician himself. Nature, grateful to him for his trust in her,
did all she could to help him in the way best known
to herself; wherefore in about a month from the day
on which Hercules carried the ' young Massa ' to
his bed, the young master was so far convalescent as
to be pronounced out of danger, and in a fair way of
recovery, with pains and prudence, and such salutary
amusements as kept his mind cheerfully engaged
without too much fatigue.

Alan had taken a great liking for Hercules, who
also seemed no less attached to Mr. Alan, and, indeed, was his chief nurse and constant attendant
night and day through the fever. Alan would look
for Hercules to shift his hot pillow, and moisten his
parched lips, and bathe his aching temples, and give
him his medicine, and what food he took to support
life, as for one to whom he could speak freely, and
open his heart, and tell his history, or, rather, such
fragments of it as most painfully pressed on his
mind, with the fear of death on it. These sudden
sympathies between natures so widely dissimilar as
were Hercules's and his young Master's, are, apparently, strange inconsistencies, but are nevertheless as
strictly real, and reasonable, and consistent with the
great law of our being and brotherhood one with
the other, as the most ordinary and intelligible things

in life. Alan Lambert felt drawn towards Hercules
from the first, and so did Hercules towards Mr.
Alan; though it would have been difficult to have
pointed out two seemingly more complete contrasts
in every respect than they were. Though such anti-
podes, their hearts warmed towards each other at
first sight. And the strange meeting under the
Abba-tree had riveted the link so tight, that nothing
was talked of among the negroes, when their 'young
Massa' got better, but "how fond he was of Hercules;" and how "him Hercules going to be
grand man now, and get de good tings, and be
put ober dem, and be rich man, just tink of dat!"

Nephew Samson did. How could it be otherwise, dinned into his ears as it was by Rosa and
Judy and the rest of them whenever he met them?
"Him Hercules de great favourite! Him Hercules
get all de good tings! Him Hercules be de rich
man now. God-A'mighty, tink of dat!"

It weighed heavily on Samson's jealous mind.
He was "the favourite," they all told him, "before
uncle Hercules came, with him fine ways, putting
'em down, so bad-mannered."

Mr. Mungo made rare fun of it, as he always did of
Samson's jealousies, which were so exceedingly gro-
tesque, at times, that it was the only way to treat
them. But on this occasion it seemed to greatly
pain Mr. Alan to hear how downcast Samson was

at the preference given to his uncle Hercules, and the slight shewn him, Samson, in never having been once admitted to pay his personal respects to ' Massa Lambert ' during his illness.

"I will give Samson an audience," smiled Alan; "to-morrow, if he will."

And when Hercules took the gracious message to his nephew, Samson hugged him to his heart, as if he could have squeezed the breath out of him for joy!

Was it true—as Judy whispered to Rosa next morning, while passing the carpenter's shed—that Aaron Pope, the Obeah-man, slept in a hut near Samson's house that night? If so, it was lucky for Samson that none knew of it but Judy and Rosa.

As it was, there were no signs but of great joy and exultation in Samson's big, black, bloated face, when, dressed in tip-top style, and flourishing his handsomest walking-cane with one hand while he made daintily visible the gay corner of his scarlet pocket-handkerchief out of his bright blue coat tail, with the brass-buttons to it, with the other, he presented himself, full fig, at Old Mill House, as in duty bound.

Mr. Alan was up, though not yet well enough to leave his room, and desired that Mr. Samson should be immediately admitted.

The meeting wants a cleverer pen to describe it than mine. On Samson's part it was perhaps a trifle too melo-dramatic; otherwise there was decided pathos in the way he ran—as soon as he caught sight of his "dear, good, kind young Massa," propped up in his chair with pillows, and looking "so pale and thin"—and threw himself at his feet, and passionately kissed his held-out hand, and for a moment or two was so choked with emotion that it brought tears into Mr. Alan's eyes. Both were deeply affected. There was deep gratitude in Alan's smile of joy that he had been saved from the deadly foe he had had such a terrible struggle with, to again taste life's sweetest delight, in the kind wishes and congratulations of his many friends which he valued so highly; and Samson's beaming face shockingly belied him if it were any other than the eloquent expression of what his thankful heart was too full to give utterance to, and which no words could have conveyed any idea of, if he had had them at command.

But by the doctor's orders, no visit, however friendly or affectionate, was at present to exceed ten minutes, and more than five of Samson's esteemed presence were gone before he found his voice. Then if Mr. Alan had been in any doubt as to whose heart was all his own in Trinidad, though no one else cared a *maccaroni* for him—there was an end to it. Samson's tongue was let loose; and Mr. Alan had enough to do to smile and listen. Till feeling tired :—

"Pour me out a glass of the Madeira there, will you, Samson?" he said, pointing to the table by the window on which were a decanter and glasses ; "and fill another for yourself. I am allowed a sip or two now, when I wish for it."

"Oh, Massa Lambert, yes, dat ar's good !" cried Samson, jumping up, and springing to the table. "But, no, no, me no want vittles, me no want drink, me only want see Massa Alan well, to talk wid Samson, talk as him do with Hercules, dat's all me want."

"Please me Samson by drinking a glass with me, as Hercules does—yes, yes—and wishing me safe out and about again soon."

"Ah, yes, Massa Lambert ! Then, sure enough, him uncle Hercules be grand man."

"I hope I shall always be grateful, Samson, to those who have been kind to me. Hercules has been very good and attentive to me in my illness, and I am sure Mr. Lyons will reward him for it. But I may not talk any more to you now. You will come and see me again."

"Oh, yes, Massa Alan ! And me be so glad dem good times coming for Hercules ; me love him uncle Hercules ; dat's right good ! and bless de Lord for it."

"Come in," said Mr. Alan, in answer to a tap at the door.

It was Hercules.

"Ah, Hercules! you are just in time to join us in a bumper to my speedy re-appearance among you, hale and hearty as ever."

Hercules smiled his glad consent; and as Samson brought the two glasses full to "poor sick Massa Alan," as he had been told to do, Hercules likewise filled himself a bumper.

The wine-glasses on the table were of different sizes, and Samson had modestly retained the smaller one for himself, while handing the larger one to Mr. Alan.

"No, no!" said Alan, as he caught sight of the extreme length to which Samson's finger-nails were grown, as he took the glass from him, but without appearing to notice it, though he felt his face turn cold as marble. "That is not fair. You know I may only drink a sip or two. Stay—yes—change with me—that will do very well, won't it, if I touch it with my lips, for luck's sake, as they do at Shiphampton. There then"—holding it out for him to take, and receiving the other in return—"now down with it!" and leaning back on his pillows, as he spoke, Alan fixed his eyes on Samson, as if to pierce his very soul.

It roused Hercules, who, till then, had been too

much engaged with his nephew's "gay best clothes and *gentlemanly* manners," to notice anything else.

"Don't you hear, Samson, what Mr. Lambert says?" murmured Hercules in a hoarse voice, "down with it!"

But Samson only grasped the glass still tighter in his great fist, without the movement of a muscle.

"Down with it!" repeated Hercules, clutching his wrist so hard that Samson relaxed his hold, and smash came the glass to the ground.

Samson cast an imploring look of dread and shame at his uncle, as he saw Hercules's eyes on his long thumb-nail; till apparently convinced, he let go his vice-like clutch.

Mr. Alan seemed too ill to speak.

"Come away," said Hercules to his staggered kinsman, who, as if rooted to the spot, seemed powerless to move. "Do you hear?"

But as Samson stood mute and immoveable, there was but one way left to save him from the black ignominy of the horrible confession that Hercules thought he saw trembling on his lips, and which would have blasted him for ever. So literally carrying him away in his giant arms—how deeply thankful Alan felt for this his second signal deliverance from the hand of the destroyer, what heart knew but his own? till came the day when he could talk of it to Hercules without the grief and pain he

then felt—far more for brutally ignorant, misguided
Samson's sake than aught else.

But though Alan mastered himself so well, till
Samson left the room, the shock was too terrible
for him in his then weak state; and causing a
relapse—for many days " it was the hardest fight he
had ever seen," the Doctor said, " between a good
constitution and what would have beaten the finest
fellow on earth, without it."

" But is there nothing due to your professional
skill?" Mr. Mungo took the liberty to ask.

" Oh, yes! Chiefly in knowing what *not* to do,
and acting in accordance."

" Always with Dame Nature's consent?"

" Just so."

Mr. Mungo looked edified. Whether or no, Mr.
Alan soon left his bed again during the day; and
then in a little while—being as a child in the
Doctor's hands—rapidly picked up his flesh and
good looks again. Whereupon a cabinet council
was held in the parlour, when he went down stairs,
as to what was next to be done, with the view of
either " shipping him back to England with all
passible dispatch, or, if he *must* stay in Trinidad, at
all events taking care he could go about, and drink
a glass of wine or water at home, without fear for
his life."

"You had better return to Shiphampton," advised Dr. Yorick.

"We shall get on better," acquiesced Mr. Mungo, "now that atrocious villain, Aaron Pope, has been caught and caged, and that reprobate rascal, Samson, provided for, where he is likely to remain for the rest of his days. No fear of his ever shewing his ugly face here again."

"Then," smiled Alan, "if that be so, I am safe?"

"Are you?" humphed the Doctor, with a shrug.

"May be till another Aaron creeps in, and then good bye to you. Popularity is pleasant, but pays its penalty here as elsewhere."

"That's the chief fear," agreed Mr. Mungo, with bent brows, "if another Aaron should come."

"Stay here," rejoined the Doctor, in his short emphatic way, "and you'll be alive—how long do you think?"

"You must not," gravely assented Mr. Mungo."

"You are a dead man if you do," added the Doctor. "Please yourself."

"I wish I could!" smiled Alan. "Poor me!"

"What," laughed Mr. Mungo, "to have freed us of two of the biggest rogues on the island? It's worth more than fifty harvests to him, as I told Mr. Lyons."

"Humph!" growled the Doctor. "Fifty harvests!

No more than that—reckoning me in? That repay us, would it, when we were all under ground? Thank you! How many times do you suppose we've been within an inch of the grave from that Aaron, since Mr. Lambert came and *took such a fancy* for him? Aye!"—with a hearty shake of both Alan's hands—"you may go back with flying colours."

"At the thought of the debt of gratitude I leave behind me," said Alan, with brimful breast, "and which I can never repay? Oh, no!"

"In the reflection, rather," said the Doctor, as soon as he could speak with his usual firmness—"of having so successfully fulfilled your mission among us, that if you come out again some day, you know where you will find hearts enough to welcome you. Aye, and true and staunch ones, too, eh, Mr. Mungo?—however—and there's no denying it—here and there, even on The Old Mill estate, ruled over by no iron-rod—no, no—a blacker heart may shew itself occasionally than any black skin, however black, that covers it. As we grow wiser, Mr. Lambert, we shall grow better at Trinidad as well as elsewhere. Tell them so in England. At present some of us know little more than do swine of anything but our appetites and how to indulge them with least trouble. We sadly want teaching. But, tell them, not with tracts and sermons only. We talk enough, don't we, of ' God A'mity ?' It's on every lip—' God bless you !—God help you !—God protect you !' It proves we are impressionable. And there's the great difficulty—how to root out old impressions as well as ingraft new ones, likely to stand."

"That's it !" cried Mr. Mungo, who, with forty years' experiences, was entitled to be heard. " What the missionaries and preachers don't do is this— they don't bear in mind the difference between an African and an Englishman. There's the mistake. They come among us, as if there were no native priests, as you may call them, no Obeah-men, no rooted prejudices to be rooted-out before sowing the good seed."

" As if," rejoined Alan, " there were no promised pleasures held out to them by their Obeahists," as Mr. Lewis says of the blacks in Jamaica ; " of here-after eating fat-hog, drinking raw rum, and dancing for centuries to the *jam-jams* and *kitty-katties*, to outshine the rewards after death which Christianity offers."

" Well, it's easier to talk than to do," muttered the Doctor, with his hand on his hat; "and, so, whoever else goes right or wrong, God help the missionaries ! say I. Any how, it's understood, I believe, that we take present sorrowful leave of Mr. Lambert as soon as he is strong enough to bear the

voyage home? Till when we must keep a tight
hand over him, Mr. Mungo; as, you know, it's
easier hereabouts to 'scotch the snake' than to
kill it?"

So, as Mr. Alan could not be in better hands,
with the view to his availing himself of the next
ship homeward, which seemed, as matters stood,
imperative, we will clear the broad waters between
Trinidad and Shiphampton with a bound, and
setting foot again in that fine old sea-port town,
see what has happened there, material to our story,
since last we left it.

CHAPTER V.

ADELAIDE AND ADA.

WHEN we left Rachel's palatial home in The Broadway, Shiphampton, for her "dear, old, wooden house," as she called it, at Trinidad, that fine old English gentleman, Sir Compton Thornhill, Bart., was in tip-top key with the three thousand pounds in his pocket so handsomely sent him by Mr. Lyons. Lady Thornhill also was exceedingly pleased with the very friendly note that accompanied the draft for the money, "conveying, as it did, such an assurance," as Clara said, "of his high opinion of Sir Compton, and regard for the family." And, of course, it soon reached Percy, through his loving sister, "what a fortunate fellow he might think himself in being a *Buck* Thornhill, and, having the pleasant prospect in view of such a munificent father-in-law as Mr. Lyons would be to him, if he pleased him."

Percy was delighted! Ordinarily Clara's letters

about home-matters had two readings. The one, before she began to cross them, Percy got through as fast as his eye could skim the lines, and glean the gist of them; but he luxuriated in the other, which, as if to make up for the stiffness of the first part, in accordance with *duty*, overflowed with affection, and that easy epistolary style which, in Percy's opinion, was the beau ideal of letter-writing. On the present occasion, however, there was not a word in the delightful double-crossed eight pages full which Percy got from his sister, the day following Mr. Lyons's "princely behaviour," but our young guardsman could sit back in his lounge-chair, with one leg across the other, and read over and over with the sincerest approval. Pressure of any kind annoyed Percy. He "hated having anything on his mind," he told Clara. "What he liked was, when he woke in the morning, to feel like he did on Sundays, when there were no duns coming. He "loved Sundays for that." It was a day of rest. Every other day in the week he was bored to death with "those devilish duns." And as it so happened that there were two or three more than usually pressing ones on the morning he got Clara's nice long letter full of "nothing but comfort," it may be supposed how happy Percy was, and how he would have "liked all other days every bit as well as he liked Sunday, if it hadn't been for those "infernal little accounts."

7—2

It gave Sir Compton supreme pleasure to pay not only his own debts, but those of his dashing son's. There was no shirking about the Squire. He was, "every inch of him," as Jerry Cobb said, "a gentleman." He "stumped-up noble," when he had the money to do it with; and "when he hadn't," according to Jerry, "you knew you had only to wait till he had, and then—there you were, safe as the bank!"

"Money makes the mare to go," they say. It certainly took the Squire into Shiphampton on *Sir Roderick's* back in such capital style that day he went to *The Old Bank* to do the needful with the Three Thousand Pound cheque in his pocket, that well the tradespeople might come smiling and rubbing their hands to their doors, to greet him as he rode up High Street, looking, they all told him, "haler and handsomer than ever."

And there was truth in it. For, notwithstanding his many "pulls," as Jerry called them, "this way and that," the Squire wore well. Owing in a great measure, perhaps, to that indomitable Thornhill pride in him, which, whether he were flush of money or short, carried him on, with head up, and chest out, and as upright, and brave, and blooming, as when he was twenty-five. Because, with his ancestral pride in himself, like the fine old oaks in his park, he was "sound at heart," as Jerry pithily put it, with a sturdy stanchness that well became Jerry's own long standing at Buck.

And where the wish and will go hand in hand with the ability, how nice it is to ride round and pay one's bills? How far the reader may deem Sir Compton deserving of any praise in the matter, there is no knowing. Clearly, "easy comes, easy goes;" and it would have been no less to the Squire's credit, if, first, with his income, he had never needed a loan from any man, and, next, if he had known, with the three thousand pounds, in purse, the delight of honestly paying one's way, if possible, with the labour of one's own hard-worked hands and the sweat of one's own noble brow. Still, it is not in the heart of all men to do as they ought, when do it they can, even with the money it has cost them no more to get than their I. O. U. and thank you. So the Squire shall have his due, for acting, under the circumstances, like "a gentleman, every inch of him," as Jerry emphatically expressed it to his stable-mates, on receipt of every farthing of his own little arrears up at the Hall next day, with ample interest over and above.

Sir Compton paid when he could, and paid well; no one had to ask him twice for money due, if he had it to give; though whether he would have been better off with twenty thousand a-year than ten, is another matter. As it was, his friends heartily wished he had it; his banker was bountiful; and his

tradespeople, in the firm belief that they should be
" sure to be paid some day," looked for his " rides
in " on *Sir Roderick*, as they would have cast eyes
at the weather-cocks to see which way the wind was.
It being a pretty well established joke among them,
that "old *Sir Roderick* knew as well as his master
did when the purse was full or empty; for, if full,
he couldn't trot along fast enough to get rid of it,
and, if empty, the snail's pace at which he put one
leg before the other up and down High Street, shewed
what was on his mind, and what he would have
given to have turned into the Old Bank for a minute
or two, and then come out and kicked up a dust
among them."

Altogether, if things had their dark side up at the
Hall, viewed with what they might have been with
better management, they had their bright side, too,
as Clara told her mother. Who, though she had
nothing to say against Rachel's goodness and beauty
and great wealth, could never be brought to acknowledge even the slightest admiration for her father.
Nay, she would not even admit that he was handsome; "unless when, drawn out of himself, his
features were animated by ordinary impulses, which
they never seemed to be otherwise. And when he
was enraged, there was an expression in them that
so far from being ' tragically beautiful,' as some
called it, was positively fearful." Still Lady Thorn-

hill could not but grant that "putting looks out of the question, nothing could be handsomer than the treatment Sir Compton had invariably received from Mr. Lyons since he made his acquaintance." And furthermore :—

"I am bound to allow, my love," she said to Lady Ada, when Percy's expected run-down was on the *tapis*, " not only that Percy has made a wise choice in Rachel Lyons, but that there is every hope of her making him a good wife, when she knows more of his disposition, and of those excellent qualities of his which are perhaps less apparent to some eyes than his follies. Of course not to his mother's."

" Nor to his aunt's," smiled Lady Ada, "if that is what you mean, my dear Adelaide."

" What I mean you perfectly well understand, Ada."

" I do, Adelaide. And you are right so far, that I disagree with you entirely on one point."

" That in his choice of Rachel for a wife Percy has not chosen wisely ?"

" Scarcely, I think."

" And why ?"

" For the simple reason, as I have often said before, because there is no love."

" My dear Ada !"

" None ! Not a grain on either side."

"Ah, my dear! you are always so positive in your opinions."

"And have often had cause to retract them? True, Adelaide! And I sincerely hope I may have reason to do so now, if this talked of union is ever to come to anything."

"Talked of, my dear! It's settled."

"Oh, indeed! How?"

"By her father—by Sir Compton—by all of us."

"Rachel included?"

The sisters earnestly regarded each other for a moment or two in silence, as if to read each other's thoughts. They were both Belmores; the same blood filled their veins; both were proud, and opinionated, and positive, where they deemed themselves right; both were actuated by 'the best motives;' and, so, of course, neither of them would yield one inch to the other, to the compromise of herself, if she could help it, though it were hardly possible that both could be right. In the present instance Lady Ada had certainly more reason on her side than had Lady Adelaide; but that tended in no wise to make Adelaide Thornhill knuckle under to Ada Chilvers. On the contrary. For, seemingly, Ada was sometimes apt to "dictate a little too freely at the Hall," which Adelaide "put up with oftener than she liked, rather than have words with Ada, when compelled to go to her for counsel and comfort." And, now, surely it was "rather too much of a good thing for Ada to tell her elder sister to her face, that a young thing like Rachel Lyons, forsooth, the daughter of a West India merchant, cared no more for the next heir to the *Buck* Baronetcy than if he had no better blood in him than she had." Adelaide Thornhill bore a good deal from Ada Chilvers, her sister, rather than quarrel with her; but she "could not submit to that! especially as there were no humiliating money-matters mixed up with it just then, as on many former occasions when Sir Compton was so troubled that, say what Ada would about their extravagances and mismanagement, she had no heart to dispute with her."

"Rachel included?" asked Lady Ada, in reply to her sister's remark that the nuptial match between Percy and Rachel was an *affaire décidée*.

"How old is she?" returned Lady Adelaide, with a smile; enough to say 'there will be time to talk of Rachel's consent when the time comes for it.'

"Old enough," smiled Lady Ada, in answer, "to have a will of her own. Yes, and a very determined will, too, if so minded."

"So much the better for Percy, my dear," rejoined Lady Adelaide, drawing herself up to her full height, which was a good inch and a half over her younger sister's, though Ada married a Lord, and

Adelaide Belmore only a Baronet; "if any other suitor should enter the lists with him. For you know, dear, how easily a silly-minded girl might misinterpret Percy's high-souled ways; to understand which requires just that firm-mindedness you speak of, in the woman of his choice, which I am pleased to hear you say Rachel possesses."

"To a greater extent," added Lady Ada, good-humouredly, "than I think I ever met with in any other girl of her age."

"Percy, then, is safe so far. It is a great thing for a young fellow of rank, my dear Ada, if he places his affections on a woman beneath him in birth, to be sure she is firm-minded, and, when she knows his ways and wishes, that she will resolutely conform to them and carry them out. Always supposing they are such as they are sure to be in Percy's case, taking after his father as he does; who, though now and then a little headstrong and impetuous—and what men are not so at times?—is the soul of honour and integrity and uprightness, left to his own excellent heart."

"True, dear! And, as a proof of it, preferred making Adelaide Belmore—with but ten thousand pounds, pin-money—his wife, because he *loved* her, to making sure of not a sixpence less than sixty thousand, was it not, with Caroline Lecroix, because he *did not*. You may well think of it with pride and pleasure, and hope Percy may be the image of his father in that, if in nothing else."

"He is his father's counterpart, Ada, in everything."

"He won't be a bit like him, my dear Adelaide if he offer his hand in marriage to Rachel Lyons."

"Why not?"

"Oh, my dear sister, how senseless, how wrong of us to be mincing matters in this way, when nothing can be clearer than that—except for the money he would have with her—Percy would as soon think of some day making Rachel Lady Thornhill as you yourself would."

It brought tears into Adelaide Thornhill's eyes, tears of pride, and grief, and vexation, to think how truly Ada spoke, and how she never would have had occasion to thus make her blush for herself, but for those deplorable 'hobbies' of her husband's which her conscience told her would not perhaps have run away with him as they had done, if his too yielding ·wife had gently but firmly checked them as she ought to have done.

"I can have but one motive, my dear Adelaide," resumed Lady Ada, after a mutual sisterly recognition of the one blood from which they sprang, "one motive alone for speaking so candidly about this, talked of union between Percy and Rachel Lyons, and you very well know what that is."

But Lady Adelaide would not trust her voice, trembling as she felt it was with the mingled thoughts she was battling with.

"Why should we have two opinions, my dear sister, on what must be as self-evident to both of us as that your welfare and happiness are mine, and mine yours; though it may sometimes please the whim in us both to see which is the taller? Suppose, dearest, we decide that grave matter thus— you shall always be so in Ada's eyes, if Ada may likewise be so in Adelaide's? Then, hear me! for I came across on purpose that you should to-day; Sir Compton's purse is replenished again?"

Lady Adelaide sighed.

"And in the handsomest way by Mr. Lyons, who will only take his note of hand for it. In short, he lends him three thousand pounds—on what security?"

It brought a flush into Adelaide's pale cheeks :—

"What security, Ada? The best he can have— Sir Compton's word of honour."

Ada smiled.

"Evidently his banker considers it sufficient," said Adelaide, colouring deeply.

"Quite so, love, if he's not out in his calculations."

"Who?—Sir Compton?"

"No, no! Do, my dear Adelaide, understand

me. You can have no higher opinion of Sir Compton's strictly honourable intentions than I have. He will pay every one to the uttermost farthing—when he can. No one doubts it who knows him. But that is not the present question."

Adelaide heaved a deep breath.

"Do you suppose for one moment, Adelaide, that a shrewd man like Mr. Lyons would lend any one living his money, by thousands, without very good reasons for doing so, or what he conceived to be such?"

"If you mean, Ada, that Mr. Lyons accommodated Sir Compton in this instance with the loan of the money, because of his friendship for him, and what he may reasonably be supposed to feel towards a family to which his own will soon be so closely allied, I agree with you, it was natural enough; nothing could be more so."

"It had its weight no doubt, my dear," smiled Lady Ada, as if she had a shrewd notion in her head beyond that, which she was half doubtful whether to out with or not.

"I can conceive nothing more natural," repeated Lady Adelaide, firmly, "than that Mr. Lyons should have acted, under the circumstances, exactly as he has done; and ought to have done, considering the position it will give him in the County, in the event of a general election, to wed his child to a Thornhill."

"Aye, my love!" laughed Lady Ada, with sparkling eyes. "And not only that! How if he calculated on what no less a personage than Ada Chilvers, widow of *The Honourable Lord Cecil Chilvers, &c., &c.*, would say to such munificence, if it ever entered his head to ask her to marry him, and be mistress of Greystone House? Do you think that had nothing to do with it?"

Lady Adelaide was evidently unprepared for the sudden blaze of wealth untold that almost blinded her! as Ada sat up in her chair with head erect and chest out, and with a "made-of-money" look about her that fairly took the shine so out of poor Sir Compton, with the three thousand pounds, *and no more*, in his pocket—*rich as Cræsus*—that though she fought against them bravely, it wouldn't do—out burst the pent-up tears with which the Thornhill bosom had been bursting ever since the money came; and well they did so. It restored the balance. The sister-hearts would be rivals only in outweighing each other in that mutual love and affection which, in truth, was at the bottom of all their little tiffs and differences, though they sometimes seemed to take such silly pains to prove the contrary.

"You do indeed surprise me! Ada," smiled Adelaide, through her tears; "though, truth to speak, Sir Compton has often joked with me about Mr. Lyons's 'sweet eye for somebody at The Priory,' as he calls it, and what a fine, great, grand lady you could be if you would. And he has made you an offer ?"

" Oh, dear, no! Not quite. You know how perverse and tiresome I can be, as Percy says, ' when I would do what is asked me in a moment, if I hadn't made up my mind *not* to do it.' "

Seemingly it disappointed Adelaide, by the cloud that came over her brow.

" It might be otherwise," went on Ada, after a moment's thought, " if I saw any likelihood of this talked-of match between Percy and Rachel ending well. But it never can."

" Percy would be greatly astonished to hear you say so," returned Adelaide, changing colour. " For we have letters from him this morning in which he speaks of it, and of arranging about the happy day itself when he comes down. Sir Compton, too, was at Greystone House yesterday, and they talked of it as a settled affair."

" My love, how call it so, when Rachel's consent has yet to be obtained ?"

" I presumed, dear, that her father's wishes and hers were one and the same. Besides which"—and it was Lady Thornhill who spoke now—"it would indeed be singular for a *Buck* Thornhill to go suing in vain to Greystone House for a wife."

" Rachel Lyons *is* a strange girl ! a very strange

girl!" said Lady Ada, rather speaking it to herself than to her sister.

"She would be very insensible, too, to what she ought to be fully sensible of by this time, I think," added Lady Thornhill, with dignity, "the sacrifices that of course Percy would make in more ways than one, when, to give her his name and rank, he relinquished the brilliant opportunities they are now offering him on all sides, to make his mother, at all events, proud of her son."

"A very strong argument certainly, from a *Buck* point-of-view," smiled Lady Ada; "but one that it would hardly do to build a feather's-weight on with Rachel Lyons, if I know her. What do you think she would do if I repeated your words to her?"

Lady Thornhill stared!

"Laugh at it. That's all I should get. No market there, I can tell you, for those sort of wares. And I could tell you something else if I liked."

"'In for a penny in for a pound,' love—go on."

"I had better not perhaps."

"As you please. So bad as that, is it?"

"Well, then, you may be sure of this—if Rachel has made up her mind to be Mrs. Percy Thornhill, it is settled, as you say; but if she has made up her mind to be Mrs. Somebody-else, or remain as she is, Percy's chance is not worth a straw."

"Is that what you were going to say?" asked Lady Adelaide, visibly piqued.

"Not exactly. But it's the gist of it."

"Why mince any words about it, love? You must be sure I have ears as well as yourself, and have heard what the silly girl said when that young drawing-master of hers was running in her head, that she 'would rather be Alan Lambert's wife, without a penny in the world, than Percy Thornhill's, if it would make her a princess.' Rhapsody! Wild nonsense! which she will blush for before long, if she don't now, if all we hear be true."

Which, in turn, making Ada Chilvers stare at the mysterious tone in which it was said:—

"Oh, you haven't seen Mr. Lyons, then," continued Adelaide, "since Sir Compton went in?"

"No, not since Monday."

"Ah, then, we are first this time. There's a sad to-do about it down at 'the works,' as they call them. Nothing is proved yet; but it's all about that there's more than two hundred pounds short, of cash received by young Lambert before he went away, and not accounted for."

"Good God, my love!" cried Lady Ada, starting from her seat; "who says so? Who dares to insinuate such a thing against as honourable and upright a young man—or I will never put trust in man again—as walks the earth?"

"Nay, my dear, I only repeat to you what we have heard—what is the talk of the town. It was in every one's mouth, Sir Compton says, when he rode in to-day. All the same, there may be no truth in it. It was not found out till last week, when young Enoch Fletcher had to go over the books with Mr. Appleby, and then it came out."

"That Alan Lambert had been guilty of embezzlement," cried Lady Ada, turning white with indignation. "Monstrous! most monstrous! As foul a charge, be sure, my dear sister, as villany ever laid at virtue's door. And what says Mr. Lyons?"

"Nothing."

"And Rachel?"

"We don't know."

"Ah me! it's a wicked world we live in, my dear Adelaide. We need have the saving sanction of our clear consciences, to keep us scathless. Adieu, my love. I may see Rachel or her father, perhaps both, this evening; and, if so, will run in again to-morrow. Meanwhile say nothing to any one about the 'fine, rich, great, grand mistress, to be! of Greystone House,' if so it please her. All will depend. If Ada Chilvers ever give her hand in wedlock to another lord and master, it will be to make those she loves best on earth prosperous and happy, as well as herself. Else, what could she wish for more than to remain Ada Chilvers? Good bye, dear."

CHAPTER VI.

MORE TROUBLES FOR POOR ALAN.

Do men, in general, see the ravages made on them by time, or climate, or sickness, or distress of mind, as the case may be, with the same eyes as their neighbours? If so, Mr. Lyons, of Greystone House, Shiphampton, must have been greatly shocked when he looked at himself in the glass, and saw what havoc only the little more than twelvemonths since he shipped off his young agent, Mr. Alan Lambert, to Trinidad, had made in his personal appearance.

If, as Rachel said, her father was "little better than the spectre of his former self," when Mr. Alan left them, what was he now? A year had added "twenty years to his score," everybody declared, as he went up and down High Street, arm-in-arm with Sir Compton, so bent and broken and thin and pale, by the side of the still upright and hale and hearty old Baronet, that the shop-

8—2

keepers would peep through the goods in their windows at him, scarcely able to credit their eyes."

" What could be the meaning of it ?"

Certainly it was a striking contrast! There was the Squire, stout and straight and full of health and activity as ever, though his hair was as white as snow, and as often as not, if his banker had failed him, it would have been all up with him; and look at the millionaire, side by side with him, who ' turned everything he touched into gold,' people said—gracious heavens! what a difference! what a spectacle!

Was it the gold-making that was to blame, or what was it? There was something wrong at the root of it. Alchemists, and astrologers, and wizards, and witches were proverbially lean, hungry, haggard folks; and could it be because of that inordinate greed of gain in Angelo Lyons, notwithstanding his princely habits, that the flesh fell so from his bones, and his eyes were so sunk in their sockets, and his cheeks were so hollow, and his back seemed more bent every market-day? and, in short, the tooth of time had apparently fixed in him so fast, as to be gnawing him to the vitals before other men of his age would have thought they had come to their prime !

His neighbours stared! as well they might. " What a fine, upright, handsome, elegant man he

was when he first came to Shiphampton, to take up
his abode among them. Now look at him! And,
yet, he rolled in riches. Not a thing on earth, that
money could buy, but what he could have if he
wished it. He was king of the town. His throne
was of gold, his sovereignty was undisputed, his
word was law, his smile carried gladness with it,
his frown dismay; yet, look at him—how shocking!"

His poor neighbours took counsel and comfort
from it :—

"What a pity!" said one of our old friends at
The Jackdaw to Simon Box. "He won't live no
time to enjoy his money, now he's made it, you'll
see. It's killing him, Mr Box."

"Well, as for that, Richard," observed the cor-
pulent chairman of *The Smutty Club*, as it was
called, in Water Lane, "we're, one and all of us,
Richard, in the hands of Providence;" emitting with
which oracular remark a huge volume of smoke from
his mouth, Mr. Box took the pipe he was solacing
himself with from his lips, and leaning back in his
chair, looked up to Heaven.

It was Mr. Simon Box's invariable rule, when ap-
pealed to by any of his younger Christian brethren
of ' the works,' touching the joys or sorrows of this
life, or any of its incidental cares or casualties,
to answer them as he answered Richard
Coles. Mr. Box referred them all to Providence,

in whose hands they were, for the instant
solution of those doubts and fears they continually
brought to him, as their occasional preacher at the
Tabernacle, next door but one to *The Jackdaw* in
Water Lane, where they held their *Smutty Club*
meetings.   It was a very proper way of disposing of
such knotty questions as seekers after knowledge,
such as Richard, would sometimes put to him at
unseasonable times—as when, for instance, Mr. Box
was at *The Jackdaw* for a little needful repose
after the toils of the day—and saved honest Simon
a good deal of trouble.

"Richard, we are one and all of us in the hands
of Providence," ejaculated Mr. Box, with a resigned
look upward, in answer to his young mate's pathetic
apprehension for the health of their opulent landlord and employer, Angelo Lyons, Esq., of The
Broadway.

"But it seems so strange, don't it, Mr. Simon?"
said Richard, contemplatively, as if more engaged
with his own thoughts than with what Mr. Box had
said—"the Governor should have fell off like that?
and see the hearty man he was when he first came!
You'd have thought, wouldn't you, nothing could
have hurt *him?*"

"What say the Scriptures, Richard?—'The love
of money is the root of all evil; which while some
coveted after, they have erred from the faith, and

pierced themselves through with many sorrows.'
Think of that, Richard!"

Richard seemingly did for more than a minute,
during which Mr. Box was also apparently chewing
the cud of it while he puffed away at his pipe. Then,
as if hardly comprehending why a man's having
plenty, and to spare, of the good things of this life
should ' pierce him through with many sorrows,' if
he got them honestly :—

"That's all very true, what St. Paul says,"
agreed Richard, with an appealing glance round at
Mr. John Strong, the tax-gatherer, who, with his
feet up on a form and his back to the wall, kept
opening and shutting his eyes over the glass of gin
and water by his side, as though, by his occasional
winks at Richard, he liked to hear him talk down
Mr. Simon, though, for his own part, he professed
to regard Simon, their occasional preacher, as "the
greatest scholar of the Club." " But it seems,
don't it, it's not riches only that ' pierce you through
with sorrows,' to look at the many as be pierced
through and through with 'em, as haven't got that to
say ?"

" Humph !" muttered Mr. Strong, in a tone that
might be interpreted either way.

" Richard," said Mr. Simon, almost in a mortified
voice, as if hurt to think it was necessary for him to
confirm what the Scriptures laid down with another

word from unworthy lips like his—" writes not St.
Paul also to Timothy thus?—' But they that will be
rich fall into temptation and a snare, and into many
foolish and hurtful lusts, which drown men in destruction and perdition."

"Humph!" repeated Mr. John Strong, as he
replaced the cold gin and water again at his elbow,
after taking a mouthful, and settled the back of his
head comfortably in his pocket-handkerchief for a
doze.

"Think of that, Richard!" exclaimed Mr. Box,
while replenishing his pipe. "Also of what the
Psalms say:—' For man walketh in a vain shadow,
and disquieteth himself in vain; he heapeth up
riches, and cannot tell who shall gather them.'"

"There's a hact!" ejaculated Mr. Strong, in his
sleep.

"Well, there's Miss Rachel, his daughter, isn't
there, anyhow, to take after him?" said Richard,
construing it literally. "Though they do say, some
of 'em, it's likely enough he'll cut her off with
nothing, if so be she won't marry to please him.
And may be it's what's fretting him into a shadow,
Mr. Simon?"

Puff—puff—puff.

"She's the extraordinarest girl! they say, is Miss
Rachel," went on Richard, with an eye to what he
had been told by his sweetheart, Susan, at The Priory.

"There's the young Squire at Buck Park head over ears in love with her, and what do you think she says?"

Mr. Simon cocked his ear.

"She'd rather beg her bread from door to door with the man she loved, than marry Percy Thornhill if it would make her a princess."

"Then, Richard," said Mr. Simon, solemnly, "it's my belief Mrs. Box didn't dream three nights running about that young chap, Alan Lambert, over in the West Indies, for nothing. Mark my words, Richard! something will happen ere long, as sure as that's a pipe in my hand. And twice last week, she says, there was a winding-sheet in the candle you couldn't blow off, blow as hard as you liked, and such a moaning in the chimney all night, she couldn't get a wink of sleep for it."

Richard changed colour.

"Didn't you mind, Richard, how that young Lambert, after he got Godfrey Forest's place at 'the works,' was never to be found no where else but at The Priory, when Miss Lyons was there?"

"Aye," nodded Richard, with a knowing wink; "and how they were always together out and about, after hours, like brother and sister. There's extraordinary! And she might be *my Lady* easy enough. Only the night before he left, they didn't get back to tea, Susan says, from old Molly's cottage, till it was dark; and then they both of 'em looked so odd-like, it put Miss Thornhill quite in a wax."

"Richard," said Mr. Box, with a depth of voice, while clearing his throat and nose of the smoke in them, that was almost sepulchral—"Richard, mark my words!—something will happen before long, Richard Coles—something nobody knows of now, not one of us—as sure, Richard, as that's a pewter-pot on the table!"

"Atrocious!" muttered Mr. John Strong, with a start—"cut their ears hoff—there's a hact!"

Which waking the burly tax-gatherer out of his doze, Mr. Box resumed his pipe. Seeing which, and that both Mr. Simon and Mr. Strong simultaneously sank into deep meditation on the entrance of Mr. Ephraim Sloper, their regular minister, for his little evening glass of cordials, wherewith to face the raw-blow off the water, Richard bethought him of his Susan, and leaving the friendly trio to their dish of gossip, hied him on love's wings to The Priory.

Mr. Sloper, though of grave deportment, as became his calling, was never without a sweet smile for his friends; and regarding Mr. John Strong and Mr. Simon Box as among his most esteemed ones, he was very pleased to meet them at *The Jackdaw* on the evening under notice, to unburthen his breast to them of something that was sorely perplexing him.

Mr. Box saw in a moment there was a weight on Mr. Ephraim Sloper's mind, by the way he put down his glass of stomachic bitters on the table beside him, without tasting it. And Simon was right.

Mr. Sloper nearly always prefaced any disagreeable intelligence he had to communicate with some scriptural or philosophical quotation, and he did so on the present occasion :—

" ' Brethren, if a man be overtaken in a fault, ye, which are spiritual, restore such an one in the spirit of meekness ; considering yourselves, lest ye also be tempted.' "

Mr. Strong emitted a low moan of acquiescence, while Mr. Box laid down his pipe, and muttering something in accordance, opened his great eyes and mouth with all due avidity for what was coming next.

" Can it be true, my friends," proceeded Mr. Sloper, after that little inward wrestling with himself which usually accompanied the sad conviction on his mind that true it certainly *was*—what he was going to say—however it grieved him to think it ; " can it be possible, what I hear of the young man, late a fellow-labourer with you at 'the works,' Alan Lambert by name ?"

It made Mr. Strong snatch up his oak-stick, and grasp it tight with both hands, and lean his whole weight on it; while, with those great eyes and mouth of his stretched to their utmost, Mr. Box should have been under the *camera*, if only to have quite satisfied him how greatly indebted those *cartes de visite* are, for the most part, to anything but your being *natural*, as silly people advise you to be, when taken, from the purest motives.

But not receiving any answer to his question, except such as amazed looks conveyed:—

"I pray to Heaven," continued Mr. Sloper, "there may be some mistake. We should be cautious how we give too ready an ear to even the praises of our fellow-creatures, much more so to those who hastily bring aught against them. Are not the eye and the tongue, my dear friends, chief members of our fleshly tabernacle, either for good or evil, according to the right or wrong uses we put them to? Then be ye not quick to see or speak but of that ye have ample testimony of, as faithful witnesses of the truth, and honest in all things."

Mr. Strong coughed, as if naturally impatient to be told "what any one could have to say against so irreproachable a young man as their late under-clerk at the works, who bore such a spotless character?"

"It is rumoured," said Mr. Sloper, sinking his

voice, from the apparent pain it gave him, "that there is a serious deficiency in Mr. Lambert's cash-accounts, now the books have been made-up by Enoch Fletcher and Mr. Appleby. I pray there may be no foundation for it. It is a back-biting world we live in, my dear friends. Offend not with your tongues, and put a bridle on your lips, that ye accuse no one falsely out of the hasty imaginations of your hearts. For what saith St. Paul:—'He is proud, knowing nothing ; but doting about questions and strifes of words, whereof cometh envy, strife, railings, evil surmisings.'"

Mr. Strong groaned. For being a functionary of the law, he blushed to think "how many got in for it, and how many got hoff, all through those quibbles and straw-splittings before their Worships and at Quarter Sessions, which was enough to make a constable hact any way but as he hought, who hadn't no conscience in his bosom, which a constable need have pretty hoften."

"It's a sad affair, very sad !" sighed Mr. Sloper, taking a sip of the bitters. " Implicitly trusted, too, by every one, as the young man, Lambert, always was."

"A most gross haggrivation that ! Mr. Sloper," said Mr. Strong, huskily.

"What's missing?" asked Mr. Box, with his eyes on the purple end of his own nose.

" More than two hundred, they say."

" There's a hact !" exclaimed Mr. Strong, with
bitter emphasis. " And with those lamb's looks
that you'd have thought as hinnocent as a babe's
hunborn ;" with which Mr. Strong rested his chin
on the knob of his oak-stick, and glared at Simon
Box in a manner any one would have supposed
Simon wouldn't have best liked, if his conscience
couldn't have stood it.

" There'll be a hinvestigation, won't there ?"
asked the town-constable, with his gaze still on
Simon's pimpled face, as if he had never seen it
before.

" It's going on now," gravely replied Mr. Sloper.

" No suspicion, eh ?" inquired Mr. Box, " against
any one else ?"

" Not that I have heard."

" Young Fletcher's all right ?"

" Young Enoch !" echoed Mr. Sloper, with a
fervent uplifting of his eyes and hands that shewed
the unspeakable joy he felt ! in the instant answer his
heart could give to it. " Heaven send ! my dear
friends, I had as much prayerful hope of every
other young Christian member of my beloved flock
as I have of him. Yes, yes ! we have built on a
firm rock there, or I greatly err ; have sown the
good seed on a soil full of fruitfulness. It is a
promising young tree. No fear ! It has taken

root where the strong winds may blow and beat against it, and the deep waters compass it round; but shall they shake that house which is built on the rock of ages, the rock for evermore ?   No, no !"

It relieved Mr. Box's breast of a heavy load, to judge by the heavings of his chest, as he listened in mute rapture to their preacher's words. For he, Simon Box, was young Enoch's godfather; and though he had confidently left the rearing of the youngster to his parents, still, he stood for him at his baptism, and would have been greatly shocked if Enoch had in any way brought disgrace on him, as his sponsor; aye, and spiritual teacher, too, extraordinary, failing Mr. Ephraim Sloper, their gifted principal.

But as Mr. John Strong could no longer repress the natural impatience he felt to know more of the particulars of this strange charge against so hitherto unimpeachable a person as Mr. Alan Lambert, Mr. Sloper drank up his bitter-cordial; and away went Mr. Box and Mr. Strong, arm-in-arm, to ' the works,' to find young Enoch, and tell him of the extremely handsome things Mr. Sloper had said of him.

Meanwhile "all to nothing the tidiest-looking young fellow," in Susan's estimation, "at ' the works,' whether with clean face or smutty," sat chatting the evening away with her up at The

Priory, by special permission of Lady Ada; who so far from expecting her servants not to have their sweethearts, like the rest of the world, *because they were servants,* positively encouraged Mr. Richard Coles to come, at fit and proper times, to see his Susan; yes, and make her his wife, too, with all convenient speed, though it robbed her ladyship of the best housemaid she ever had. Nor, by all accounts, cared Lady Ada a jot what Richard and Susan talked about in her kitchen, or when bidding their good-byes at the gate. Her Ladyship did nothing that she was ashamed of, out or at home; and if they liked to make her or her affairs the theme of their discourses, they were quite welcome to the good it would do them, if they told the truth; and if not, the loss lay entirely with themselves. She supposed that servant-girls were no less human flesh and blood, like their mistresses and large and little Misses, because they wore plain caps and aprons, and were not allowed flowers outside their bonnets, nor to be seen going up or down the front-stairs when there were back-ones. Wherefore, being flesh and blood like their betters, too many of them, and without education to teach them right, where they went wrong, her Ladyship concluded they must have sweethearts, and husbands, and homes of their own, as the natural consequence. Which was all the more reasonable, when, if they might not follow the examples of those above them, what bad examples they must be; how absurd, on the face of it, to look for more self-denial from the poor and ignorant of this world than the wealthy and wise.

So it may be imagined how comfortable Mr. Richard found it at The Priory, under Lady Ada's genial dispensation, with free leave to pay his fit and beseeming visits there, and make honest love to Susan as much as he pleased.

"Oh, Mr. Richard!" exclaimed Susan, as soon as she saw him that evening, "what is all this terrible to-do down town about Mr. Lambert?"

But as Richard had only just been told what had happened, as he crossed the fields to The Priory, he could give her no more information than she already possessed.

"You don't believe a word of it, do you, Richard?"

"It don't seem likely anyhow, does it?" he answered; but with so perturbed a brow that Susan turned pale.

"My Lady says it's the wickedest thing she ever heard of," said Susan, as soon as the colour returned to her face. "Just as if a good, kind-hearted, generous gentleman like Mr. Alan would stoop to such baseness!"

"Don't seem natural, does it, Susan?"

"It's the blackest baseness, Richard, ears ever

heard of. Two hundred pounds missing? A wonder they hadn't said five. There's nothing too bad they won't say. See how they went on with their bad-treatment and lies and malice before he left. Wasn't it enough to curdle the blood in your veins? They're evil-minded enough for anything."

"Who?"

"Those that should know better, Richard, than to be picking holes in other people's manners, when they can't see to mend their own. I've no patience!"

"Well, true, there be two or three queer ones among us," granted Richard, with evident regret.

"You never said a truer word than that, Richard. There are! And shall I tell you what's my opinion of this missing money? It's all got-up, as I tell my Lady, got-up, Richard, as sure as that's a fender! Can't you see why?"

But though Richard opened his eyes wide enough, it was clear to Susan that he was still in a fog; which, indeed, Richard was apt to be when asked to suddenly embrace all the facts of a case, not one of which but, if left to himself, he would have taken time to turn over and over before coming to any conclusion about it.

"Law, Richard, how dense of you!" cried Susan, with an intelligent sparkle of those bright brown

eyes of hers that fully made up, in his estimation, for
any want of acumen in his own. "Can't you see?
Got-up by—I shouldn't wonder a bit—that limb of
mischief, young Enoch Fletcher, out of spite and
revenge."

"Revenge!" echoed Richard. "What for?"

"For that night, don't you remember, he was
in the 'lock-up' for making a disturbance round
Mr. Lyons's house on the night of the ball? Aye,
and for something else, too, as likely as not."

Richard might well stare.

"Who's to know," went on Susan, after thinking
a moment, "what's in the crafty head of a sly,
slinking, hypocritical creature like that young Enoch,
who can't look you in the face when he speaks to
you, and whines through his nose so, it's quite painful? Do you suppose he hasn't heard that Mr.
Lambert may come back to Shiphampton, now
they're quiet again over there? Leave him alone
for that. There's nothing he's not up to."

Richard smiled.

"Then isn't it just what a limb of mischief like
him would do, to get this missing money, or anything else, up, that he thought would best help himself, to keep him in, I mean, where he is—getting a
pretty picking, by all accounts, one way or another?"

"He'd never be that base, would he?" demurred
Richard, doubtfully. "If the money's not been

taken, how could he prove it. It would come to nothing, then, wouldn't it?"

"Certainly not? Law, Richard! can't you see? It would bring suspicion on Mr. Lambert, wouldn't it?"

"Not if no one believed it, surely?"

"That wouldn't matter, Richard. You can't get pitch on you, can you, without its sticking to you? Very well, then, and so does suspicion."

"Not when you've washed your hands of it?"

"That take away the smell of it?" laughed Susan, at her lover's simplicity. "Get once sus- pected, Richard, and people's eyes on you, and their tongues at work—it's not one white-washing, nor two, nor three, Richard, will set you straight again; no, not if you were as spotless as driven snow."

Richard turned white. The bare thought of it— as Susan put it—thrilled through him with a force that almost took away his breath. Seeing which, Susan asked him if it were true what people said about Mr. Lyons's housekeeper, Faith Lincoln, being "jealous of Mr. Lyons's frequent visits at The Priory?"

"They do say so," replied Richard. "And what then?"

"Then it's like her temper," rejoined Susan, with a toss of the head; "which, by all accounts, is un- bearable at times."

May be," suggested Richard, "it's her African blood. Leastways, there's dark blood in them all there."

"At Greystone House? Yes, so I tell my lady. Can't you see it plain in the housekeeper? What eyes she's got! And so they have all, except Miss Rachel's, and hers are a heavenly blue, like her mother's. Yes, they say Faith Lincoln's in a terrible way about Mr. Lyons being so much up here of late."

"What odds is it to her?"

"Jealousy! nothing but jealousy! Richard—that green-eyed monster!"

"Because she thought to hook him for herself?"

"Nothing else."

"The cheek of that!" and Richard laughed out loud.

"Well, it's my opinion Richard"—and Susan sunk her voice—"if anything's to come of it between them, here, and at the Hall, the sooner the better."

"Oh, indeed!"

"They can't keep it up much longer there, as they're going on. Those racers of the Squire's are running them to ruin. Haven't you heard?"

"Nothing particular much, since I saw Jerry. It's all right, he says, about *Flower-of-the-Flock.* That would help 'em, wouldn't it?"

"Nonsense! Trust to that, and where will they be this day year? Shall I tell you who knows?"

"Him that finds the money?"

"Aye! aye! And somebody else, too, *there*"—pointing to the drawing-room—"who, if she would only say *yes* to him, as he wants her, might set them all on their legs again safer than ever."

"Oh! and won't she?"

"If she don't, Richard—God help them!"

"But won't she?" persisted Richard, paling at his own thoughts in connexion.

"Not if Faith Lincoln can help it."

"She can't, can she? He'll never dash them, and himself, too, will he, for her?"

"Well, they say she's got such a hold over him, he's like a child in her hands; unless it's when his blood's up, and then curb him who can. He's fearful! they say, when he's in a fury. Then, none of them can do anything with him, not even his own child. If ever"—again pointing to the drawing-room—"she's mistress of Greystone House, she'll have some tempers to deal with, Richard, you'll see! And she must be, Richard—must as sure as you're born—if ever Miss Rachel's to be brought to say *yes* to Mr. Percy. For they say she can't a-bear him! that she'd rather beg her bread from door to door, with the husband she loved, than marry Percy Thornhill, to be made a princess!"

"And I don't blame her," smiled Richard, while stealing his arm round the waist *he* loved best, preparatory to the good-night kiss; "don't blame her a bit, if she don't like him. It's what any plucky woman would do. It's what you would do, wouldn't you, Susan?"

"What, Richard?"

"Say *yes* to no man on earth—*but one*—when he asked you to give him the sweetest kisses you could, before saying good-bye?"

"Oh, for shame!"

"And then to fix the day, you know, as soon as he could manage it, for coming to the scratch—ch, Susan?—when he could have as many sweet ones as he liked, without asking?"

"Oh, you wicked man!"

"Good night—God bless you!"

Which, in due course, bringing us to Greystone House again, let us see, in the next chapter, what twelvemonths' development of the beautiful bud had done for lovely Rachel, 'The Rose of Shiphampton,' as Mr. Nestor Blythe and Miss Jane Rosse called her; and what chance there was, if any, of the young Squire of Buck Park ever calling the precious flower his own.

CHAPTER VII.

IF time had dealt by no means leniently with her
father, it had developed the beautiful young bud,
Rachel, his child, into a most beautiful flower. She
was, indeed, 'The Rose of The Broadway,' as people
called her; and well Angelo Lyons might be proud
of her, and, in her ripening charms, have little care
or concern for his own looks, when he gazed fondly
on hers, and saw the sensation they created wherever
she went.

And Rachel's captivations lay not only in her
lovely face and figure; she was very loveable as well
as lovely. She had a good heart as well as charming
form and features; and a mind, if overshadowed at
times by 'those strange yearnings,' as Lady Ada
called them, still so intrinsically right-principled,

and abounding in generous emotions, that even
Percy Thornhill, partial as he was to more gaiety and
fun and merriment in a woman, than fell to Rachel's
share, could not but compliment himself on his
choice of a " decidedly superior girl," for his bride-
elect, as he called her, to Clara and his mother,
when they sat in cabinet-council.

If Rachel were incomparably lovely in Alan Lambert's eyes, when he sailed for Trinidad, and the
beautiful bud had then but partly given promise of
what another summer would do for it, with what
feelings would he have contemplated her now, ex-
panding into riper womanhood, the delight of all
beholders, and given in wedlock, by universal rumour,
to his noble rival?

How thankful we ought to be that not only the
future of our hopes is hidden from us, in great mercy,
but, oftentimes, as much of the present, as, if
brought face to face with us, would oftener defeat
than help us. Wise were they who said—' Possess
ye your souls in peace,' and ' maintain the even tenor
of your way.' And how would it be possible to so
do, if the ' book of fate' lay open to us? or, if, at
every turn *yea* and *nay* were staring at us, and
tempting us, not necessarily to elect wisely, but,
rather, through our blindness and perversity, to
make choice of that which, had it not been mercifully denied us, would perhaps have been our ruin?

Though unseen, there is a goal to which we press on, because we hope to reach it, because we think we ought, and because, too, it may be now and eternally needful that we should so think and act. And though we never reach it, what then? No less must we press on. Have we no earthly mission, no appointed task to do, no everlasting end to attain, no divine law to fulfil? So, in great love, we are led on, blindfold, that we may go on, and not stop, when other work but our own must be done—His work, His will, His ways fulfilled, before we can attain to His end.

Could Alan Lambert have been the little bird, at Trinidad, he often longed to be, when he would have "given worlds to wing it across the broad waters and perch down within eye and ear reach of what was going on, in his absence, at Shiphampton and The Priory," how much nearer would it have brought him to the goal in view? The great ocean rolled between him and the idol of his heart; till sometimes he felt it was the impassable barrier to his ever beholding her again. And then if, like the bird that skimmed the billows, he had had wings to fly to her, and resolve the doubts that tortured him, notwithstanding how he trusted her, "Oh, how happy he would have been!"

It was not to be. So there was no help for it but for him to hope, and press on, and persevere,

" come what might," as he kept constantly saying
to himself, in the full belief that nothing *could*
come but what he prayed for—with such faith as he
had in himself, and her, and the urging Spirit that
worked within him. Alan's youthful ardour would
have found wings for itself to surmount all obstacles;
his heart sometimes sank at the thought of " how
cruel it was of fate to have severed him from the
only being on earth he loved, and who loved him."
And could he have done so, he would have flown
back as fast as wings could have carried him to
perhaps the certain downfall of his dearest hopes
and aspirations, because he would blindly see and
would hear what the present was doing for
him; as if it mattered one iota what intervened
between the longed-for object and His appointed
end—to bring us to which, a far better friend than
we supposed Him to be in Whom we put *such trust ;*
said *nay* to our every prayer to Him to crush us.

As it was, Alan had no alternative but to call to
mind, in moments of anxiety and vexation, "that
last evening at The Priory," and the solemn pledge
it gave him that, whatever other doubts or distrusts
he might have to deal with, least of all need he fear
that he would have to pay his respects, on his return,
to Lady Percy Thornhill, *née* Rachel Lyons, his
" own Rachel."

And was it not this same constant thought that

more than any other reconciled Rachel to her father's evident determination to so separate her from Alan, and Alan from her, as to remove the only obstacle he saw to her union with Percy Thornhill? Did it not support and console her under every trial? was it not the antidote to her every care? the secret charm that kept the brightness of her eyes undimmed, the native bloom unsullied on her cheeks, her brow without a cloud to hurt, in short, her heart so satisfied with and sure of its object? that well Lady Ada might wistfully watch her, and wonder "how it would end for them at Buck Park if her nephew Percy's tender hopes for himself were destined to disappointment?"

To render which "impossible," Percy took Clara's advice; and the month's "courtship in earnest," as he called it, that followed, while down at Buck, on leave, was an eventful episode in Percy's life, deserving of far more notice than can be now afforded it, considering who were the chief actors in the little thrilling home drama it gave rise to, and the important interests involved in the issue.

Clara Thornhill had had her eyes about her since Alan Lambert's departure for the West Indies. That event greatly relieved her mind; but it in no wise satisfied Clara that it would make the way to Rachel's heart any easier to her brother Percy. On

the contrary, she thought she knew enough of
Rachel Lyons to be sure that if 'absence made the
heart grow fonder,' that strange organ in Rachel's
breast would beat none the less for Alan, poor and
dependent as he was, because of the opportunity his
absence gave his rival to outshine him. Nevertheless, "Percy must try—Percy must do his best—
Percy had made great conquests—Percy was a
million times better-looking than Alan Lambert—
Percy was a born-gentleman—Percy was in the
Guards—Percy was next heir to the Baronetcy—
Percy was a Buck-Thornhill." And as nothing
more could be needed, in Clara's estimation, than
that, it was as well Rachel did not see the sumptuous
toss of the head Miss Clara gave the " bare idea of
a mere merchant's daughter being such a little fool
as to say anything but yes, if you please, and thank
you, too, if asked to do so by her brother,"—that is,
if it were true, as Lady Ada said, that Rachel
had an incontrollable way of laughing in people's
faces who said or did anything that highly amused
her.

Clara perfectly well saw what "an egregious little
fool Rachel Lyons would be to prefer being Mrs.
Alan Lambert, or Mrs. Any-one else, to being Mrs.
Percy Thornhill, and, in the natural course of things,
my Lady." But however palpable this was, it was
no less so that Rachel was " a strange girl, with

very singular notions, and a most determined will of
her own, where she set her heart on anything in
earnest." It was also evident that she scarcely
exhibited as much regret at the loss of her young
drawing-master and sketching companion, as was
consistent with her professions of esteem for him
while he was with her, and her "known regard for
him," if Clara's shrewd suspicions ;were correct.
From which Clara not illogically deduced that
Rachel was a vast deal fonder of him, and he of her,
than any one knew of but themselves, which was
the reason she bore the separation so well, because
of their mutual trust in each other and the comfort
it afforded them. In truth, if Rachel had any
design, by the cheerfulness with which she talked
of Mr. Alan's anticipated settlement in Trinidad, to
throw dust in Clara Thornhill's eyes, she rather
overdid it. For it set Clara thinking "why it was
she now seemed so satisfied with what, when it was
first mentioned to her, turned her pale and took
away her breath, so that for a little while she
sat like an image, as if unable to move or to speak."

Clearly, in this instance, Rachel was no diplomatist,
however "deep and dark" it pleased Clara to often
call her, when she could not make her out. Rachel
was neither. A more truthful, open-hearted girl
did not live than Rachel was with those she felt she
could trust; but Clara's pointed, penetrating,

persistent way always shut her up, and gave to her look and manner that "mysteriousness," as Clara called it, which kept them so ₍apart; though Clara would have been very angry with any one who had told her that, least of all Rachel's loving friends did Clara Thornhill understand her.

At all events, Clara was not far wrong in con- jecturing "how ninety-nine girls out of a hundred, in love with a man as Clara believed Rachel was with Alan Lambert when he went away, would have behaved when he was gone ?" And the reasonable suppositions it gave rise to in Clara's anxious breast for her listless brother, so opened her eyes to the necessity of rather more energy on his part, if he meant to make 'The Rose of Shiphampton' his own, to say nothing of the immense fortune she would bring him some day, that Percy got such a letter from her as really did affect him. For it touched his pride, it wounded his self-love, it fairly hit, and hit hard, the only part in him that was vulnerable ; under the smart of which, off he went post-haste for a month's "blaze-away" at the Buck pheasants and partridges ; and, this time, to "really and truly make love in downright earnest," he informed Clara, "for her comfort;" and assuredly a considerable relief to her it was. For affairs at home wore a serious aspect ; expenses went on ; creditors pressed ; and where were the funds to come from now, if their banker failed them? as fail he, certainly would but for his "great friendship for the family, and his laudable desire to give his daughter the noble name of Thornhill?"

"This is acting like my own dear, noble, bonnie, brave brother!" was Clara's ardent welcome, as they threw their arms round each other, on his arrival; in the certainty that "now he was there," and "in downright earnest," too, the deed determined on by him was as good as done. "So good-bye for ever to anybody and everybody else's insane hopes in that quarter, now a Thornhill was come; at the beckon of whose little finger alone what spinster in the county but would have been overwhelmed with joy! at the thought of what Sir Percy Thornhill, to be, had it in his gracious power to raise her to, and do for her, if such had been his will?

"Depend on it, Percy!" encouraged Clara, "Rachel only requires you to be yourself to her, to immediately accept you. You have never yet been what I call *yourself* to her. I mean, you have not even taken the pains you ought to have done—and which every woman demands from the man who seeks her in marriage—to do yourself justice in her eyes. All men must do that, my dear brother. It is a compliment to ourselves that we expect. Not but that we are quick enough to give your mighty Highnesses all conceivable merit due to you, and more; but you must take some pains for yourselves. Else, how are we to know you are sufficiently anxious about us, and in earnest?"

Percy gave deep attention, while eating his luncheon, to what his sister said.

"Earnest is the word, my dear Percy. It is wonderful what is done by it with us women. With patience, it has gained crowned Queens upon their thrones. My dear boy, shall I tell you what won't do at Greystone House, so don't try it?"

" What, Clarie?"

" You won't be angry?"

" You ninny!"

" That sublimely easy, indifferent manner you have—mind, I know it is high class—that exquisitely epicurean air of yours, which, if not understood—as how do you expect it can be in a commercial place like this?—would induce a belief that you are as elegantly apathetic as you seem, about what, in fact, but for your polished breeding, you feel every bit as anxious and agitated about as the coarsest nature among us."

" Good!" laughed Percy, with the glass of sherry to his lips—" your most obedient."

" You own it's true?" smiled Clara.

" It must be, if you say so."

" And you will be sure to bear it in mind, my

dear boy, when you see Rachel? I assure you, you must do so with her. She don't understand your high-class unexcitability. She takes it for want of earnestness. What do you think some one heard her say?"

"To my disparagement? Impossible to conjecture."

"That you never seemed in earnest but when you were in a rage; and not quite so then."

"Ha! ha! ha!" laughed Percy; "only then? By George! that's droll. I must pop the question in a storm, then? Thunder and lightning, eh? Ha! ha?"

"My dear boy, you must be in earnest with Rachel Lyons. It is your only chance."

Percy rather winced at this.

"You will never win her otherwise."

"You said I must be 'myself' just now."

"And I repeat it. Don't I know my own brother? Don't I happen to know what you were before you went in the Guards? Mind, I am not saying but that it has wonderfully improved you. Of course, it has! But that's not the question now. The question is, where are you when you are at Buck? Not in St. James's, or at Windsor?"

"That's clear."

"Well, then, being at Buck, and at The Priory, and at Greystone House—how then?"

" I must do as they do there, I suppose ?"

" Just so; if you really mean to do the business while you are down, on which, you know, Percy, as well as I can tell you, depends just this"—and, for a moment or two her lips trembled so she could hardly speak—" whether—"

" Oh, yes! I know—never mind about that—all right enough—don't fear," interrupted Percy, tossing off another bumper of wine, for luck's sake. " You shall see !"

" Oh, Percy !"

" Nonsense !"

" I wish I could so regard it."

" What !—about those mortgages ?"

" Yes; and much more besides those."

" My debts ?"

" Which press, don't they, as much as ours do here ?"

" What then, if I propose, and Rachel accepts me, and it has her father's consent? Won't that do ?"

" Very well! Only—"

" Croak! croak! croak! I'll tell you what, Clarie, you mustn't get into *that* habit. You have no idea how it plays the deuce with a woman's good looks, to be always whining and pining herself into shadows for nothing. It points the nose, and sours the eyes, and screws up the mouth, and wrinkles the skin, sooner than anything. See the Governor, how jolly he is—past—what's his age? Never mind. Supposing he gave way to the ' blues,' do you think he'd carry the face he does? There now—to shew you what nonsense it is to be always fidgeting yourself into fiddlestrings—hang me! if I couldn't have gone and thrown myself into eternity from the top of the Monument that morning before I got your letter to say how handsomely old Crassus had come down with the Three Thousand! Supposing I had done it, without waiting for the post to come in— you would have called me rather precipitate? Very well, then, please not to dash a fellow with your *ifs*, and *buts*, and *onlies ;* when, only have a little patience, and—I say, Clarie—by George! I'm in earnest, now—only let Rachel say *yes*, and shall I tell you what you shall have on your carriage-panels and the family plate, when it's my Lady Clara Chilvers says this, in May Fair, and my Lady Clara Chilvers does that—can't you guess?"

"Get along with your rubbish!"

"Rubbish? Hark you!"—and while what he whispered in her ear, as he kissed her, brought the colour to her cheeks :—"It's a fact!" he declared, with an earnestness that sent every drop of blood back again to her heart ; "he said it, as I hoped to be saved!"

"Who—Montagu Chilvers?"

"Yes, Montagu Chilvers, next heir, but one, to the Earldom—that—"

"Stuff and nonsense!" with her arm round his neck, and her hand on his mouth, but not so as to stop his tongue.

"That he 'hadn't seen such another splendid girl as Clara Thornhill since he danced with her in Belgrave Square; and if he had enough to make both ends meet, like a gentleman, he would run down, and never leave her till she made him the happiest or the most miserable of men.'"

It richly deserved a good hard pinch of each cheek, and Percy got them. But though her eyes sparkled, there were tears in them, and she sighed.

He took up his hat and gloves for a stroll, till dinner, through the stubbles and turnips; but she clung to his arm.

Percy, though somewhat self-willed and shallow, was not insensible to his sister's devoted love for him; and, for a moment, her upraised look of mingled admiration and anxiety, as she leant on his arm, as though it were now her main reliance, touched him keenly.

"What more could my pet of pets desire than such a brilliant future for herself and all of us?" he asked her, with fond smiles, as she walked with him to the courtyard, to join the keeper with the dogs and guns.

"Only one thing," she answered, keeping back all she could the tears from her eyes.

"Ah! that I will come to the scratch in good earnest with old Crassus?"

"With Rachel, you mean?"

"It's not one and the same thing, then? Think of the saucy independence of that! Oh, I must coax her over first, must I?"

"How else, Percy dear, are we all to be as happy as you speak of, and as you alone now can make us, if you will? But though she spoke so confidently, Percy was not so blindly self-sufficient but that he could see what paled her face, as she said it, and made her arm tremble in his, notwithstanding he was such a support to her. Aye, and presently afterwards sent him, with Ben, into the stubbles and turnips, so confused, what with one thought or another, that though the birds kept rising all round them, within range, not one could the young Squire bring down; which was enough to make Ben stare with surprise! knowing as he did what "a crack-shot Mr. Percy was both in field and in covert."

And, next day, Percy, having donned the easy undress suit he thought he looked best in, a dark mulberry tweed which Clara said "amazingly became him," walked into town to have a chat with Mr. Lyons, and show himself to Rachel, and, furthermore, transact to the best of his power the

all-important business he had come down for, and
meant to carry out with flying colours.

With his interview with Mr. Lyons we need concern ourselves no further than to record that it was
as gentlemanly and friendly a declaration of mutual
attachment and implicit trust and confidence, &c., &c.,
as ever took place between father-in-law and son-in-
law, elect, for sufficient reasons on both sides. They
were delighted with each other. And more than
once, when Percy recollected how he had called
" such a princely fellow," as he found him, ' old
Crassus,' and other facetious names, before he knew
what " a brick" he was, it pained him so, that he
felt quite small—small at the thought of " what he
himself then and there had of the current coin of
the realm in his pocket, or elsewhere, to shew
against the sort of cheque, payable at sight, " old
Crassus " could have drawn for Percy Thornhill, Esq.,
or order, on the *Old Bank* opposite, had it pleased
him to do it.

Maybe it was rather a snobbish notion of Percy's.
And very likely the consciousness in his own mind
that it was so, tended in some measure to enhance
the " placid dignity with which ' old Crassus' sat
and calmly listened to him and his London and
Windsor chit-chat," as Percy afterwards told Clara,
" with the air and manner of a monarch, rather than
of a merchant." So that when Percy rose to shake

hands, and go to Rachel and Miss Falconbridge in the boudoir, well he might take his seat on the ottoman near Rachel, like one duly accredited to her by no less a person than her father, and feel all the consequence and encouragement it gave him.

And so they were very merry together, and ran on with all sorts of gossip and fun and nonsense for a good half-hour, before Miss Falconbridge suddenly bethought her of something she wanted to tell Faith Lincoln. When, left alone, up came the colour into Percy's cheeks, and away it went from Rachel's; and for a minute or more they sat with their eyes on anything, seemingly, but what was most apparent to them, viz., the fact that the vital moment had come for that *yes* or *no*, on the issue of which hung far more than both of them liked to think of, if unpropitious to themselves.

"Had you good sport, shooting, yesterday?" asked Rachel, by way of breaking the awkward pause caused by Miss Falconbridge's departure, in the way she thought would best put the young squire at his ease.

"I did not touch a feather."

"How was that?"

"I'll be hanged if I know."

"Then it was from no skill of yours that papa got the brace of pheasants and leash of partridges this morning? Leash is the correct word, is it not?"

"Quite so! Yes, quite! No, indeed, I wasn't up to the mark at all. I don't know that I should have hit a barn door if I had tried. Fact, by George!"

"Perhaps you were tired after your journey down?"

"Not in the least; I never felt fresher; but somehow they all got away."

"What a good thing for them."

"Ha! ha! ha! Don't look at all bad, though, do they, hanging in the larder?"

"I dare say I shall greatly relish some of what you kindly sent Ben with to-day, when they are roasted," smiled Rachel. "Clara's a great sportswoman, is she not?"

"Another Diana! Which Rachel Lyons is not, I believe. But—but—that don't matter, does it?"

Rachel shook her head, with tightened lips, feeling, perhaps, inclined to laugh. When ensued another more awkward pause than the last; during which, after crushing his felt "wide-awake" hat up into a ball, Percy seemed to be trying to make up his mind not to sit "spoonying there any longer, but to out with what he had to say like a man," or, rather, as Clara had admonished him to bear in mind, "like the son of his father, in short, like Percy Thornhill." But though his breast heaved with all a Thornhill's heroism, not a word could he speak to the purpose. His tongue, which had been rattling on so valiantly with the father, was as if paralysed when it had to find words for—one would have thought—as simple and easy a question as man could put to a woman. The simplest mode of speech would have done for Rachel; high-flown addresses, or flatteries, or empty compliments were not at all in her way; so Percy had but to say what he had to say naturally and earnestly, and there would have been an end to it, as far as that went.

What tied his tongue? It could not have been because he thought he was distasteful to her, for it would have been contrary to the man himself for such a preposterous notion to have entered his head. Who was he? and who was she? Oh, no! Percy Thornhill never supposed that. Nor could it have been from any real fear of his power to "smash that confounded young upstart, Alan Lambert," with a word, however much thoughtless encourage· ment Rachel had good naturedly given him. For Clara had kept from him the worst she had heard; and even if he had known it, it would have gone into one ear, with Percy, and out at the other, for any doubt it would have occasioned him of his ability to crush the insolent insect that was stinging him, when it pleased him to stretch forth his hand and do it. Then what tied his lips? Was it that he had no love for Rachel, and so, when it "came to the scratch" with her, as he termed it, and the

word must be said that then and there did the deed
that made over the young Squire of Buck, and next
heir to the Baronetcy, to a "mere merchant's daughter," he bethought himself whether there was " any
hurry?" whether it wouldn't be better to be "quite
sure about money-matters first," before irrevocably
committing himself? Certainly this might have
occurred to Percy; but it was not what kept him
with his hat crushed up into a ball, and his eyes on
the "rum shape" he had squeezed it into, without
a word at command, when he was to have had
"something to tell Clara," when he got home,
that would have shown her "what Percy Thornhill
could do."

What had Clara whispered in his ear at the lodge-
gate, when he was mounting his horse to go and do
the deed that was to be the earthly salvation of them
all at Buck Park?

" Be in earnest with her."

It rang in his ears all the way into town, and
all the time he was in the dingy back room with his
(to be) father-in-law; though no one would have
thought so, to have heard him run on. And now it
unnerved him so, just when it ought, in sporting
phrase, to have been "the spur to carry him on and
safe over," that, but for the merest accident, a foot-
step overhead, there is no knowing what would
have been poor Clara's disappointment and chagrin

when he went back, empty, and told her what a muff he had been.

As it was, the possibility of Miss Falconbridge's speedy re-appearance saved the poor "wide-awake" from further mal-usage ; and looking up at Rachel with all the earnestness he could summon to his aid :—

" My dear Miss Lyons," he began, " you form a very erroneous opinion of Percy Thornhill if you think he is in earnest only when he is in a rage."

" Good gracious ! Mr. Thornhill," cried Rachel, reddening, " who has been so silly as to think it worth while to repeat to you what I must have laughed at while I said it, to have said it at all ?"

" Of course ! of course !" said Percy, visibly re-lieved, and with sparkling eyes. " I knew that very well. I don't of course mean to say but that there's many a wiser head than mine, and that it's likely enough you know it without my telling you ; but this I do mean to say, my dear Miss Lyons, there's no truer, nor warmer, nor stauncher heart than Percy Thornhill's, where it takes, and means to be so, and nothing else, whatever some may say of it who don't know."

" I am sure I have never heard to the contrary," simply rejoined Rachel, though evidently confused.

" Well, then," said Percy, after taking a deep breath, " you won't think any the worse of me for

one thing—and that is for telling you truly and
earnestly what I came here for this morning ?"

' She looked full at him.

" I came to ask you rather an important question
—important to yourself, I fondly hope, as well
as to me—I mean, if I thought otherwise—that is,
if it were not for your happiness as well as my own,
I would tear the tongue out of my head rather than
say another word to you about it;" with which
fixing his eyes on hers, he took another breath while
waiting to see what impression it had on her.

It blanched her face; till the heart, in return for
the sudden load laid on it, sent the blood back to her
cheeks and temples with an impetuosity that filled
him with renewed hopes, by reason of what he concluded such beauteous blushes signified in budding
woman :—

" I mean it, my dear Miss Lyons !" repeated
Percy, with increased emphasis, in conformity with
Clara's counsel ; " yes, that I would die sooner than
continue for another instant to hope even for the
greatest happiness that could happen to me on earth,
unless it insured yours also ?"

Rachel stared at him.

Percy saw he must be less round about and more
explicit. Evidently his earnestness was telling for
him, and now was the moment to " hit while the
iron was hot, and clinch the rivet." So, still with

his gaze on her, and modulating his not unmusical voice to its softest key, in harmony with the touching expression he threw into his eyes:—

"Need I tell you, dear Miss Rachel," he said, with a depth and decision of tone it was impossible she could misinterpret, "how long and how truly and ardently I have admired you as I never admired any other woman in my life; how from the first time we met, but one vision of perfect earthly joy has filled my heart; how sincerely I wish I was more worthy to offer you this hand, in pledge of how much I esteem, how much I love you! Yes, and—and—if you will be mine—if you will be Lady Thornhill, some day—how my life shall be devoted to make you the proudest and happiest wife, as I should be the proudest and happiest husband under the sun."

This was indeed "coming to the point" in good earnest; and for a moment or two neither of them seemed to exactly know what to do next. When the tread over-head giving warning again that in this life all we can depend on is the opportunity in hand:—

"Speak, Rachel! dearest Rachel!" entreated Percy, with as little doubt in his own mind what would be her answer, as that it was a Buck-Thornhill who put the question. "Will you be mine? Oh, yes, you will! You cannot have a doubt.

Your father gives his warmest sanction to our union; so do my father and mother; Clara would be heart-broken if I returned to her with any other than your consent to make us happy; and, for myself—how I love you, Rachel, and what I will do for you, if you will let me, actions will prove better than words.   Rachel!"

She averted not her eyes from him; though, in his ardour, he drew near her and would have clasped her hand in his, had she not avoided it by rising, as if to lay down the piece of silk embroidery she was working on the table.   But having by this little device obtained full command over herself:—

" You make me an offer of your hand in marriage, I believe, Mr. Thornhill, if I understand you rightly," she said to him, kindly, but firmly, and with so sweet a smile, that, might he have followed his own impulses, rather than Clara's counsel, he would have caught her to his breast and crushed every hope for ever.

So he only bowed in reply.

" I sincerely thank you, Mr. Percy, for such a flattering mark of your approval and preference," she continued, " which I shall ever think of with pride and pleasure ; though "—and her voice faltered a little—" scarcely with the gratitude, may be, that you think I ought to feel for so great a token of kindness and condescension on your pa t."

"Not of *love*, you think, Miss Rachel?"

"Oh, Mr. Thornhill, do not ask me that?"

"Why not?"

"I hardly know how to answer you. But can love spring from so short an acquaintance as ours? How often have we met? Till now have we ever conversed on any but the commonest topics? We have never before exchanged a mutual thought, perhaps, or real sympathy? So how talk of love? You do not even know me; nor I you. How can you love me, if you have yet to learn my disposition? You know nothing of it. It might alter you if you did. I think it would. But I sincerely thank you, Mr. Thornhill, all the same; indeed I do!"

"Is that all, Miss Rachel?" and there was such genuine grief and mortification in the tone in which it was said, that more than ever was Rachel resolved to so frame her present replies, that, while she promised nothing, she would so far yield a daughterly obedience to her father's wishes as not to act counter to them, if, with time, she saw reason to embrace them.

"Is that all the hope I may take home with me?" asked Percy, sadly.

"I think it is as much as you could fairly wish me to give you," replied Rachel, looking towards the clock on the mantle-piece, as the footsteps above grew louder.

"You do not refuse me, then?"

" I say only, that, as there can be no love between us, any further present mention of it by either of us would be foolish."

" Which encourages me to rely on what a better knowledge of each other may obtain for me in your estimation ere long?"

" Anyhow, Mr. Thornhill"—and for the first time she did not care to encounter his eyes, by the way she dropped hers, as she spoke—" I should prefer to be two or three years older than I am, before I thought of doing anything that would take me from home—from my dear father, whose health is much broken, and causes me great concern."

" Ah, Miss Lyons!" said Percy, as he agitatedly moved towards the door; " would you have said the same to *some one else,* if he had made you the offer of his hand and heart as I have just done?" and the imperial look he gave her was, as she afterwards told Jane Rosse, her bosom-friend, " the only genuine touch of real feeling she had ever seen in a Thornhill. And why? Because of wounded pride, and of the impossibility of his adding, with any grace, ' I am a Buck-Thornhill, Miss Lyons; and you would have been my Lady Thornhill, Miss Lyons ; no little, Miss Lyons, I imagine, to weigh against your money.'"

Percy stood at the door, as if hardly conscious of where he was, or what he was doing. He looked dumbfounded. Not small. That was impossible for a Thornbill. They never looked small, for they never felt so. There was that wonderful self-sustaining power within them, which kept them up, and going gallantly on, come what might to defeat them. But Percy had been cautioned by Clara that Rachel had a peculiar way of laughing at those who plumed themselves on their blood and birthright, "as if they came from any other first parents than her own." So he merely threw out what he thought would be a clincher for that "up-start under-clerk of theirs," Alan Lambert, in case he had anything to do with her dutiful desire to stick to home for two or three years to come, as she prettily put it, out of love for her father.

Rachel distinctly heard what he said, and understood it, too, though it suited her to stare at him, as if to comprehend his meaning. Then, as if sorry to see him so crest-fallen all about one who so little deserved it :—

"I would have said the same to the person you speak of, or to any other," she smilingly replied, "who had asked me what you have so kindly done, Mr. Percy, had we known no more of each other than you and I do. Personally, I can have but one feeling towards you"—offering him her hand— "and every member of your family. And when you tell Clara what I say, make it clear to her, won't you, how proud and pleased I am to know you think so well of me, and would make me such a fine, grand body; but that, however desperately in love I was with any one, I must remain Rachel Lyons, till—oh, it is impossible, Mr. Percy, to say when— till my dear father—"

"Give his consent," interrupted Percy, with a bitter smile, as he let fall her hand, "to your accepting some one else? If so, my dear Miss Lyons, I may still indulge a hope that my petition, though in vain to-day, may have better luck to come, if all we hear of that favoured person be true."

"Favoured person! Mr. Thornhill? What do you mean?"

"Nay, Miss Lyons, if it be so, all I can say is he will be fortunate if you have no reason to think less highly of him than you do now."

"Of him—of Mr. Alan Lambert, do you mean— my father's confidential agent now in Trinidad?"

"You anticipate my meaning."

"I do. And why should I not? Yes, why? You allude to the atrocious charge of embezzlement made against him by some wicked persons at 'the works?'"—and the curl of the lip that accompanied the look of scorn she gave the bare idea of it, was so like her father's, when his blood was up, but under stern control, that Percy felt for the moment almost

11—2

a sense of relief in the thought, as he gazed at her, that, by her own resolve, he had yet some time before him before he "booked himself for good."

"No one will be more rejoiced than myself," said Percy, loftily, "when these shocking accusations are disproved. They are most disgraceful."

"They are," said Rachel calmly, but with a face like marble, "alike to their zealous believers as well as their inventors. Letters are on their way out to Mr. Lambert. We shall soon see."

"If they bring him back?" rejoined Percy, carelessly. "Perhaps they may."

"Not at all unlikely," agreed Rachel, with perfect command over herself.

"They *must*, I should think," said Percy, narrowly scanning her.

"Of course they will," returned Rachel, with a placid smile, "if the public establishment of his innocence require it."

"In which of course you believe, Miss Lyons?"

"As firmly and sacredly, Mr. Thornhill, as I do that there is a just God above us, however we may appear to question it sometimes."

Pondering on which, and much else of moment in anxious connection therewith, the young Squire rode l ack slowly to Buck, as grave as a judge. So grave, that when Clara saw him coming up the drive, "an instinctive presentiment," to use her own words, " came over her, that there was more trouble in store for them — trouble, trouble — nothing but trouble—Oh, God ! what would be the end of it ?"

CHAPTER VIII.

IN WHICH AUNT ADA IS FOUND TO BE A PERSON OF NO LITTLE CONSEQUENCE AT BUCK PARK.

RACHEL's rejection of Percy Thornhill was a stunning blow to them at Buck Park. Sir Compton heard of it with raised eye-brows, and that peculiar little shrill whistle of his which usually denoted one of two things with him—either that he "didn't believe a word of it," or that he did, and "what an infernal mess it was to be in!" In the present instance it partook of both disbelief and dismay. The poor "old boy," as his hunting friends called him, sat all of a heap in his chair, tapping the upraised toes of his boots with his stick, and emitting that little whistle, while Lady Thornhill made it as palatably clear as she could to him what had happened—how "Mr. Lyons had behaved in the handsomest way to Percy, their first-born, and next heir to the baronetcy; but how his daughter, Rachel, had thought proper to give herself great airs; to the extent of telling Percy, in return for his splendid offer of marriage, that 'as there could be no love between them, from their little knowledge of each other, she could give him no other promise than that she would prefer to remain at home for two or three years longer before she bestowed herself in marriage on any man.' "

" Two or three years—two or three years, eh ?" the Squire kept musingly repeating to himself, as his loving Lady went on with her account of Percy's " noble generosity," and its strange reward. " Two or three years ! By when, eh—who's to know— what may befall—what may happen, eh—something will, of course—always does—sure—sure—said that, did she ?—two or three years !"—and as if fairly at fault, the " old boy " drew himself up and sat back in his chair, as upright, and with his chest out, as when he was thirty. But it wouldn't do. His pride gave way—he closed his eyes, as though, by the sigh after sigh that escaped him, to shut out what was floating before them—till, muttering " what's to become of us now, if *Flower-of-the-Flock* cheat me, too,"—his chin dropped—nature asserted her rights—and he slept.

There was trouble, and perplexity of mind, and anxious faces from heavy hearts at Buck Park. The Squire woke from his sleep in his chair with so great a numbness of one leg and arm, that he was "sure he was going to have a fit of the gout." He had had several touches of it before then; but this numbness was a new feature, and brought Doctor Bruce to his bedside next day. Whereupon it was soon in every one's mouth that the Squire was "laid up again with the gout." True, Sir Compton was laid up, but not now with "the old enemy;" though the Doctor, when asked about it, deemed it best to let them all have it their own way, and call it "gout," or the "rheumatics," or "lumbago," or "because of his getting in years." What mattered it, so that he himself, Doctor Bruce, knew why the "fine old boy" was laid on his back, and what was the cause of it, and what would cure him best, and dry the affectionate tears that were being shed for him down stairs.

No, it was not the gout this time that brought the Doctor's carriage every day to Buck Park for many more visits and consultations than any former illness of the Squire's had called him there for. It was, simply, from a shock to the nervous system that Sir Compton was then suffering, as the Doctor explained to Lady Thornhill and Percy and Clara, "caused by divers other disagreeables he had had to manfully contend with of late, besides this last blow to his pride at the innocent hands of Miss Rachel. Quiet of mind was indispensable to his

recovery, if recover he did; but with that, and,
haply, a turn of the tide in his favour, he was heart-
of-oak still at the core, and possibly might live till
the grey hairs began to think of peeping here and
there even out of Miss Clara's bonnie brown hair,
before he went the way of all flesh."

With her beloved husband to principally think
for and look after, Lady Thornhill had the less time
to devote to her own ills and ailments; the consequence of which was, she found solace even in that
wherein some of her sympathizing friends feared for
her most. " For every creature of God is good, and
nothing to be refused, if it be received with thanksgiving." Laying which to heart, there was cause
for rejoicing even in this fresh affliction of the sick
pillow she sat by night and day, to the exclusion of
those other crushing cares, as they seemed, but
which were, as well as this present pressing one,
causes for great joy and gratitude, if meekly received,
and with that thankfulness which, "with prayer,
sanctifies all these His dispensations for our use
and behoof."

And there is no cant nor sermonizing in this,
honest reader, not one word of it but what the
novelist may put down, if so it please him, in his
novel, and you may read therein, if you will, without
loss; however some silly, hypercritical folks may tell
you "it is out of place to write of holy truths in

fiction." Give no heed to such doctrine. No error can be greater. It is nowhere out of place, where we meet the Creator face to face in His works—and where do we not so meet him ?—to hail Him, whoever and whatever we are, with all our hearts and souls, and praise and glorify Him. It is nowhere inconsistent or out of character, whether in God-fearing verse or prose, or fiction or fable, for the pen to do honour to The Great Power from which it derives any skill or ability, while amusing you, dear reader, wherewith to acknowledge the Mighty Master Hand in all and through all; careless for aught but how best, in the fulfilment of the given task, to speak His praises and proclaim His incalculable mercy and goodness wherever it can. Tells the molehill of its Great Maker any less than the mountain ? Then, though the author of this homely story neither writes history, nor of the lives of great men and women, nor on the wonders of science and art, nay, not even "artistically," may be, in his own humble way—surely he is as good as a butterfly on the wing, to speak of Him who made him, and in Whom he rejoices ? And, thus thinking, he will so take leave to speak to the best of his poor power, whenever and wherever he can, in discharge of some part of the precious debt due to himself.

Poor Clara ! What she felt when Percy told her of the result of his interview with Rachel, none knew but herself. For, though proud, she was generous, and loved her elegant dashing brother with an affection that, while it did not altogether blind her to his faults, shrank so from seeing him cast down, that of course it was to Clara he went in trouble, which made it no easy matter for her to preserve the golden medium between feeling and duty.

What was to be done now?

" I will never demean myself so again !" exclaimed Percy, bitterly. " I could kick myself when I think of it. The insufferable assurance of telling me to my face—or what was the same thing—that I had no love for her. What did she mean by that ?"

" Nothing, my dear brother, worth your fretting about. Merely her strange way of talking."

" No, no !" cried Percy, as he stamped up and down the library, " that won't do—won't do at any price. She meant—shall I tell you what ?"

" Oh, my dear Percy ! don't, don't vex yourself any more about it."

" I must—I can't help it. Do you suppose I'm to be told to my face that I'm mercenary, that I came there, not from any love for her, but only for her money ? Stand that, can I ?"

" You misunderstood her ; you did indeed, Percy ; she never dreamt of any such thing."

" What— haven't I eyes and ears ? Am I blind and deaf ? Am I such a fool that I can't credit my own senses? Then, again, the cunning of putting it off for two or three years, till she's older—isn't it as plain as a pike-staff what's at the bottom of that?"

"She is so blunt and *gauche*," sighed Clara, at the sight of her brother's pained brow. "You took her by surprise, perhaps, and she knew not what else to say."

"Didn't she? There I differ with you, Clarie, differ *in toto*. Not know what to say? Not Rachel Lyons? Whose child is she? All bosh! Don't talk such rubbish."

"Whether or no, Percy, it won't help us any, your putting yourself into these fevers? If Rachel cares for you—as of course she does and must, naturally enough—it will end all right when her father talks to her; and if she don't—which is ridiculous to think of—why then"—with another deeper sigh than the last—"all I can say is she is not worth another thought, not she!"

"It's all very well to say that, Clarie; but—who's to stand waiting her time? Two or three years—there's cheek! Submit, will I, by Jove! to any nonsense of that sort from *them?* You'll see! Who are they? Disgusting! I call it, for a Buck-Thornhill to knuckle under to any man."

"But you don't, my dear brother; you never did, and you never will; it never was so said of a Thornhill of Buck, and it never shall be!"

It calmed him a little; and he lay down on a settee by her side, that she might put her fingers through his curly hair, which always soothed him.

"Percy, dear," she said, after a mutual brown study, while she made him a fresh 'brutus' to her liking.

He heaved a deep breath.

"I won't believe," she went on, "but that Rachel was taken a little by surprise, and will give in when her father speaks to her."

"No such luck, Clarie."

"Have patience, Percy. Even if she liked Alan Lambert, of what good would it be if it hadn't her father's consent? Is it likely he would give her to him? Never! And if not, would Rachel disobey her father? All she has of her own is about Two Hundred a-year that came to her from her mother. Do you think for one moment she would forfeit all his immense wealth for the sake of a pauper dependent like Alan Lambert?"

"Yes, if it went with the whim."

"Stuff and nonsense! She is flesh and blood of Angelo Lyons, is she not?"

"Which is why I say she would do it, if she chose. You should have seen the curl of her lip when she was taking his part about that missing money. Hang me, then! if I didn't feel half glad I wasn't booked. It was her father's look exactly,

when you might take your oath he meant to have
his own way all the time he was giving you yours.
Entre nous, Clarie, there's a look about that gold-
making father of hers the most peculiar I ever saw,
when your eyes are not on him, and his jaw falls,
and he's thinking. Only fancy, if he hadn't a
shilling—how we should love him !"

"But he has, my dear boy. Many more than
one. I only wish you and I had half as many."

"Well, but you really have a notion, eh, Clarie,
that Rachel will listen to reason when her father
talks to her about it ?"

"I think I know, Percy dear, what would wonderfully help us."

"Eh—do you—what ?"

"If Aunt Ada would have him."

"Angelo Lyons ? By George ! yes, you're right,
Clarie ;" and the force of it instantly brought Percy
on his legs again ; and away he went up and down
the room, as if out of his wits with delight.

"On condition," proceeded Clara, with measured
words, as if they were too precious to be lightly
uttered—"on condition, don't you see, Percy, that,
first of all, Rachel said *yes* to her nephew, when his
loving aunt would graciously say the same to her
father. Whereby you will observe, Percy dear,
there might be two fashionable weddings in one
family on the same day, and dear Rachel would not

only then have a husband, but the second mother she so often says is the image in many respects of her first."

Percy—great, tall Life-Guardsman as he was—literally jumped for joy! like a great boy. And when his father was asleep, and he could get his mother all to himself for an hour, he put her in possession of "the sanguine hopes" he still had, from what Clara had said, that the speedy union of the two families might be brought about, which would put an end to their troubles.

Comfort, from whatever source it may come, or however speculative and problematical it may be, is pleasant hearing in times of emergency, when even a straw to catch at is better than nothing, and forlorn hopes are hugged to the bosom as best friends.

It did indeed seem feasible enough, as Clara suggested, that "if Aunt Ada would be Rachel's mother-in-law, who would have such influence with her as she would?" And the more Percy and his mother talked it over, and put it in all its lights, the clearer it became to them that "the sooner Aunt Ada was sounded, as to her feelings thereon, the better."

"You see, my dearest mother," said Percy, "what a brilliant thing it would be for my aunt, to be mistress of such wealth as Angelo Lyons's! And it isn't as if he came from a wrong stock.

There's good blood in the Lyons's. Old Nathan, of
Market Street, knew his father, when he was at the
Hague and in Italy, picture hunting, and says he
was a most gentlemanly man. Anyhow, if my
aunt stooped a little to have him, Angelo Lyons is a
princely fellow with his money; and keep him up
to what Basil Horne, of Barbadoes, says he would
do for her if she would have him—by Jove! talk of
giving her a coach of gold to ride in, what's that,
by George! to what she would have if she were
Queen of Diamonds at Greystone House? Don't
you see, my dear mother, how it would be the
making of my aunt, with the pittance she has to live
on, for a woman of her rank and position?"

"Which would scarcely be improved, she might
think," demurred Lady Thornhill, drawing herself
up, "by such an alliance. Ada Chilvers is proud,
and looks high, as the Belmores always did, as well
as the Thornhills."

"Yes, my dearest mother, that's all right enough;
but I can see nothing *infra dig.* in Aunt Ada marrying the father, if it's not so for me to marry his
daughter."

Which making his mother wink, and her cheeks flush
at so fair a way of putting it, Percy kissed away the
little confusion she was evidently in, to quite reconcile
it to her mind, whether, being both a Belmore and a
Thornhill, she ought to stand out rather more than

she was doing, for conscience-sake, or give in with the best grace she might, as there really appeared to be no alternative.

"I'll tell you what it is, my dearest mother," coaxed Percy, with her hand in his, and putting the diamond and ruby and pearl and emerald rings on her taper fingers in the way he most liked to look at them—"times are not what they used to be. By George! you must have something more than a great handle to your name now a days. It's not 'what have you got?' now, I can tell you, but 'what are you?' Blood's a splendid thing, of itself, and beats all the rest hollow; but you see there's not that class-exclusiveness that there used to be in your day and my father's."

"It seems so, indeed!" sighed his mother.

"When I said _your_ day, mother dearest," with a contrite look up at her, "of course I meant long before yours, come to the truth of it. For, pos! I can see no difference in you—and that's as true as I'm sitting here—ever since I was a boy, and used to tell the fellows at Eton what a splendid woman my mother was! and how she might have been a duchess if she had liked—and you know it's true, too."

"Silly boy, silly!"

"Then, I say, my dear mother, you will, won't you?"

"What?"

"Have it over with Aunt Ada when she comes to-morrow?"

"Not as easy a matter, Percy, as you seem to think. Your Aunt Ada sees with her own eyes, no woman better; and will do so now, I daresay, in preference to mine or any one else's."

"Still, you may sound her a bit, and see how she takes it? It's all nonsense for her to pretend to be indifferent to old Crassus's tender attentions—that's all bosh! She rather admires him."

"My dear boy, what language! You must not speak so. It is most unpatrician, Percy. You never hear your dear father do it"—and the recollection of who that father was, and what he was, and where he was, was too much for the pent-in flood, and, giving way, Adelaide Thornhill burst into tears.

Percy loved his mother tenderly—how tenderly he thoroughly knew at that moment, when, putting his arm round her, he felt the throbbings of her heart, every one of which was as if to tell him 'who she, too, was, and what she was, and where she would inevitably be before that day twelvemonth, if the dark cloud then over them did not pass away— in short, if it pleased Heaven to bring them, for their extravagances, to ruin.'

"My own dearest, best of mothers," whispered Percy, with his lips to her cheek, "I feel sure—I never felt surer of anything in my life—that when Aunt Ada sees the enormous consequences to us all of her accepting Mr. Lyons's noble proposals, she will not refuse him. She has the tenderest regard for my father, and must see how he is suffering from anxiety of mind more than anything else, and how ill and care-worn you are, how unhappy we all are. And do you think, with the power aunt has to put things straight, she won't help us all she can? Of course she will. It would be contrary to nature not to do it. Then, don't you see, my dear mother, how happy we should be? Of course Aunt Ada would make her acceptance of Mr. Lyons contingent on Rachel's acceptance of me; which she could do very well; for, recollect, Rachel did not refuse me, but only wished not to leave her father, which was natural enough. Else, of course, had she rejected me"—and Percy's eyes shot fire at the bare thought of it—"there would have been an end of it. But I take it, my dear mother, Rachel Lyons—mighty little Miss as she is, in pounds, shillings, and pence —knows better than that a good deal."

When an upstairs bell recalling Lady Thornhill to her sick-room duties :—

"I will try and have a talk with your aunt about matters, if I can, next time I see her," she promised, as Percy walked with her to see his father. "I can but hear what she thinks of it. She has a

12—2

kind heart, has Ada Chilvers, though you wouldn't think so always, when we try for the upper hand together, because Adelaide is the elder, and Ada married a Lord. But it's in the family—in both of us—in all of us—here, as well as there."

" What, mother ?"

" *You* to ask such a question ! Too much pride by half. Ah, me! what ruinous sums many will give for the experience that robs them of every shilling, who would look on both sides of a sixpence before parting with it, though it would make them as wise as Solomon, and purchase them the peace of the Saints."

Percy's grave looks, in reply, said "very true" to this remark of his mother's; but, whether he fully appreciated the force and meaning of it, as applicable to themselves, there is no saying for certain. He dutifully listened to the good words, as they fell from her lips; and then drawing a chair to his father's bedside, no son, in the pressing hour of affliction, could have manifested more heartfelt sorrow for it, or seeming determination to lay the lesson it taught to heart, and profit by it, when it was over, than Percy Thornhill.

Sir Compton was sorely beset. Debts and duns are hard to deal with, without the ' one thing needful ' in such cases ; but when, in addition to them, comes illness, and the break-up of the nervous

powers wherewithal to go on with the battle, and
fight it out, then find the stoutest and strongest
what that wonderful *nerve* in them has done, when
it can do no more. The poor old Squire—literally
poor now in everything but his unflinching integrity
of *intention* towards all men—lay on his back, help-
less. His purse had money in it, his mind was
healthier, perhaps, than it had ever been in his life
before—if his constant mutterings about "what an
egregious fool" he had been, might be taken as any
test,—but, when his right arm wanted to be shewing
Lady Thornhill and his children what valiant things
he yet meant to achieve before his last sands had
run through, and the only chance of reparation for
past errors was gone for ever—it all but fell powerless on the quilt. It would have been inexcusable
of the Doctor, had he disguised the fact from his
family and friends that the 'fine old boy' had so far
succumbed to circumstances as to have partially
surrendered the loss of nearly the whole of one side
to the stern calls made on his moral manhood.
The body had yielded to the mind. It lay like a
fine old oak struck at last by the storms it had
weathered so long; and, though but the wreck of
its former self, with all its greenness still about
it, and only wanting the power to right itself again
in the old soil, to flourish as well as ever.

Poor Lady Thornhill! The 'fine old tree' was

prostrate; and she could only think of it now as of
what it used to be when it was the universal pride
and joy of every eye and heart, and had no rival at
Buck for beauty and nobility. But, in its decline,
was its greatest grandeur for her; its most touching
glory lay in its fall; it never was so worthy of loving
admiration and honour as now. And so Percy also
thought, notwithstanding his heedlessness. For
was he not a Thornhill? And when did Clara's
eyes, too, sparkle more, and her proud, handsome
nostrils expand to fuller extent, than when she
heard her beloved brother called "a chip of the old
block," and "his father all over?"

The Doctor did all that doctor could for his
"fine old patient;" but it was beyond the art of
man to restore its wonted vitality to the hand which,
when it would have gladly clasped the sorrowing
son's that grasped it, lay in his warm clutch cold
and motionless. It was more than Percy could, at
first, realize. He had heard of paralysis, and
thought he knew what it meant, and how exceedingly distressing it must be to lose the use of
one's limbs; but, hitherto, when Percy grasped his
father's hand, he felt the life-blood of his sire instantly mingle with his own; by which he feared for
nothing for him, but that he might possibly be
"shorter of ready money than Sir Compton Thornhill ought to be," which, indeed, was Percy's only

trouble. Now, whether his father had his pockets full of gold, or not a halfpenny in them, what mattered it to Percy, so that he might feel that honoured old hand move in his again, and grow warm, and give joyful promise of again being the same open, honest, heartfelt, generous, gentlemanly hand it had ever been to every one who knew him.

Ah, is it not the lost sheep that the shepherd is most anxious about, when, to recover it, he regards all else, in his own thought for the missing one, as comparatively nothing worth his caring for? If Percy could but have felt his father's hand warmly respond to his, as of yore, what would all the wealth of the world have been worth to him in comparison?" And, perhaps, his father read his thoughts, and that was the reason why he turned his face away, to hide the tears in his eyes. But, if so, it was only to let his mother, who sat on the other side of his bed, see them the better—see what his heart was saying to itself it would willingly give for that palsied hand of his, in his child's grasp, to be able to begin life again; and, then, "oh, what was there that it would *not* do, that it would *not* be tempted by, that it would *not* be the senseless slave to, for the true joys that would flow from prudence and forethought?"

And what was Clara's heart fullest of, while she kept the Doctor from hurrying off to his other patients with her anxious questions, till he would give her one word in answer to them, on which she might build till she saw him again? Clara's whole thoughts were on Aunt Ada, and "whether she would accept Mr. Lyons, who only wanted the slightest encouragement from her, to make her mistress of all he possessed? If so, it would do more for her sick father—troubled as he was about money-matters—than all the Doctors; which she knew was Doctor Bruce's opinion, though, of course, he could not exactly say so."

And when Lady Ada's next day's sisterly solicitude for her troubled relatives at the Hall brought her face to face with the stern facts of the case, and she heard from Doctor Bruce what fears he had for his prostrate patient, and "how indispensable a mind at ease was to his recovery"—then, of her own accord, Ada Chilvers shut herself up with Adelaide Thornhill for an hour or more in Sir Compton's dressing-room, to talk about something that deeply concerned herself as well as them.

" Yes, my love," went on Ada, after breaking the ice, in her own semi-serious, semi-smiling way, of what she had to tell her sister; " it is as I foresaw—Mr. Lyons was at The Priory last night, and made me an offer of marriage, with such splendid settlements, my dear, if I will accept him, as may well dazzle if not induce me to think twice before I reject so sure a means, I don't doubt, dear, of effectually helping you all, and myself, too, into—what was it Mr. Basil Horne, of Barbadoes, said I should ride in if I would have him ?"

" A carriage of gold !" and Adelaide clasped her hands tight in her lap. " Oh, and Mr. Lyons will give you—what ?"

" Two gold carriages, he says, love—double, treble, he declares, my dear, to what any one else on earth will give me, if I will be his wife."

Adelaide Thornhill's lips turned ashy pale, so that, though she tried hard to pronounce the words of congratulation that trembled on them, not a syllable could she pronounce, and Ada had to anticipate her :—

" I know what it is you want to say, my dear sister, but will not. The same as I had on my lips when Mr. Lyons entreated me to answer him. Are we not sisters, Adelaide ? Are we not both of us Belmores ? Are you not a Thornhill also ? and am I not a Chilvers ? So now, my love, candidly, what's to be done ? for every right sense of politeness and gratitude demand from me *yea* or *nay*, you see, with two gold carriages at my disposal stopping the way, and which I must be pleased either to accept or decline."

" Who more competent to decide it, and decide wisely," returned Adelaide, as cheerfully as she could speak, " than yourself?"

"Still," smiled Ada, "what would Adelaide, the elder, say to Ada, the younger, if she did so decide, without first coming to my Lady Thornhill?"

"Ah," laughed Adelaide, with swimming eyes, "and what would Ada, the younger, say to Adelaide, the elder, if—a Thornhill though Adelaide be—she were to presume to dictate to a Chilvers? What— a poor my Lady Adelaide, who, if every one had their own, can't say to a certainty whether this day six months she may be lawfully worth a wheel-barrow, to venture to compete any longer with a grand my Lady Ada, with two gold coaches to ride in whenever she likes? Oh, no! no! Ada must tell Adelaide now, not Adelaide Ada, what she must do, and Adelaide will be all obedience, as in duty bound." But though she struggled hard to say it so valiantly, what must the 'grand my Lady Ada,' with the 'two gold coaches' of her own, do—as soon as she saw herself in undisputed possession—but, throwing herself into her sister's arms, clasp her to her breast in a way so excessively unusual for any one to do, who had any sort of fine carriages of their own, that well they might both of them taste a mutual joy in that mutual embrace which they had never tasted before, full as both of them were with the sufficient means thereunto to heart-bursting.

And when the tear-minglings were dried away with kisses; and the cabinet counsel that forthwith

ensued was over; and the sister-hearts took their
seats by the sick bed-side, with beaming looks never
seen in mortal faces but when they are heralds of
glad things,—the poor ill-at-ease Squire, on his back,
and grievously assailed from without and within,
forgot how it was with his nerveless right hand:
till, determined not to be beaten, he raised his left
from out the bed-clothes, brushed a tear with it from
his cheek, smiled, as if grateful that he still had
that to trust to, and holding a hand of each of them
grasped in it till he fell asleep :—

"Yes," said Ada to Adelaide, with the good-
night kiss, "it shall be as I told you, love. I will
have my ' gold coaches,' please Heaven! And then
it will be hard indeed, dearest, if Adelaide Thornhill
need put down her 'wheelbarrow,' if it please her
to keep it."

CHAPTER IX.

IN WHICH, THOUGH 'TURNING EVERY THING HE TOUCHES INTO GOLD,' MR. LYONS CAN HARDLY BE SAID TO LIE ON 'A BED OF ROSES.'

WHAT Mr. Lyons thought of Rachel's rejection of Percy Thornhill will be best understood by what he did. He heard of what had passed between them from Rachel's own lips with his usual calmness, listened attentively to what she had to urge in its justification, said neither yes nor no to it, kissed her on parting, and having dressed himself to his liking, walked across to The Priory, and asked Lady Ada to be his wife, and a second mother to his motherless daughter.

Lady Ada was not taken by surprise. She had long expected to formally hear from her strange friend's lips what he then came to tell her, and received his declaration of love, and of what he would do for her, and those nearest and dearest to her, if she would accept him, with perfect grace and good breeding. But though she did not say *no*, neither did she say *yes* to his prayer.

They sat talking till within a few minutes of his leaving; when, with his characteristic brevity, he asked her—

" Will you be mine ?"

" To ride in my ' coach of gold ?' " she smilingly answered, to the which he had jokingly alluded when laying all his treasures at her feet. " Ought that alone to tempt me, when you know that, had I been as avaricious as we keen-eyed widows are said to be —and unhappily are compelled to be sometimes— I need not have gone about till now in my basket chair, if there is faith in Barbadoes ?"

" Well, then," he laughed, "supposing I say you shall have *two* gold coaches—how then ?"

"Oh, one for me to go to church in, to be married ?" she asked frankly, " and the other for Percy and Rachel ?"

" Even so, if they will."

" They ! If *she* will, you mean ?"

He smiled.

" Rachel has said to the contrary, has she not ?"

" Hem !"

" Is it not so ?"

" That the silly child must run to her father before she could understand what it all meant, and whether he would part with her to any one living? Seemingly."

"Oh! and how now?"

"Will you be mine?" he repeated.

They looked fixedly at each other.

"And a second mother to Rachel?" he added, with an air and tone of such admiration and earnestness, that it was impossible she could doubt his sincerity.

"One word from your lips"—and he raised her hand to his, as he said it—" will suffice."

"To give Percy what, of course, he must have with Rachel's hand, if he have it at all, or of what worth would it be to him?"

"Anything—everything in my power that you can ask—yes."

"Ah, but that may not include what I mean."

"My every shilling shall be at your disposal."

"What then, if it would not buy me what I want—what I must have—must—ever to say that one word you ask for."

"And," he added, while drawing a paper packet from his coat pocket, and laying it on the table; "I also freely give you what you will find there, to make any use you please of—either to increase your personal securities, as Mr. Salisbury may best advise you, or to throw it in the fire, if you prefer it—immediately you are mine."

She blushed.

"You would like to talk it over with your sister, Lady Thornhill?" he said, with the air of one who could afford to be generous, and wished to be so in this instance. "And, pray, convey to her my deep sympathy in her present affliction, and confident hope that now it rests with yourself alone to make Buck Park the happiest home in the world to them; that when Sir Compton recovers he may have one little source of anxiety the less for, if I may so far flatter myself, your noble trust in me, even to committing to me what, but for that trust, I might have asked for in vain, though I could have made you mistress of all the wealth of the world."

"Still, you will not understand me," she smiled, as he shook hands. "My 'gold coaches' are safe enough; I have no fear about them; but Rachel is her father's child; and you know how iron-willed he can be, if he has steeled his heart to it?"

"True," he granted, as if it suddenly occurred to him what she meant—"without her heart, of what value would her hand be to Percy? It rests with yourself."

"I am not sure of that."

"It does."

She looked thoughtful.

"Say but that you will be mine," he fervently added; "let me tell Rachel that you will be that

mother to her, in reality, which she has so often
wished you were, and Percy need not fear. Why
do you hesitate?"

"Because I think I know Rachel better than
even her father does, in some things. She would
tell me what she would not say to you."

" As how?"

"For instance"—and Lady Ada spoke the firmer
for her knowledge of the man she addressed, and the
necessity of being brief and clear with him—"what
would you say if she told you she would rather earn
her bread by labour, with the man she loved, than
marry Percy Thornhill?"

"Laugh at it."

"The very last way, I should have thought, to
treat her."

"Which proves how much she needs a mother.
No doubt you judge her best."

"Has she ever told you the same thing?"

"About her 'rather having Alan Lambert, if he
were a pauper, than Percy Thornhill, if he could
make her a princess?' Not exactly in those words.
But I have eyes and ears like other people, and—am
her father."

"And, therefore, must remember whose child she
is, and how hopeless it would be to force, if you
cannot lead her."

"It rests with yourself," he said again, as the cloud on his brow passed away.

"I should be happier if I could think so."

"You can prove it if you will."

"How?"

"By the one word said, without which all our hopes will be in vain."

"What a mighty creature you would make me out! And it's not at all pleasant, I can tell you. I don't like it. It makes me giddy. Mountain-tops always did, and looking down precipices. Giddy heights don't suit me. I declare my head spins round with the bare thought of it. 'Two gold coaches' to ride in! Gracious goodness! what have I done to deserve it?"

"Nothing yet," he smiled, so fondly, that she could not but smile, too. "But you will have done all that is needful, I hope, by the next time we meet; which shall be the day after to-morrow, if you please. Then we will talk about the 'giddy heights and gold coaches,' and see what can be done to reduce them within reasonable limits, if they bother us."

It was a precious budget-full for Aunt Ada to take with her to the Hall next day; and how she acquitted herself under it the reader has been told. It now only remained for her to pronounce that one indispensable little *yes* to what "the richest commoner in the county" had asked her, and what on earth was there, that wealth could buy, that she could not have for the asking, as Mr. Lyons told her, " demand of him what she would."

" *Yes*, then," she said to him on his next visit: " provided always, one of my ' gold coaches' shall take Rachel Lyons, in bridal apparel, to be the wedded wife of Percy Thornhill, when the other conveys Ada Chilvers, widow, to the altar, to be Ada Lyons."

" Agreed !" he promised, with, for Angelo Lyons, an amount of emotion that made his lustrous black eyes shine so peculiarly bright, that she could not encounter them. For it was when they so shone that he seemed to Ada Chilvers inspired by that " mysterious spirit," as people called it, within him, which setting all her art to fathom it at defiance, sometimes filled her with anything but admiration for him ; nay, so repelled her, that she would have quarrelled with him many a time for what she thought was at the root of it—his " irreligious free-thinking," as she mildly termed it—if it had not been for Rachel.

Ada Chilvers, however, had now said the word that spoke for itself, and signified, if it meant anything, that she had made up her mind to take Angelo Lyons for better or worse, in the fond hope, may be, of using that reclaiming influence which she flattered herself she would have over him, as his wife, and the mother of Rachel, to his great joy as well as her own.

"I go home to crown my proud conquest," he said, grasping her hand. "Then whom need I envy?"

"Ah, but you may be 'reckoning without your host,'" she smiled—"'counting your chickens before they are hatched.'—Is that business-like in the Broadway?"

"They tell me," he said, with the little subdued laugh that always denoted in Angelo Lyons how safe he felt in himself, "that 'all I touch turns to gold.' That don't look, does it, like bad marketing? At any rate"—admiringly regarding her—"I have abundant reason to crow over my beautiful bargain to-day! And when Rachel hears me—no, no—don't fear—I shan't kill my goose to get at the golden eggs."

But though he spoke so confidently, his face was deadly pale, and more than once his voice slightly trembled, when dropping his eyes on the carpet, he seemed, by his manner, as if scarcely sure that he had said and done all he ought, as a lover; and, yet, as though it would have been inconsistent with his character to have said or done more. There was no hesitation nor awkwardness in it; but only that habitual constraint which always, more or less, withheld him, whether at home or in public, from being sociable, even in his easiest moods. It was a curious courtship that of Angelo Lyons and Ada Chilvers's; but as Angelo Lyons was such an universally strange creature, Lady Ada laid it all to one cause; and knowing how the most irreligious husbands had owed their present and eternal happiness to the Heavenward precepts and examples of their wives:—

"Henceforth it shall be my first earthly loving task," she said to her sister Adelaide, "to not only be to him a wife, and a second mother to his child, if I go with him to the altar, but the means, with God's help, of bringing him to the knowledge of his fatal errors; which done, how richly I shall be repaid, my dear sister, for any self-sacrifices I may make for it."

Had Angelo Lyons forgotten, then, his troth to the woman he had, in less prosperous days, vowed he loved more than any other woman on earth, and would make his wife as soon as circumstances permitted him to marry? Oh no! Angelo Lyons was no more the man to forget that, than that he had a right hand and a left which had done this for him or not done that, and were consequently first or last in his silent esteem, as the case might be. He perfectly well recollected "those happy hours," as he called them, at Tobago and at Trinidad, when there was no female face or figure, in his sight, to equal

Faith Lincoln's. And perhaps he treasured their memory none the less because since then he had become a rich man, and, may be, more for his daughter's sake than his own, desired that his wealth should lift him into the social position he was ambitious to fill for her sake. That he greatly prized Faith Lincoln, was well known; he made no secret of it; he told every one, as did Rachel and Miss Falconbridge, "what a treasure she was to him; how faithfully she served him; what a superior person she was; and how glad he should be to see her in the position of life she was entitled to by birth."

And Faith knew it, and pondered over it; and quelling as best she might the all but hopeless thoughts that, spite of hopelessness, would sometimes sparkle in her flushed cheeks and handsome eyes, after he had been talking with her, kept her own counsel, and made no complaint.

On consenting to take charge of Miss Lyons, when a child, Faith had solemnly resolved that, come what might, she would be true to herself, and neither in wish, word, nor work, be any bar to Mr. Lyons's attainment of that high social position which she foresaw would be his chief aim and end when the Balfour estates fell in to him. And she had kept her vow. What struggles it had cost her to do so, who knew but herself? If anyone knew, it was the man she most tried to hide them from. Perhaps he saw deeper into the truth of it than she herself did, and, so, had smilingly evaded as long as he had the many tempting snares laid in Shiphampton and about to entice him into matrimony. And this had kept alive those inextinguishable ₁sparks of hope in Faith's fond bosom which sometimes sweetly whispered her that "should he remain a widower till his daughter was married, who could tell what he might not do in his loneliness for her who seemed so essential to his comfort at all times?"

And the quenchless sparks glowed on with more or less brightness and intensity till came the rumour to Faith's bewildered ears of "what a grand favourite of Mr. Lyons's Lady Ada Chilvers was; and how remarkably handsome and interesting she thought him; and how pleased he was to have found such an affectionate friend for his child in one whom Rachel so greatly esteemed."

Then came a change, indeed, over the spirit of Faith's dream. But "he shall not see it," she said to herself; "though it break my heart, he shall hear no murmur from my lips; I will be true to myself; or how else would he care for me as he does?"

And Angelo Lyons *would not* see it; lest, perhaps, it should clash with his fatherly duty towards his child, and his splendid views for her when she was old enough to appreciate the world's ways, and the value of social position.

Still, so long as Mr. Lyons was kind to her, what complaint could Faith Lincoln make? Nay, his kindness rather increased than diminished; nor did it escape her how he would sit and earnestly watch her when she was at work with her needle, or, while he was walking up and down the room with his hands behind him, keep his eyes fixed on her when he raised them from the floor. Or, if she rose to leave him when he seemed weary, how he would stop, and almost querulously ask her 'why she did so?' and 'whether she was tired of him?' and 'why it was she was so altered?' And then, if he saw she was pale, or out of spirits, how he would hold her in conversation, just as he used to do in the West Indies; when if anyone had told her that the time would ever come that he would thus deal with her, while his heart was with another—" sooner would she have believed that white was black, that light was darkness, that truth was a lie, that virtue was villainy, that her own heart was false and faithless."

Angelo Lyons would only see—whatever else his eyes told him—what duty demanded of him for the sake of his child. Her welfare and happiness must be his first consideration, whatever it cost him. To which yielding implicit consent, Faith pursued her one fixed plan, strong alone in the conviction that

she, too, was doing her duty, and that, in his knowledge that she *was* so doing, rested her sole power
over him, her sole hope in him, indifferent as he
seemed to be to ordinary moral emotions, or, indeed,
to fears in any shape.

But well-armed as Faith thought she was against
all assaults from that proud, passionate heart of
hers, "come what might," Angelo Lyons's lip qui-
vered a little, as she followed him into his room,
after his return from The Priory on the evening
in question, and in as gay a tone as he could as-
sume, he bade her sit down, and listen to what he
had to say to her. He reckoned on that strong
armour of Faith's to keep her scathless; but his lip
slightly trembled as he told her to take the chair
near him, for he had "something of moment" to tell
her. Which proved how wisely she had judged
him, when, on her knees, she made a solemn vow to
Heaven that, come what might, she would be "true
to herself—he should never despise her, though
the consequent self-struggle for the victory might
be her death."

Circumlocution, or superfluity of words, was no
part of Mr. Lyons's usual system; and on this occasion he seemed to wish to be as brief and explicit
with his housekeeper as possible, as if he had made
up his mind as to what he meant to do, and nothing
more was, therefore, needed than for him to apprize

her of it, with all due acknowledgment of her interest in him.

"You know," he began, after pushing the lamp
on the table a little more behind him, to avoid its
glare, "what passed between Mr. Thornhill and my
daughter when he was here last?"

"Yes, Miss Lyons told me."

"Which means—what?"

"Of course, that she did not accept him."

"Why not?"

"Because she will only give her hand, I suppose,
where she can give her heart."

"Hem—because, you mean, that smooth-faced
youngster, Alan Lambert, is running in her head."

"Poor young man! His face, surely, is but the
index of his mind—placid, because at peace with
itself?"

"Why so eloquent in *his* praises?"

"I speak as I think and believe of him."

"Hem—that, but for Alan Lambert, the next
heir to the Buck Baronetcy would have a better
chance?"

"May be."

"Hem—that if Percy Thornhill could make
Rachel Lyons a princess, she would prefer the
pauper, Alan Lambert, to him?"

"As to that," smiled Faith, "if every one had
their own in this life, it would often be difficult to

determine who was rich, and who was poor; but, in this instance, nothing can be plainer."

"Which is beside the question," said Mr. Lyons, looking at his fingers. "Rich or poor, do you deny that the result would have been different for Percy Thornhill, if there had been no Alan Lambert?"

"I cannot say."

"Well, then, hear me—it is my wish that Rachel should accept Mr. Percy Thornhill; it is indispensable to my views in her behalf that she should immediately do so; it would mar my plans if she did not; I expect cheerful obedience from my child in a matter so nearly affecting her welfare as the prudent choice of a husband, with the wealth she will have, and of which I may be allowed to be a better judge than herself—and I will have it."

Faith was silent.

"I will have it!" he repeated, in the tone which he never spoke in but when he meant what he said.

"You should not have to say *will*," observed Faith.

"Nor shall I, if she be wise."

"She is your own flesh and blood."

"Somewhat self-willed, eh?"

"And like a rock, where she thinks herself right."

It was complimentary, and he looked up from his hands in his lap, and stared at her!

"Don't you admire her for it?" Faith asked him.

"For being like me?" he smiled. "Greatly! Now we shall do business. Think alike—act alike. Yes, it happens very fortunately!"

Faith saw where his thoughts were.

"If I told you," he went on, after absently musing for a moment or two, "that I was likely to marry again, what would you say?"

"Would it affect your fixed purpose, one way or the other," she replied, with a face like marble, "say what I would?"

"I should be glad to have your concurrence, Faith, in whatever I might deem it desirable to do in such a case, far more, I need not say, for my child's sake than for my own."

"And you have it," she replied, with a stern calmness that astonished him; "if it will be for your happiness and hers."

He sat and looked hard at her, as if, though her words were intelligible enough, he had scarcely received quite the answer he expected. Then recollecting himself:—

"They are in great trouble at Buck Park," he went on. "Sir Compton is very ill. Nothing but an easy mind can save him, the Doctor says. And where that's to come from now, pressed on all sides as he is, is the marvel."

"Unless," anticipated Faith, without the visible thrill of a nerve, though the heavings of her heart

almost choked her, "Rachel Lyons will give her
heart, with her hand, to Percy Thornhill—and—
and—her father will give his to—to,"—but there
she stopped, and gazed at him in a manner that so
confused him for an instant, that he was not aware
that she had swooned; when, rushing to her, he
caught her, as she was falling, in his arms, and,
pressing his lips to her cold cheek, again, and
again, it seemed by the way he bent over her till
life returned, that, iron-hard as he was, even
Angelo Lyons had his weaknesses, notwithstanding
the pains he took to prove how case-hardened he
was.

Faith Lincoln was not given to fainting fits, and
Mr. Lyons had to account for so unusual an ex-
hibition on her part as seemed best to him. He
had intended to elicit from Faith how she felt
towards Lady Ada, before acknowledging to her that
he had offered her marriage, and been conditionally
accepted; but was glad, as it happened, that he had
said no more about it. And he went up to bed
very sorry for what had occurred; but by no means
out of conceit with himself when he looked in his
glass, and saw that, "spectre" as he was, as people
whispered each other in the streets, "one heart, at
all events, knew of none other to equal him"—
falling asleep to the soothing influence of which,
his dreams ought to have been happy, if fond,

devoted Faith were the burden of them, and what it was evident she suffered for him.

But it was not fated that Angelo Lyons, Esq., millionaire though he was of The Broadway, Shiphampton, and with every worldly antidote to care, one would have thought, that human heart could wish for at his command, should sleep soundly that night. For scarcely had he dropped off into his first fitful doze, after hearing the hall-clock strike twelve, one, and two (for Mr. Lyons was a light sleeper) —when stealthily crawling from the chimney on to the floor of his room, came noiseless feet, creeping, and creeping, and creeping on; till, within spring of the bedside, they stopped, stood stock-still for as long as it seemed the question with them, by the indecision they manifested, what next to do, whether to retrace their steps, or, now they were there, to accomplish what they came for?—when the deep breathing of the sleeper decided it; for with a leap, old Bony, covered with soot and dirt as he was from his chimney-sweepings, lighted on the beautifully embroidered white satin quilt that sumptuously enveloped the slumbering form of the wealthy master, and crawling on to his chest, thereon settled himself very comfortably, as if that night quite at home in the Broadway.

"Hem—hem—don't, don't—who's there?— hands off," moaned the sleeper, as if with the im-

pression of some night-mare delusion; but old
Bony moved not. On the contrary, he lay stretched
out on his belly, full length, and as if so well satisfied with his bed, after the cold comfort he had
come from up above, that it would require more
than " hands off !" to dislodge him. A lull of nearly
a minute ensued, when Mr. Lyons breathed harder
and harder, and evidently was struggling to shake
off somebody or something, but could not. When
by a desperate effort he woke, and starting up " hell
seize you, you devil !" he said, through his clenched
teeth ; and grasping his grim bed-fellow by the
throat :—" Hands off," growled Bony, as well as
he could express himself, with the choking grip
round his windpipe—" it's my turn now;" and
digging his claws deep into the naked flesh of his
foe,—though it was just with life in him, and no
more, when Bony crawled away up the chimney again
from the death blow, he had left his marks behind him ! And very ugly and painful marks they
were ; so ugly and so painful to think of as well as
to bear—seeing that this was not the first serious
fall out between Bony and the master—that woe-
betide old Bony if he ever showed his gaunt, grim
face again in Greystone House, with such a price as
was set on him, from that day, dead or alive.

It must have been a savage fight between them ;
nor had Bony, seemingly, any intention of giving in,

till leaping from his bed, Mr. Lyons literally drove him back the way he came at the poker's point. After which Mr. Lyons went to the secretary book-case in the corner of his room where he kept his money and other valuables, and bathed his wounds with some tincture he found therein. Relieved by which, he drew his keys from his coat pocket, unlocked first one private drawer, then another, till he came to the secret one he wanted, that flew open on his touching a spring, and possessing himself of the snuff-box (to all appearance) that excited Faith's curiosity so much on a former occasion, he re-locked the secretary, put the box under his pillow, and lying down again—all was still and quiet in Grey-stone House as if nothing had happened.

And when Mr. Lyons came down to breakfast next morning, Faith was shocked to see how ill he looked, how dreadfully pale and hollow-eyed, and how much less firm his step was, and how his voice failed him, and what absent answers he gave to her questions, after telling her of his encounter with Bony, as if his mind were wandering. She had often of late noticed this wandering of his mind, but never so much as now. And it struck her the more because of the many times he had forgotten things, since his frequent visits to The Priory, which, till he went there so much, engrossed his chief attention. Indeed, she had often regarded him with pain when thinking "how it would have fared with him, with his strange ways, if he had been poor instead of rich, and his eccentricities had been called madness, which they certainly would often have been of late, but for the gold that governed all things."

Anyhow, his manner this morning was stranger than ever, so strange that when, on going into his room presently afterwards, the housemaid put into Faith's hand the jewelled box she had found under his pillow, while making his bed :—

"This proves it," said Faith to herself—"proves where his thoughts are—with her—her whose image haunts him—Ada Chilvers—Ada—Ada"—and hearing a footfall, she thrust the box in her bosom— "not Faith now—no, no, no longer Faith—and not to tell me what he had done—to think to blind me —*me*—*me*—who—Oh, my God! my God!—he must be mad—he must! he must!" and shutting herself up in her chamber, what followed Faith's secret possession of her mysterious " bosom-treasure" will be seen in another chapter.

CHAPTER X.

TELLS, BESIDES OTHER MATTERS CONNECTED WITH
THE STORY, OF A 'CURIOUS QUESTION OF IDENTITY'
OF NO SLIGHT IMPORT TO THE PARTIES CON-
CERNED.

How the cleverest plans of the wealthiest and migh-
tiest may be thwarted by the slightest incidents.
Even the opulent Mr. Lyons, of Greystone House,
was a creature of circumstances. When he left Lady
Ada Chilvers, after obtaining her conditional consent to his offer of marriage, he made sure of returning to her in less than eight-and-forty hours,
crowned with success. He was " certain of Rachel,
now Lady Ada Chilvers would be a second mother
to her;" and with regard to what Faith Lincoln
would naturally feel on the subject, he had " too
firm a trust in her discreet attachment for himself, to
believe but that she would wisely merge any personal

ambition of her own in the one paramount aim and end she well knew he had in view—the welfare and happiness of his child."

Faith heard what it pleased Mr. Lyons to communicate, and swooned when she saw what he cautiously disguised from her, as well as what he disclosed. Faith had not been blind or deaf for the many months during which scarcely two days passed but Mr. Lyons found time to dine or drink tea at The Priory. And did not Molly and Hester live close by? and was not Susan, the Priory housemaid, a great favourite of theirs, and as big a little gossip in her own innocent way, whatever she thought to the contrary, as was to be found in Buck? Was it likely, with so much at stake as Faith Lincoln had in the issue, that she should have shut her eyes and ears to what was going on at the Hall, and The Priory, even to the knowledge of how soon she would have to realize as best she might what " even to think of turned her cold as marble ?"

But as it happened that Mr. Lyons fell ill, notwithstanding his iron frame, after his night encounter with Bony, and so continued for some time, Faith's last spark of hope burnt on ; the brighter because of her knowledge of Rachel Lyons's character, and the certainty she felt, that, though her father turned her penniless into the streets, she would never wed Percy Thornhill. Rachel had solemnly declared she "never would," and whose flesh and blood was she that she should be worse than her word when she had made up her mind ?   Had she not also acknowledged to Faith, in confidence, what had passed between Mr. Lambert and herself on the evening before he left them for Trinidad ?   Yes.   And Faith had "formed a very erroneous estimate of Rachel's iron will, like her father's, when she was resolved, if Percy Thornhill ever called her his bride." And if not, and " it depended," as the gossips said, " on Miss Lyons being Mrs. Percy Thornhill, whether Lady Ada would ever marry such a ghost of a man as her father"—then—

"Ah me !" said Faith to herself, as every day brought her additional assurance from Rachel's own lips of where her heart was—" who can say in this world of constant chances and changes what may happen ?   He came home from her, full of confidence, with all his plans perfected, and his reliance on himself so great, so sufficient, that I, *even I* must congratulate him on his good fortune, when it pleased him to tell me of it.   Now look !"

Faith might well exclaim !   It was indeed a sad spectacle, to see to what the lust for gold, and what gold could buy, had brought its worshipper.   Look at him !   Who that knew him when he first came to Shiphampton, to take possession of his vast wealth, would have recognised in that apparition of what he

11—2

then was, the tall, handsome, elegant Angelo Lyons?
It staggered his friends!

" Is all right at the core with him ?" one would
say to the other, as he bowed them out of his bank-
parlour, with those affable, hollow eyes of his, and
oily tongue, or made his usual sauntering circuit of
the streets on market-days.

Whether or no, Mr. Lyons looked ghastly now,
on his back, under the Doctor's hands, fretting at
his tardy recovery; and though " so wandering in
his mind," as Faith expressed it, still so keenly
sensible of what was happening round him, and so
acutely alive to every sound and movement, even to
the whisperings and moanings of the winds, that
they were obliged to put bags up his bed-room
chimney, and stop the ticking of the clock in the
hall—it fidgeted him so.

A strange incident, also, occurred the day after
Doctor Bruce dropped in to see him, by Faith's
request, rather in a friendly than a professional way,
which greatly affected him when the Doctor thus
mentioned it to amuse him :—

" What news ?" asked Mr. Lyons.

" Most wonderful !" answered the Doctor, drawing
a chair to the sofa-side on which reclined his princely
patient in a sumptuous amber-silk wrapping gown.
" Haven't you heard ?"

Mr. Lyons shook his head. He was deadly pale

and hollowed cheeked, appeared very weak, breathed heavily, and replied to what was said to him more by nods than words, as if it pained him to talk; so the Doctor had the conversation pretty well all to himself:—

"Oh, they didn't tell you?" he went on, after his patient had sucked the piece of orange he gave him to moisten his mouth. "You never saw such a rumpus as there was yesterday round the Town Hall. There was that poor, crazy, jabbering wretch, Abel White, the 'black,' who was had up years ago on suspicion of murdering Mrs. Balfour and her niece—with his face all over mud and dirt, running after those idle young rascals who ought to be sent to the treadmill for hunting him about as they do. It's a gross shame! For I'll be bound for it he had no more to do with the murder than you or I had; or do you think he would have found his way back here again, of all places on earth, after the narrow escape he had?"

"Most strange," said Mr. Lyons, faintly.

"And as to his being 'cracked,' as they call him, he's as sane on every point but one—that lost knife of his—as Master John Strong himself, the hardest-headed fellow in the borough. Enough to drive any man mad to be hunted and hooted as he is."

"What brought him back here?"

"A dream he had, so they say, that he should

find his knife in Shiphampton. You know how superstitious those West Indian negroes are? May be some of them at Tobago, who wanted to get rid of him, put it into his head—one of their Obeah-villains perhaps, for what he could get by it?"

"How long has he been here?"

"Heaven only knows. He is so dogged in his answers, you can't get anything comprehensible out of him. And no wonder, bullied and badgered as he is. Clearly he's all in the clouds when he talks of his ' knife.'"

"He cannot have been here long?" observed Mr. Lyons.

"For months past, John Strong thinks, hanging about here and there; though, grown old as he has, and in the queer dress he wears now, nobody knew him till the other day when he was taken up for following and annoying a gentleman down by the water."

"Why?"

"Because he 'thought he knew him,' he said, ' and wanted to see his face.'"

Mr. Lyons muttered his surprise that it was allowed—" Where were the police?"

"We'll, he's safe out of harm's way now," continued the Doctor, musingly, as if recalling something to mind. "But I do think he must be a little crazed on one point, or he never would go on jabbering as he does about that 'lost knife.' It's never out of his sight. But, still, I can't think it has anything to do with the murder. Would a murderer act as Abel White does? would he come searching among the crowd that pelts him blind almost, for the instrument that, if he's guilty, might hang him?"

"Scarcely."

"Not unless he were out of his senses. And really it looks something like it, to see and hear him. There he goes on from day-light to dark, with his great beseeching eyes on the ground, looking for 'me knife,' as if his life depended on it. Perhaps because they tell him 'he will be hanged for it some day.' There he goes on, on, from morning to night, prying into every hole and corner for it, with such a piteous face, that any one would think he was broken-hearted. And if they ask him 'what are you looking for, Abel?'—'Me knife, me knife,' he says, 'dat me cut me food wid dat the young lady gib me at de great house dere when me hungry, and me neber see no more when de tall big man come by de house and knock me down; and den dey say me kill de young lady and de old lady dat gib me food, which am de great lie, de great lie! me no neber hurt nobody, kind to Abel—that's how he talks.'"

"Poor Abel!" said Mr. Lyons, feelingly.

"So say I!" echoed the Doctor. "He had far better have stayed where he was. Guilty or not, now they have got him again, they'll lead him a dog's life here. What caused such a rumpus at the Town Hall, was his telling the Mayor he 'should know the tall, big man again, if he saw him, who came out of the house where the murder was, and ran against him, and threw him down, and made him lose his knife.'"

"Hem—said that, did he? Poor crazy-brained black!" muttered Mr. Lyons, with a deep-drawn breath, as if fatigued.

"Yes, and the best of it is," smiled the Doctor, "if he sees a tall man in good clothes, off he goes after him, to look in his face; which the Mayor says must be put a stop to, for it's getting insufferable. Only the day before yesterday he dodged Mr. Chittlewits's brother, our Tory member, up and down High Street, to note his face, till Sir Peter got quite nervous. And John Strong says ' the vagabond was caught the other day half-way up your garden-wall, close to the yew-trees, getting over to try and find where the tall man came from who 'killed de ladies, and den made him lose him knife down dere.'"

"Poor Abel!" repeated Mr. Lyons, visibly pained. "And what does the Mayor mean to do with him?"

"Ship him back to Tobago, as soon as he comes out of the Infirmary."

"In there, is he?"

"Yes, in the cholera ward; and very bad he is, too. They took him in last night in a deplorable state. It's infamous, if he's innocent. I daresay Miss Lyons will see him to-day. And, by the bye, I must have a serious word or two with her about that. She is indefatigable—a treasure of a girl! They look to her, in the sick-wards, as they would to an angel of help, and counsel, and comfort. What a blessed mission to fulfil! if undertaken and set about and carried out as she does it. Who, to see her at their sick bedsides, would suppose she was the richest heiress in the county? Being a bachelor, though past my prime—which is surprising, eh?— don't I know where I would look for a wife if I were a Prince, possessed of every virtue under heaven, and with riches untold? Ah, you may well be proud of her! But we must not let her kill herself to save others. The genuinely good and true and useful in this life are too few to be careless of them. Is she come home?"

"No."

"Then I shall take the liberty of riding round and fetching her forthwith," said the Doctor, shaking hands; "or we shall soon have to nurse the nurse, which won't do. We must keep the

Mayor up to shipping that crazy fellow off again to the far West as soon as possible, or there will be no peace in the town. God help the poor defenceless wretch in the rabble's hands of Shiphampton; though, if they had the right man, the veritable arch-villain himself in their clutch, by Heaven! it would be a sight for sore eyes, wouldn't it, to see them tear him limb from limb? Good bye."

It was true that the " black," Abel White, the once strongly suspected assassin of Joyce Balfour and her niece, Ann, of the Broadway, had found his way back from the West Indies to Shiphampton, in search, as he told the Mayor, on being questioned, " ob de tall big man dat killed de ladies dat gib him de victuals, and den knocked him down and made him lose him knife." That Abel must have been crazy to have shown his face again, however altered, in a place from which he had so narrowly escaped with his life, seemed certain. Though there were many who thought the contrary, and that it was the best proof of his innocence, and of his sleepless anxiety— which had unsettled his mind—to clear himself of the fearful stigma attached to him wherever he went. And this not improbable view of it was strengthened in the opinions of his friends—among whom were his worship, the Mayor, and the Doctor, and Mr. Nestor Blythe, the " old church " curate, no small authorities in Shiphampton—by the very circumstance that, his enemies said, "told most against him," viz., that he, Abel White, would know the man again, if he saw him, who came out "ob de great house," &c., &c. For he adhered so persistently to it, and to the one same story he told from the first, that at last even the rabble held back and listened to what the Mayor, and the Doctor, and the Parson had to say about it. Till struck down by the cholera, poor Abel found a present safe asylum from the storms without in the new Infirmary of which Mr. Lyons was the munificent president; and where, under Rachel Lyons's judicious, gentle sway, he might be sure of having that "oil poured into his bleeding wounds" which, alike ministering to flesh and spirit, must have been a happy release for the poor "black," though it was the last drop of joy left him on earth out of all his great cup of bitterness.

There was much sickness in Shiphampton, as was usual there in the autumn, and Rachel Lyons had enough to do. But where our tasks are pleasures to us, how easy of accomplishment they are, how well we can afford to blushingly smile at the "great difficulties," as we called them, for want of knowing better. Rachel was happy. Not an hour of the day but told of work done, good work, useful work, profitable work, Christian work, charitable work, blessed work! How, then, could the Doctor be surprised, if, on trying to carry away his "too zealous young nurse from her perilous duties," she bade him "be of good cheer; for she had an amulet against all ailments—but the one it pleased the Great Disposer of events to bring on her,—and when that came, in what would she be better off than the poor "black" there on his sick-pallet, if she had not equal faith and trust in the Almighty Hand that could raise her up as well as cast her down?"

The Doctor was silenced; and blushed to think of "the heroic fearlessness of those who, with their camphor-bags round their necks, and sovereign essences to their noses, thought themselves brave and safe."

The cholera raged with its customary virulence in the closely-packed labourers' tenements alongside the river, of which Mr. Lyons was the landlord; and some sovereign shield, indeed, ought Rachel Lyons, his daughter, to have had, to pass scathless, from death-bed to death-bed as she did during the worst of it. It is a wonderful power that inspires, and impels, and sustains the practical and unflinching nurse, who sees no danger but in the non-fulfilment of the duties of her calling, whether embraced for pay, or, as in Rachel Lyons's case, for the gratification of as pure and noble an impulse as it is possible to conceive the heart of woman can be actuated by, for the sake of its sorely-smitten fellow-creatures. Rachel was in her element. The Doctor expostulated; her father, knowing whose child she was, kissed her with pride, while asking for " the absent roses " from her cheeks, and why she was " so self-willed and imprudent ?"

To which she would smilingly reply :—

" My dearest father, to ask that ! 'What is to be will be,' you often say, don't you ? Oh, yes ! Well, then, why fear ? What matters it how the ' roses ' go, or when they may return ? It don't concern me a straw. Are there no sins and wicked-nesses in houses, to look at which, outside and in, where seems there a crevice through which sin, or sickness, or sorrow, in any shape, could enter ? And are there not homes, open to every angry assault from without and within, wretched to witness, but in which, though poverty-stricken, the love and peace reign which nothing can take from them ?"

" Yes," said Angelo Lyons, with his thoughts only on those pale cheeks in which the father's eye was alone concerned for the missing roses ; " but what has that to do with such wilful disobedience as my Rachel's, after the Doctor's orders ?"

" This, father dear, don't you see ?—that being somewhat of your opinion in the present instance, that ' what is to be will be,' I say to myself, what matters it whether I stop at home or go out—where I go or what I do, whether I run away from the danger or into it, so that I find that feeling of strength and security which it is so nice to feel, ten times stronger, hundreds of times, thousands of times, when I am up to my ears in those 'dreadful perils,' as Lady Ada terms them, than when I am shut in safe and snug, as they call it, at home, where no harm can come to me?"

It procured her another kiss, where the treasured roses were not; for well the father knew to whose child he was speaking, and how fruitless would be further words from him, in the teeth of his own examples. And, so, the doctors were baffled; the sextons got rich; the death-bells tolled on; it was one continuous funeral dirge from week's end to week's end; the town was aghast; proud man, the lord of the earth fell, powerless, before the Great Lord of Heaven, whose wisdom and goodness in all and through all were vindicated. It was His will—and it was well! But though no rose, nor sign of one, was to be seen in Rachel's face; though she went out, on her self-sought missions, early, and came home late; though no perils daunted her; though she seemed to court danger rather than to avoid it; though her father was wracked with anxiety; and the Doctor shook his head; and Lady Ada foretold the worst; and loving friends on all sides predicted what " next would happen :—"

" Fear not!" Rachel said to them, cheerfully. " Why should you fear, while I am as strong as I

am? Oh, you cannot think how safe I feel! How
could I know what strength I had till I tried it? or
what would be given me till I wanted it? I know
now. I will give in when I can do no more. Pray
wait till then."

Which somewhat calling off her father's musings
from himself, and his money-makings, he got better;
so much so, as to take carriage airings to The Priory
and Buck Park; and then in a little while to show
himself again, though looking miserably ill, round
the market on Saturday, to the delight of his many
friends.

The "black," Abel White, though "all but
dead," people said, during the ten days Miss Lyons
had nursed him, woke up one morning such "a
miraculous resurrection," that joy spread through
the infirmary. Not a sick sufferer but was eagerly
looking for Rachel Lyons; not a tongue but was
echoing her praises; not a fainting soul but took
courage—"now that the Great Giver had sent them
such a ministering angel to help them." But Abel's
delight, whenever "Missie Lyons" approached his
bed, was, amidst many a heart-rending scene, the
most pathetic of all. What he said, or, rather, jabbered, while grasping her hand in both his, with his
great imploring eyes strained to their utmost in
speechless expression of a fulness of joy and gratitude that could find no articulate words, was unin-

telligible enough. But said the big tears that rolled down his cheeks nothing? though they so choked his voice, that, as he pressed the "angel-hand" he held in his to his lips in mute adoration, his heart seemed bursting? Oh, yes, they told their own tale better than if Abel had been the ablest orator that ever sat up in a sick bed, after being "saved from the dead," with lips that could never say enough in behalf of his God and doctor, when he was well.

But the best of nurses are but mortal; and there is a point beyond which even such "ministering angels" as Rachel Lyons may not hazard their precious faculties with impunity. Else, what would be their far more exceeding glory, when, joined to their sister angels in heaven, there shall then be no limit to their power, no end to their eternal joys, in the fruits of their missions fulfilled?

Abel, the recovered 'black,' was bathing his "saviour's" hand with his tears—for Rachel had enlightened him to the knowledge of Whose "feeble ministers" she and his other nurses were—when Doctor Bruce came into the ward to see the convalescents. The Doctor spoke kind words to his negro patient; and then he looked fixedly at his nurse. There was that in her deadly pale face, yet burning eyes, which needed no further proof, and would brook no delay:—

"My carriage is here," he said to her, with an

earnestness of tone and manner that for a moment brought a little glow to one cheek; "I am going past Greystone House and will drop you."

"Oh, thank you! Doctor Bruce," she replied, pressing his hand; "but I don't think I can go with you now. In an hour I shall be at liberty. Why do you look at me so? Ah, I know! But don't fear. The roses are nothing to go by. If you see my father tell him I shall be home very soon."

"Come with me now."

"And return after luncheon? They might not like to part with me then. No, I will finish what I have to do now; then I shall have a whole half holiday to myself, sha'n't I ?"

Compelled to be presently satisfied with which, the Doctor walked moodily on from the Infirmary towards the thick of the market, followed by his carriage, in the hope that he might see Mr. Lyons and deliver Rachel's message to him. He found him arm-in-arm with the Mayor, among the sheep and pig-pens, gaining golden opinions from the farmers and country-folk for his "not a bit of pride in him," as they expressed it, and "affability."

"Ha! Doctor, what tidings to-day from my people?" asked their anxious landlord, leaving the Mayor, with the litter of little pigs he was sweet on, to link his arm in his medical friend's.

"On the mend," said the Doctor, gravely;
"decidedly so in Balfour's Buildings; but—in short,
is Rachel Lyons to be the next victim, or is she
not?"

Her father stared, transfixed, at him.

"We must act, not talk, and promptly, too,"
added the Doctor.

"What do you mean?" asked Mr. Lyons, with
a face of leaden hue and quivering lips.

"That if I could have had my own way—which
you know is easier said than done with a Lyons—I
would have brought her away with me from the
Infirmary, and taken her home, and put her into a
hot-bath and a hot-bed with all possible dispatch.
But, alas!"

"She would not?"

"She must finish what she had to do, and then
would be home, I was to tell you, very soon."

"Why did you not insist on her immediate
return?"

"Because, if I had, she would have been there
again in the afternoon; for she said so."

At which moment up came Mr. Nestor Blythe,
the curate, full of glee at the "wonderful bargain"
the Mayor had got with his little pigs:—

"Dear, dear! Mr. Lyons, how glad I am to see
you out again! Your presence quite enlivens us.
Poor Sir Compton will be rejoiced when I tell him

I met you. Mr. Chittlewits was saying how sadly your illness had pulled you down. He is very busy with his little pigs."

Mr. Lyons listened.

" Six and an odd one for two guineas—incredible ! I think I saw you with him at the pen? Dear, dear ! and Giles Todgers asked him two pound ten. I hope Miss Lyons is well ?"

" Will you do her a great service, Mr. Blythe ?" interrupted the Doctor, as Mr. Lyons was about to express his anxious fears to the contrary; "a very great one ?"

" Indeed will I !" cried the curate, with beaming face ; " as who would not who knew and appreciated Miss Lyons's worth as much as I do. What can I do for her ?"

" Let my carriage," said the Doctor, with a tight grasp of his arm, " take you to the Infirmary, where she is now, and must not remain another hour, if we can carry her away. She may listen to you, though I tried in vain but now to bear her off. Be gentle; but if nothing else than force will do, use it, bring her away, take her home, where I shall wait for you; and then if she won't listen to reason, we must mercifully tie her down and otherwise deal with her *secundum artem*."

Mr. Lyons gasped for breath.

" Dear, dear ! I am apprehensive," demurred

Mr. Blythe, "lest my utmost endeavours should prove ineffectual; in which case much precious time would be lost; the consequences of which might be"—

"Fatal," anticipated the Doctor. "True!"

"Then let us waste no more of it," said Mr. Lyons; "but go at once and see what we can achieve between us;" and off in the Doctor's carriage, less than five minutes sufficed to take them to the Infirmary; with what result may be sufficiently told in very small space indeed.

"Have the kindness," said Mr. Lyons to a warder, "to let my daughter know that I am here and wish to speak with her."

Having communicated which to his wife, that worthy matron came forward with great dignity and courtesy combined, to express her "deep regret at the sudden indisposition of Miss Lyons, but sincere hope that it would pass over with a little rest and care."

Mr. Lyons's lips were white.

"Where is Miss Lyons?" asked Mr. Blythe, in evident alarm.

"We persuaded her to lie down for a while, sir," answered the matron, "before she left, as she seemed so poorly."

"Can I go to her," asked Mr. Lyons, impatiently.

"Oh, certainly, sir! if you will be pleased to walk this way."

It led down a passage, and past a common assembly-room for the convalescent in-door invalids, to the nurses' parlour, on a sofa in which Rachel was trying to get rid of the stunning head-ache she had been battling with all the morning till she could bear it no longer.

"Oh, my dearest father!" she cried, on hearing he was at the door, and rising to meet him, "how very kind of you to come for me! But is it wise of you to venture out so far? Then you have not seen Doctor Bruce?"

"Yes, I have," with a fond kiss; "and borrowed his carriage to take you home with me."

"How good of him!"—and shaking hands with the nurse in waiting; "Good bye, Martha," smiled Rachel. "I shall come again to-morrow, if I can. See to Abel White—that one of you read to him out of the story-book I gave him, which he likes so much; and mind he don't fret any more about that hapless 'lost knife' of his, which he will be sure to do now he is getting well."

"Sure, sure! Miss, it shall be seen to," promised Martha; and leaning on her father's arm, Rachel could not resist the pleasure of a peep into the in-door invalids' room, as they passed it, the door of which was open; when drawing her father's attention to Abel, in particular, who at the moment had his back towards them, but instantly after, being apprised, by the glowing faces round him, who was there, he gave a scream of joy! and bounded towards his ' saviour.'

Mr. Lyons moved on; but Rachel seeing Abel's downcast look, held out her hand to him; transported by which, Abel sprang towards it, to grasp it in both of his, and press it to his lips; which compelling Mr. Lyons to stop :—

"Me God! me God!" yelled Abel, starting back at sight of his face—"see—see—him de man, him am—him am—de man, de man dat came out of de great house dere where de ladies killed—him am—and knock me down—him am—and make me lose me knife—God-A'mighty! God-A'mighty!" over-powered by which wild fanatic outburst, as it seemed, Abel stood, with the froth on his trembling lips, and strained eye-balls fixed on their object, rather like one phrenzied than in his sober senses.

"He raves," said Martha, indignantly catching him by the arm and pulling him back.

"Dear! dear!" exclaimed Mr. Blythe, hurrying forward at the sound of the hubbub; "what's the matter? I pray you, tell me!"

"A little mistake of our invalid friend's here," smiled Mr. Lyons, with perfect composure, "on a curious question of identity, similar, seemingly, to the one he got locked up for the other day, poor fellow! That 'lost knife' of his sadly unsettles his brain.   Doctor Bruce should see to it.   A stop must be put to it."

"That's true, sir," said the warder.   "He's as mad as a March-hare when he gets that 'knife' in his head.   It's my belief he'd be best in the Lunatic.   Anyhow, it was as much as Sir Peter Chittlewits could do to shake him off in the High Street."

But Abel would not be silenced :—

"Me no mad," he cried, getting free of those who were dragging him away—"me see de man's face dat come out ob de house and knock me down—me did ! me did !—him de man dere—him am ! him am !—God A'mighty strike me down dead ! if"—

"Hush ! hush ! Abel," said Rachel, placing her hand flat on his chest, to keep him back; "you know not what you say."

"Me does ! me does ! Missie," cried Abel, more impetuously than before, as Mr. Lyons drew his daughter to the door—"me no mad—no, no !—me see him face—him de man—him am, him am—de same man dere—dere—or God A'mighty kill me dead—dat"—

"Abel, he is my father," said Rachel, in the sweet voice that had so often calmed his wandering brain and soothed his woes.   No sooner had she uttered which, with a pitying look at the poor dumbstruck 'black' that thrilled through every heart, when falling on his knees at her feet—

"Me God! me God!" sobbed Abel, with his eyes buried in his hands, as if to shut out the agonizing conviction of his ill-manners and ingratitude —"what me done?—what me say?—bad Abel—cruel Abel—wicked Abel!" when with a dismal cry of misery indescribable, he gazed up into his 'angel-saviour's face,' lifted his clasped hands above his head, muttered something that no one understood, fell full-length on the pavement, and was carried, a jabbering idiot, to his bed.

CHAPTER XI.

TAKES THE READER TO " THE JACKDAW;" AND THEN
TO GREYSTONE HOUSE; AND SHEWS HOW MR.
NESTOR BLYTHE WAS DEXTEROUSLY EXTRICATED
FROM A MOST PERILOUS POSITION BY MISS ROSSE.

RUMOUR gathers as it goes; and soon nothing
hardly was talked of in Shiphampton and for miles
round but Mr. Lyons's strange adventure at the
Infirmary, and the various comments it had given
rise to. It was rare food for busy tongues. As
usual, the gossips differed. Some professed to see
in it only additional proof of Abel's lunacy; while
others, with raised or knitted brows, were very saga-
cious, and though they preferred saying nothing,
evidently meant a great deal by the whimsical faces
they made, and the grunts and shrugs they gave to
questions they would neither say yes nor no to;
that, happen what might, " who could tell but that
it was just what they thought *would* happen ?"

That Abel's strange accusation — to use plain English—had caused great sensation all over the town, was not to be wondered at. True, he had followed more than one tall well-dressed man, before he was taken ill, because he said he bore a resemblance to the individual his mind was always full of, who "made me lose me knife." And, consequently, if he could not let even their irreproachable Tory member, Sir Peter Chittlewits, alone,—who could call themselves safe from Abel White, that stood six feet high, had dark complexions, and Roman noses, and handsome clothes on their backs? Still, it had been proved in evidence before the magistrates that Abel White was the identical 'black' to whom Mrs. Ann Balfour gave the bread and meat and milk and water with her own hands shortly before the murder; and " was it likely that he could have invented the story of the tall man coming from the house and knocking him down, unless something of the kind had occurred?"

" It's my hopinion," said Mr. John Strong, the town constable, to his friend Mr. Simon Box, at *The Jackdaw*, over their social evening pipe, " God's ways arn't man's ways, Simon. And, as sure as that's a bacco-box, there's more in what that nigger says than's come out yet, Simon."

" Else," said Simon, meditatively, " what shut him up all of a moment when he came to know who it was he was tackling so? Didn't you mark that, John?"

It was a fresh light to their pipes, and they puffed away in concert.

" Yes," resumed Mr. Box, after turning it over, " I'd like that explained."

" Threw Abel all of a heap, didn't it?" agreed Mr. Strong.

" That's what roused me more than anything, John."

" Gagged him at once, eh, Simon?"

" But mind you," observed Simon, casting a look heavenward, " there's nothing, John, to be said against the girl—she's an angel."

" A hangel!" echoed Mr. Strong, " that'll be a harch-hangel in heaven, Simon, if ever there was one."

" That's true, John. And you see there's no saying how he might feel—black nigger as he is—when she clapped her hand on his breast and said ' it's my father, Abel'—after the angel she's been to him all through. Anyhow, it doubled him up?"

" Simon," said Mr. Strong, in a cloud of smoke he gracefully wreathed round his head as he lay down his pipe, " the ways of God arn't man's ways. It's my hopinion, Simon, nothing happens, as you may say, but something comes of it. It's what hought to be preached on hoftener than it is, Simon.

For hinstance, there's that missing money down by
the water, I'd like that hexplained. That's something, isn't it? Well, and it won't be none the
worse, will it, for young Enoch, where it is? Then
there's this nigger-business—do you think it's going
to hend in nothing? How many years, Simon, has
John Strong been town constable? Thirty-two,
Simon, come next Shrove-tide. Then, as sure,
Simon, as that's a pipe in my hand, shall I tell you
what—the law's the law, Simon Box. And if you
think John Strong's not wide awake, Simon, though
maybe he shuts his heyes when he's minded, I'm
hanged if you know John Strong, then, so that's
flat! Eh, Simon, you'd not like to be in the shoes
of him, would you, who did it, if John Strong knew
it? Cut their ears hoff, too!—there's a hact!"

Mr. Box groaned.

" Simon !"

" What, John ?"

" It's an hexpression of countenance, that of the
landlord of your house and mine, Simon, that's
not everybody's taste. What a heye he's got!"

" When he's put out any—yes, hasn't he ?"

" They're the most deceiving heyes in the world,
Simon. They melt and freeze you. And what's
the reason of that? Why, because of course there's
something at bottom you can't make out, something
that blows hot and cold as you may say. And why

not, if all's right here ?"—and Mr. Strong laid his
hand on his breast—" Simon, I should like that
hexplained."

" Maybe he's got a weak stomach that won't
digest his food, John, to judge by his colour."

" Or a hinward grief, Simon, that heats him
away. Simon, those slave-masters have done a
queer thing or two in their lives."

" So it's not money alone, is it, John, will make
you fat ?"

" Without hinward peace ? Pshaw !"

" He's never been gay like, has he, since he
came ?"

" It's my hopinion, Simon, you may scrub and
scrub for ever, where a murder's been, and you'll not
scrub it hout. There's those stones there get redder
and redder, they say, that he wouldn't have meddled
with. That's so hodd, too ! letting *them* bide.
Why ? I should like that hexplained."

" Only to think !" exclaimed Simon, turning
white, " of letting them blood-red stones stop.
Maybe he's not quite right in his head, John ?"

" Not him ?—not Angelo Lyons right in the head,
Simon ? Humph !" and Mr. Strong smilingly
fixed his hat on his own, at the thought.—" Right in
his head, Simon ? Aye, aye ! right enough there.
Don't tell me of heads, Simon. What's heads
without hearts ? Answer me that ! But mind you,

his girl's a hangel! like her mother; else, who'd ever go near the hunked house who could help it? Anyhow, the nigger turned him as white as a ghost, Dick says. So that shews, don't it, there's none of us, high or low, rich or poor, Simon, but shrinks at a hawful haccusation like that? And to cut their ears hoff, too, Simon—there was a hact!"

Which being Mr. John Strong's usual way of winding up his somewhat rambling discourses on the subject, little more could be gleaned from them than that the town constable rather liked hearing the sound of his own voice, especially when and where he had friend Simon to sit and listen to him, talk as long and as loud as he would.

Abel, the 'black,' woke from the deep sleep into which his surcharged brain and weakness combined threw him, a confirmed idiot. He gazed about him, as if in search of somebody, or something; grew thoughtful; and then laughed; and then frowned; and then, when anyone spoke to him, jabbered a pack of "unintelligible nonsense," the nurses said, "that no one could make head or tail of."

It greatly grieved Rachel Lyons, on her invalid couch, to hear how the wandering brain of her "poor African," as she called him, had seemingly lost for ever what little self-control it had. He often asked for 'Missie Rachel,' Martha said; and would look eagerly towards the door when he heard any

one coming; and was never without the story-book
she gave him, either in his lap or on his pillow;
though as often as not he was reading it backward
or upside-down. But the pictures in it were his
delight. Especially those in which he saw his
'Missie Rachel' in the lovely, struggling girl who
heroically fought her up-hill way through perils and
perplexities to fame and fortune. And he would
sit and gaze on her sweet smiling face—smiling at
him, Abel—" bad, cruel Abel"—he would keep
muttering, till the tears rolled down his cheeks;
when he would clasp the book in his hands, and
letting his head drop, notice no one, nor move
nor speak till the benumbing fit was over.

Nor was Mr. Lyons less hurt, seemingly, than his
daughter at the sad accounts Martha daily sent
them of the 'black.'

" What had we best do with him?" he asked the
Doctor.

" Either return him, under proper care, to his
own country," said Doctor Bruce, " or get him
into the County Lunatic Asylum, of which you are
a governor."

" Good!"—and, as soon as the Doctor gave the
order for it, away went Abel to his last home
on earth, loaded with presents, and kindest promises
from 'Missie Rachel,' and as handsomely provided
for by her father for the rest of his days as if he had

been the whitest-skinned imbecile ever consigned to a mad-house, because of his special claims on the tender care and solicitude of his friends.

But though Abel was thus safely disposed of, the town-talk went on; and Mr. Lyons found himself far more the theme of public curiosity and conjecture than was agreeable to him when he went through the streets. He was immensely popular; and no doubts were entertained that his return to Parliament, as their Borough Whig-member, at the forthcoming general election, would be ' a triumphant walk-over.' But the penalties he had to pay for it, in this instance, were rather severe; considering the no notice that was taken of his friend Sir Peter Chittlewits's share of Abel's marked attentions; though it was as much as the town constable could do to make Abel understand that Sir Peter was a knighted M.P., and " above doing a bad hact."

Of course it reached that fine old English gentleman, Sir Compton Thornhill, on his bed of pain and sorrow, what the town was in a buzz about, and greatly it amused him. Oh! could he but have jumped out of the flannel bandages that bound him prisoner, and ordered *Sir Roderick* round, and cantered-in to Greystone House, "what a glorious treat he would have had!" But though the Doctor bade the Squire be of " good cheer," and "compare his actual with his possible state, in the which there was a world of comfort," it required Lady Thornhill, and Clara, and the nurse's united help to get him propped up near the window of his room, that he might see what was going on out of doors; and how the old oaks looked; and what the rooks were doing; and where the wind lay; and what sort of a scent they would have had with the hounds, if he had been drawing the Buck-covers?"

Percy had returned to barracks soon after Mr. Lyons's illness precluded the hope of his winning over Rachel till her father was better. But as it was an understood thing between his mother and Aunt Ada, that "Ada Chilvers's acceptance of Angelo Lyons was to depend on Rachel Lyons's acceptance of Percy Thornhill," Clara wished her brother "good-bye, and God speed you," in the certain expectation that "before many weeks Rachel would yield to the tender pressure on all sides, when the sooner matters were summed up and settled the better."

Meanwhile, during her father's slow recovery from the extreme prostration he was suffering from, Rachel had enough on her hands, what with one charitable call or another, without troubling her head about *affaires du cœur*, though with as emotional a heart, loving reader, as ever beat in woman's bosom. She had not positively refused Percy's "noble offer," as Clara called it, to make her Lady Rachel some day; and so Clara felt convinced that "when Rachel saw how her father's happiness would be sacrificed by her rejection of Percy, her love for her parent, if for no one else, would outweigh all other considerations; and then—"Oh, my poor head! my poor head!" exclaimed Clara, from the depth of her wounded pride, "how glad and thankful I shall be!"

Had Clara, then, wholly dismissed from her mind all fears on Alan Lambert's account? If now and then the thought of his possible return to Shiphampton, to clear himself of that strange missing money affair in young Enoch Fletcher's office, troubled her dreams, there was the consolatory reflection, against it, of Mr. Lyons's weight in the scale, and "how unlikely it was that Rachel would act in opposition to her father's wishes. Added to which, Mr. Mungo's last letters from Trinidad were full of gloomy fears for the continued good conduct of the negroes under him, when Mr. Lambert left. For, said Mr. Mungo, in his postscript:—

"Immediately it was known by the negroes that they were likely to lose Mr. Lambert, things changed. It fell like a thunder-bolt among them. The works were abandoned, and it was as much as Mr. Alan could do to prevent an open rebellion. They swore they would 'see and speak to Massa Lyons himself before they would work any more.' If it had not been for Mr. Lambert's firmness and kindness, Heaven only knows what would have happened. He tells them he will not leave them just yet, if they will return to their duties, and give up any Obeah-man who has led them astray; as two Obeah-men were found lurking about the wood near Samson's dwelling, after he was packed off to Jamaica, vowing vengeance against the overseers for what they had done to him. How it will end remains to be proved. Those Obeah-villains seldom threaten in vain. There's a lull now, and Heaven send it may last. Anyhow, Mr. Lambert, though he had purposed to leave by the next ship, will stay with us as long as he can. All will depend. His simple denial of the alleged 'non-entries' in the day-books of certain orders said to have been omitted by him while in office at Shiphampton, will be found in his letters inclosed; and will, no doubt, amply suffice, till he can personally refute such a monstrous charge as it involves against—as far as our experience of him goes out here—his unblemished honour and integrity. I hope to send brighter tidings in my next."

Clara, therefore, had no further apprehensions of Alan Lambert's immediate return, the fear of which, and of how it might prejudice Percy in Rachel's eyes, had been a sad thorn in her pillow. For well she knew what a sly, crafty, hypocritical young fox Enoch Fletcher was, and how Rachel indignantly resented any and every insinuation, however slight, that seemed to give credence to his wily ways. Right or wrong, Rachel always inclined rather to the weaker side than the stronger; it was in her nature to do so; and, in the present instance—of "as foul an accusation as ever was trumped up against an honest man, unable to defend himself—" they were "no friends of Rachel Lyons's who put her to the blush to refute them."

So, now that Mr. Lyons was well enough to visit again at The Priory and Buck Park, what was there to prevent matters being brought to a close as soon as Sir Compton could attend to them? which Doctor Bruce said he would be able to do very soon, "if they kept him amused."

" And, then, if Percy could run down again for a fortnight, everything could be so nicely settled !" said Clara to herself; and an end put to the present dreadful state of suspense, which—putting myself out of the question—is killing dear papa, and wearing poor, dear, patient, uncomplaining mamma into her grave."

But what thought they about it at Greystone House, while Clara was thus arranging it all so easily ?

Faith Lincoln alone, among them all, 'maintained the even tenor of her way,' with a heart whose secret throbbings she dared not yield to, lest they should tempt her to be false to herself, and the solemn vows she had made to Heaven, never to swerve from her purpose, never to desert the one fixed aim and end of her life, come what might, so that she sank not in his sight, whose esteem—insensible as he appeared to its appeals—was "more precious to her than his love, for it was by that alone she held him. What his lip professed to contemptuously curl at in others, he valued in her, or how could she ever have had the influence over him she had? In his respect for her lay her only power over him; and if it galled him a little sometimes to submit, she kept her ground with him; else, with what eyes would he have regarded her, if she had fallen under that 'iron will' on which he prided himself, instead of firmly and fondly compelling it to bend to her own?

But though no human eye but Faith's could see the vulture that had been ceaselessly gnawing at her heart since the night she was carried senseless to her bed—and by him, too, whose lips, while they kissed her cold cheek, pronounced her death-doom,—who, in Greystone House, carried, to all appearance, the index of a heart at ease in their faces, as did Faith Lincoln? It amazed even Angelo Lyons. And if he could not decipher her, who could? That Faith was a changed woman since that unhappy night, he plainly saw. Not changed as towards him, but rather as towards herself. Indeed she seemed to regard him with a deeper feeling of interest than ever; and if there were, at times, a shade more seriousness, amounting to almost melancholy, in her tone and manner when they were together, it rather added to than took away from her attractions. For Faith never looked handsomer, or more engaging, than when there was that settled pensiveness of expression in her thoughtful face which harmonized so well with her sombre character, and gave to her deportment its chief grace in Mr. Lyons's eyes.

But it puzzled him, now, to comprehend her. Her looks, and tone, and manner had, if possible, a deeper feeling in them for him than at any former time; but there was a visible change in the way she approached him, and listened to what he said, and replied to his questions; as if her mind were not exclusively centred in what she was about, and hardly knew sometimes whether to look grave or gay. Her cheerfulness, too, when he made her smile, was forced; and she would keep her eyes absently on him so long, after he dropped his on his hands or the carpet, that many times it sent him pacing up and down the room, with his arms behind him, till she ceased measuring him from head to foot. When sitting down again, as she went on with her needle-work—which he was always pleased to see her with, while he went on talking—he would scrutinize her in turn, if he could do so unobserved.

And when in the solitude of her own room, after these mutual scrutinies :—

"Ah, he may narrowly scan me with those deep-seeing eyes," she mentally ejaculated, with heaving bosom ; "but he little knows what it costs me to disguise so. Oh, that I could be true and candid with him! What is it ties my tongue? Great God !"—and she shuddered—"deeply and devotedly as I loved him, as I love him still, and shall ever love him—though"—and her face became ghastly, as she clasped her hands tight, as if in prayer— "though none would look upon him but myself— oh no ! never, never was he wicked—terrible as he is in his fierce anger and resentments, he is not a villain—he is not cruel—say what else they may of him, they can never lay *that* to his charge."

Poor, fond, devoted Faith ! How willing may be the spirit, but how weak the flesh. Nor could it long escape deep-seeing eyes like Angelo Lyons's, that even the loving fidelity *he* had trusted most to, though he would not own it, was not proof against the last cruel wrong that breaks the stanchest heart.

But whose merry voice is it we think we hear, blithely inquiring of Faith, as they go up stairs together, while Mr. Nestor Blythe takes charge of the ponies at the door, "how her dear darling

Rachel is? and when she will be well enough to have a ride with her to the vicarage?" Who that ever heard gay, joyous, light-hearted, laughing Jane Rosse's cherry tones merrily ringing in hall and bower, could mistake them for any other?

"Oh, my sweetest, dearest girl!" cried Jane, rushing up to Rachel, who in a loose purple cashmere *robe de chambre*, exquisitely embroidered by Miss Falconbridge, lay on a couch reading one of Lady Montagu's volumes of letters; "how glad I am to hear you have cheated them all who said you were going to die, and leave your poor little Janie heart broken. What a good creature you must be to get well so soon! So there's a kiss for it—and another—and another—how nice, isn't it?"

"Indeed, yes—very!"

"Well, then, now hear, darling—but first of all, how do you like my new bonnet?"

It was a drawn cerise-velvet one, lined with white satin, and being trimmed in accordance with Jane's complexion, became her exceedingly.

"Charming, dearest!"

"Yes, isn't it? And how do you think I got it?"

"There's roguery in those eyes," laughed Rachel, "so who's to say but yourself?"

"I wish, dear, you could jump up and look out of window," said Jane, gravely.

Rachel contrived it with a little help, and peeped into the street.

"Do you see?" cried Jane, blushing up to her ears.

"The Broadway beneath?"

"Oh, you silly girl! what's that to do with my bonnet? Yes, the Broadway beneath; and somebody, darling, that's waiting there with the ponies, to know how you like his present. A fact, sweetest! On my word of honour, I hadn't the remotest conception Mr. Blythe meant to make me an offer till the day before yesterday; nor do I believe he would have done so perhaps for weeks, months, years to come, may be, but for the most comical incident you ever heard of, darling, that happened while we were botanizing in the oak-grove. You know, dearest, the postern-gate which papa had spiked at top, to keep the boys from getting over and stealing the fruit? arrow-spiked, darling?"

"Quite well."

"Nearly at the bottom of the cherry orchard. Well, then, dearest, there was the most beautiful bunch of holly-berries you ever saw in your life, nodding at me on the other side of the gate, where the hedge joins it, just out of reach, the most provoking thing you can think of, for stretch his arm out for it as far as he could, Mr. Blythe couldn't reach it. You know his indomitable spirit, my dear, when his blood's up. 'Beat me, shall it?' said he, and—law, my dear, you should have seen him, sedate as he is, —up he leaped, and over the gate he went before I could say a word. It was marvellous! But—and now comes the comical part of it—getting back, he slipped somehow, which forcing him to sit down on the spikes, to recover his balance, they held him tight, dear—tore his clothes shockingly—yes, dear—but that was not the worst—it was full five minutes before he could get off, and then not before I had mounted on the camp-stool, and with my scissors 'extricated him,' as he called it, 'from his perilous position.'"

"You brave girl!"

"I could have rescued him, my dear, in half the time, but for the fit of laughing we both had while I was getting my scissors out of my pocket. 'Nay, nay, Miss Jane,' he kept saying (you know his funny way), 'I pray you, leave me to my fate. Dear! dear! how extraordinary! Be so good as to return home-ward, Miss Jane, and I will tear myself away, and presently rejoin you, if, peradventure, my nether garments will beseemingly permit.' But wait, love, that's not all. I kept snipping, and snipping, till with one other great snip, off he jumped, and grasp-ing me by the hand till the tears came into my eyes, at the thought of his torn and tattered condition— 'My dear Miss Rosse,' he said, turning as white as

a sheet, and then very red, and then white again—
you know, my darling, what a feeling heart his is?
—in short, dearest, he made me an offer, on the
spot, of his heart and hand, in the most noble and
gentlemanly way. Yes, and then walked with me,
love, just as if nothing had happened, to the vicarage,
and sat down to dinner in a pair of papa's trousers,
nearly half-way up his legs—he is such a tall creature.
And this morning, dearest, what must he do, after
papa and mamma had given their consent, but present me with this love of a bonnet of his own
choosing—'in gratitude for the fearful perils from
which I extricated him,' he says—and—and—now
don't it become me?—wasn't it kind of him?—isn't
he a good kind creature?"

"Just the one to make my dear Jane happy now
and hereafter," said Rachel, with her arms round
her friend, and her eyes full of glad tears. "What
could you wish for more?"

"Yes, yes!" laughed Jane, clapping her hands
for joy, "that's exactly what dear mamma says.
And not only that, darling—I take it to be a mutual
affair, entirely so! Shew him anywhere, if you
can, a tidier little body than Jane Rosse will make
him for a wife, if he know when he's well off. It
has papa's warmest sanction, dearest. And what
do you think Mr. Blythe has made papa promise—
for you know, love, how long Nestor has been

courting me, though we kept it so dark?—that we shall be married on the same day you are."

" Oh, Jane! when will that be ?"

" As soon as your little Ladyship pleases; which makes it so nice, don't it, for me and Nestor ?"

" How can you talk so, Jane ? If you are not Mrs. Nestor Blythe till I am Mrs. Percy Thornhill— if that's what you mean—you will never be !"

" Then what shocking, shameful stories people tell !" cried Jane, with flashing eyes. " It's quite dreadful ! Only just now we heard for certain at Mrs. Bliss's, where Nestor bought my bonnet, that it was all settled."

" What, dearest ?"

"That you had accepted Percy Thornhill, and that Lady Ada Chilvers was to be Lady Ada, of Greystone House."

"Jane, you must have known better than that," said Rachel.

"I never could conceive, Rachel, that you were in earnest about Mr. Alan Lambert."

" Am I in the habit, Jane dear, of saying what I do not mean ?"

" No, love; but there are some things too extraordinary to believe possible. And pardon me, dearest, for saying it, but this admiration of yours for a penniless stranger, like Mr. Lambert—however good-looking, and noble-minded, and kind-hearted, and amiable, and agreeable, and all that, he may be—always seemed to me so wrong of you, with your brilliant prospects, that I assure you, dear, it did not surprise me in the least to hear you had come to your sober senses, and accepted what will make you mistress bye and bye of Buck Park—your lawful *right*."

Rachel smiled.

"Added to which, love," went on Jane, with lengthened face, "see what is in every one's mouth about Mr. Lambert and this missing money at 'the works.' How shocking!"

"Of those who are at the bottom of it, Jane, for, perhaps, their own wicked ends! Yes, very! Hark you, Jane dear! I love Alan Lambert much more for it. So the gossips are out for once."

"You are a strange girl, Rachel."

"I gave my heart to Alan Lambert, as you well know, Jane, before we parted; I pledged my faith to him to that effect, when he, too, plighted his to me; his traducers may have a purpose of their own to serve; I have only to be true to him and myself; then how ask me to marry Percy Thornhill, though it would make me a princess? Oh, Jane! I thought you knew me better!"

Jane heaved a sigh.

"But," said Rachel, fondly kissing her, "as I know of nothing that would make me happier than to have dear Lady Ada for my second mother, surely, Jane, there might be *two* marriages on the same day at the 'old church,' leave alone mine? So you and Mr. Blythe would not be without company, would you, if you are resolutely bent on lovingly helping each other off the hooks through life, as Darby and Joan should do. And which, dear,"— with another good bye kiss for kiss—"mind and ask Mr. Blythe (when you tell him what a sweet pretty bonnet I think it) if he hadn't resolved on all the while you were 'extricating him from his perilous position;' so as to make him feel free to insure such an expert little housewife as Jane Rosse, for his own, when he got down, with all seemly despatch?"

It sent Jane merrily laughing back to Nestor; though scarcely as well pleased as if she had managed the *three* grand weddings in one; but, still, positively resolved that, come what might, nothing should prevent her and Nestor being as happy as two turtle-doves—Heaven willing—for the rest of their days."

" *Telle est la vie!*" mentally ejaculated Rachel, as she lay down again, with Lady Montagu's volume— "hopes and fears mingled, joys and sorrows combined, blended sunshine and shade, wheel within wheel, everything coming, nothing certain but death. My 'lawful *right!*' Ah! happy Jane! what a treasure

to its possessor, in this scheming world of untruths
and trials, such a sunny, smiling, ever buoyant
heart as yours ! How little, at this joyous moment,
you would understand the 'strange thought,' as
you would call it, with which I concluded my last
letter to 'poor, penniless Alan.' But he will not
misconstrue it :—

> " What matters it, if peace be mine,
>   What ties may hold me here,
> Whether in worldly eyes I shine,
>   Or 'nobody' appear?
> I know I 'somebody' must be
>   In His all-seeing sight,
> Who lived for me, Who died for me,
>   That I might have my Right."

To the blissful tune of which Rachel closed her e   s ;
and then read on ; and then closed them again ;
till giving way to the heaviness that stole over
her, she fell asleep—presenting a form so calmly
beautiful to look at, as she lay, that even Faith, who
knew her so well, held her breath as she gazed on
her, at the saddening thought of " how nature
often seemed to lavish her choicest loveliness on the
flowers that soonest fell."

CHAPTER XII.

'MAN proposes, but God disposes.' The cunning schemer, less with an eye to the future than the present, lays his plans, pursues, and brings them to perfection. But the *fiat* has gone forth; and just perhaps as he is in the zenith of his triumph, when his cup of joy is so full that a drop more would overflow it, it is dashed from his exultant hand, and the subtle simpleton stands aghast—not astounished, for none, even in thought, are atheists—stands aghast! Which is a state of mind compounded oftener than not of that crushing consciousness, and self conviction, and condemnation, which tremblingly acknowledging the Avenging-will, has no refuge but One whereunto to fly in its dire extremity. And Oh, how acutely it will then understand 'depart from me, for I know you not,' when not a face will know it, when every door is shut against it, when an ignominious grave is yawning for it, beyond which there can be no appeal.

While Jane Rosse and Rachel were pleasantly chatting together about the 'new bonnet' and Mr. Blythe, Mr. Lyons was reading, with perturbed brow, the letters just brought him to The Old Bank, from Trinidad. It was a very comfortable parlour, that parlour of The Shiphampton Old Bank in which its head and principal, Angelo Lyons, Esq., usually sat for an hour or two, in the morning, transacting business, and skimming the cream off the daily papers. It was an oak-pannelled room of rare antiquity, but neither smelt of the dry-rot nor varnish; the ceiling also was of old oak, fancifully carved and richly gilded, but there was a large bay-window to it, which admitted light enough; and the worm-eaten floor had a superb Turkey carpet over it, and the dark purple cloth window curtains, though sombre, were modern, as also were the large leather-seated chairs from Gillow's, and the solid tables, book-cases, &c., &c., to match. Nothing could be pleasanter than your first impression on entering the comfortable parlour of The Shiphampton Old Bank, after Mr. Lyons had re-constructed it.

It was elegant, but homely, with an air about it, look where you would, that bade you welcome. It put you at your ease; it asked you to feel yourself at home. Wealth shook you by the hand, and your heart swelled. You sat down and were in no hurry to get up again; you felt that your banker was your friend; that his money was yours, and yours his; that your best interests were mutual. And when you quitted that comfortable bank-parlour, not the least pleasurable of your reflections was the certainty left on your mind by that last genial smile and gentle pressure of your rich banker's long white fingers, 'how proud and pleased he would be to see you there again whenever you pleased to drop in.'

Mr. Lyons's brow might well be perturbed at the calamitous accounts brought him by the just-in mail from Trinidad. Mr. Mungo was well nigh driven frantic with the terrible doings on The Old Mill House Estate, which it was his sad duty to tell of.

"When I last wrote," his letter went on, after expressing the great grief he felt at being the herald of such deplorable tidings, "I had sanguine hopes that we should prevail on the negroes to resume their work, and go on quietly. And so they did for a little while. Till it being absolutely necessary to make an example of Rosa and

Judy, for partly harbouring a reputed Obeah-man, who came, as he said, 'with a message for them from Obeah himself, which it would be worse than death to them if they disregarded,'—there was a general turn-out of the hands, and a round robin brought me that 'if Rosa and Judy were punished, I had better look to myself.' Of course, to have yielded to threats like this, would have been the same thing as laying down all power and authority; so Rosa and Judy were punished with the utmost leniency, and I have now to acquaint you with the lamentable results.

"For a week after Rosa and Judy had acknowledged to Mr. Lambert the greatness of their offence, and how justly they had been punished for it, nothing could be more satisfactory than the general conduct of the negroes was. Indeed, they were so studiously 'good-mannered' that I began to have my suspicions. But Mr. Lambert was more confident. He had visited them at their homes, made them presents, nursed their 'pickaninnies,' and addressed them twice in public; and went to bed, after his last talk with them, immensely pleased with their behaviour. Next day Old Mill House and outbuildings were burnt to the ground; and I will leave you to imagine the state of consternation we are in. As yet no lives have been lost. Fires are breaking out nightly, how or by whom done no one can tell;

though there can be no doubt that the Obeah-men
are at the bottom of it;' and, if so, we may think
ourselves fortunate if we have seen the worst. All
order is at an end. In all my long West-Indian
experience, I never witnessed such a state of anarchy
and insubordination as we are now in. The negroes,
mad with drink, are more like devils than men. In
short, when or what will be the end of it, Heaven
only knows; for to call in the arm of the law would
add fuel to fire, till everything was destroyed. Even,
sir, if you could come out at once to us, I dread to
think what might happen before we saw you. I
have scrupulously obeyed your instructions through-
out; but *your presence alone* can restore order.

"We saved what we could out of Old Mill House,
after saving ourselves. In the endeavour to rescue
from the flames such articles of furniture, plate,
pictures, books, &c., as he thought were most
valued at Greystone House, Mr. Lambert narrowly
escaped with his life. Though so meek and gentle,
he has the courage of a lion, in times of need. I
may mention one instance—Mr. Alan *would* return,
when the house was blazing (though we did all we
could to dissuade him) to fetch away the portraits of
Mrs. and Miss Lyons hanging in Miss Rachel's
room, and was dragged out, senseless, with them in
his arms. He is a noble young man, and much
beloved. Even the frantic blacks stop their howl-

ings and blasphemies when they see him, and fall on their knees to kiss his hands. But Rosa and Judy, whose pickaninnies he often nurses, have told him to 'go away, or he will be killed.' Nothing daunts him; and he goes about among the worst of them, as unsuspicious and unconcerned as a child. But we watch him closely—as we know how the Obeah-men hate him, and to what lengths they will go, if enraged—and intend, whether he will or not, to ship him off home to England, if needs must. So you may see him any day after the receipt of this (if in time for the mail), or before, if we see necessity.

"For myself, I shall stay and take my chance, in the knowledge that I have endeavoured to do my duty to the best of my power. An overseer's life in Trinidad, as elsewhere, is no sinecure, as you well know. But, if I give you satisfaction, I shall not flinch from fulfilling, as I best can, the kind trust you place in me. Still, the *Massa's* own little finger will do more with his negroes than a thousand agents; and Heaven send we may have the joy, sir, of seeing you soon.

"Some pieces of old plate and several coins and trinkets, &c., were picked out of the *debris* of Old Mill House by Hercules, of whom I wrote to you in my last. He is exceedingly well-behaved; though at times gloomy and taciturn, almost ferocious to look at, when his moody fits are on him. I think there must be something in his past history that troubles him. But Mr. Lambert has taken a great liking to him, which Hercules returns. He helped to nurse Mr. Alan in his illness, and was very anxious to get him well. He talks, sometimes, of going to England, where he has friends, and settling there, with the money he has saved. His nephew, Samson, vows vengeance against him for helping to get him sent to Jamaica. Some say, 'if his uncle had turned up before you gave Samson the head-carpenter's place, he would have poisoned Hercules to get him out of his way.' And I believe it. Also that Mr. Lambert is a marked man. For which reason we shall take leave, as I said before, to pack him off to England again with all possible speed—please Heaven nothing too dreadful to think of happen to forestall us, which God forbid."

A striking photo-likeness might have been taken of Mr. Lyons's once eminently handsome, but now wretchedly thin and careworn face, as he sat with Mr. Mungo's calamitous letter grasped in one hand, while he vacantly gazed on the filbert-shaped finger-nails of the other, absorbed in thought. Gentleman was unmistakably stamped on him, the well disciplined gentleman, and that happy combination of the man of fashion and the man of business, which, more than anything else, made him as popular as he was in Shiphampton. It seemed impossible for any man to be absolute lord and master of the where-withal to be supremely contented in this life, beyond what Angelo Lyons was. If *he* had not 'the key to happiness,' who had? What earthly thing was there, purchasable with money, that he could not have? He had but to speak the word, and the world's costliest treasures lay at his feet. 'I will,' and it was done. Enough almost, in all conscience, to turn the heads of nineteen country-town *Mayni Apollines.* out of twenty? But it never so served Angelo Lyons. The richest commoner in the county was the most urbane; the millionaire Mr. Lyons, of Greystone House, was at once the humble servant of all who had dealings with him, and their princely lord.

As he sat, buried in thought, after thrice reading Mr. Mungo's letter from beginning to end, who would have recognized, at first sight, in that bent, broken old man, as he looked, though not much past the meridian of life, the tall, upright, hale, handsome Angelo Lyons they shook hands with when he was the pride and boast of the borough for manly beauty and grace? There were the fine Roman features standing classically out as originally cut by the master-hand, still faultless; but where were the flesh and blood that gave them their life, and character, and expression, and used to so charm

every eye? Was it the man, Angelo Lyons himself,
or his spectre, reclining back in his chair, with head
so bowed that his chin nearly touched his chest?
while tightening the letter in the grasp that seemed,
to use a vulgar phrase, to have 'doubled him up,'
his face became so cadaverously pale for so long as
he kept his vacant gaze on his nails, that, but for
the twitching of his lips when he was muttering
something to himself about 'that fellow Hercules,'
and 'Ruth Lyons,' he might have almost passed for
one of Madame Tussaud's wax figures, dressed for
show.

There could be no mistake about it—once seen,
face to face, Angelo Lyons could not be easily forgotten. There was that in him, and about all his
actions and words, which indelibly stamped itself on
the mind. He fixed you. Perhaps the impression
was too vivid. You could have taken pen or pencil
and traced it in a moment from memory. There it
was, clean and clear before you—the lofty forehead,
the arched eyebrows, the Roman nose, the classic
mouth and cheek and chin, the well turned head,
and proud neck that would have graced a Tarquin.
Nor was there any lack of fire in the eyes; they
were full of fire, but wanted warmth; and the smile
of the mouth, when it did smile, though fascinating,
quickly passed away; indeed, was seldom called up

at all but in obedience to the ruling will or the whim of the moment.

Lady Ada's idea of Mr. Lyons's face, when she first knew him, was that it was "painfully expressive." And if this could be said of it when all tongues were speaking in admiration of it, what was to be thought of it now, when it was even the theme of startled observation by the street-boys as they passed him, who knew him as well as they did the town hall.

Our smoky-faced friends of "The Jackdaw," Messrs. Strong and Box, minced no words about it.

"Did you see him crawling up to the Bank this morning, Simon?" quoth the town constable. "Simon, what is it corrodes his bliss?"

"Aye, John, what? Mayhap that 'skeleton in the closet,' as they call it, which we've all got, high and low, rich and poor, somewhere or other, staring at us in the dark depths of our hearts, John, like a law of nature—to tell us—what? Why, in course, that all is vanity!"

"Hawful!" ejaculated Mr. Strong. "You'll see, Simon! It's my hopinion he's got a secret grief he's hobligated to come face to face with, whether he will or no, and that's what's tackling him."

"It can't be want of money, can it, John, turning into gold as he does everything he touches? The 'skeleton' don't come that way?"

"Well," said Mr. Strong, gruffly, " there be two ways, Simon, to look at that—it might and it might not. It's the last straw, isn't it, breaks the camel's back ?"

" Sure."

"Well, then, a man may load himself so with riches, mayn't he, that down he goes? Because why? Because he's that covetous, Simon, he'd never know when he'd had enough—till it broke him. Simon, what't your ' skeleton ?' Not wanting hany hother woman for your wife, eh, but the one you've got? nor hoverrunning the constable? nor robbing others hof their lawful own to henrich yourself? Then, Simon, what is it ?"

" I'm blessed if I know, John."

" And why not, Simon ? I'll tell you. Because it's all lies about those 'skeletons in the closet,' we've got. We haven't. Where's yours, Simon? where's mine ? where's the skeletons in the closets of lots more hof us, who've got tidy wives, and snug homes, as times go, and pay our way some- how, and send the little ones to school, and haven't no illness to speak of, and hought, instead of talk- ing of ' skeletons,' to go down on our marrow- bones and thank God we're as well to do as we are ?"

" You should hold forth about it, John," advised
Mr. Box.

" Though, mind you, Simon," pursued Mr.
Strong, " I'm not prepared to say, by no means,
but there *are* ' skeletons' in some closets, and terrible ones! It stands to reason, and nature, there
should be. Else, Simon, what's your conscience for ?
Love another woman more than your own wife (as
one of them great writers says, I've read of), hor
spend more than you hearn, hor go never to church
or chapel, hor rob, murder, and such like—there
you are ! there's your skeleton ! and get away from
it if you can. Simon, I don't henvy no man with
his ' skeleton' in the dead of the night. It's then
it tackles him. Do you suppose there's no skeleton
in Greystone House, made of gold as it is ? Then
what's bent and broken him ? I'd like that hexplained. And don't you mark now how he keeps
his heyes down when he's talking ? Carry that ghost
of a face, need he, if he hadn't no hinward grief,
nothing corroding his bliss ? Pshaw !"

But we must have done with Mr. John Strong
and Mr. Simon Box's ' Jackdaw' speculations, *in re*
their wealthy governor's altered appearance, and
return to the ' Old Bank' parlour, where we left
Mr. Lyons, though so bent and broken, undeniably
" the strongest man on his legs in Shiphampton,"
in his commercial friends' eyes, as far as pounds,

shillings, and pence went, notwithstanding the spectre he looked.

Mr. Lyons had closed his eyes, after deeply pondering on Mr. Mungo's disastrous epistle, as if thoroughly prostrated and inclined for a doze, when in walked his solicitor, Mr. Salisbury.

"Ah! taking forty winks before turning out again?" laughed the privileged man of law, as he seated himself facing his opulent client. "What news?" with a glance at the newspaper.

Mr. Lyons handed him his Trinidad overseer's letter to read.

"Humph!" exclaimed Mr. Salisbury as he came to the end of it—"what incarnate fiends they must be out there! Shocking! shocking! And what do you mean to do?"

Mr. Lyons looked at him, as if to say it was just the question he had been putting to himself, to no effect.

"Evidently," observed Mr. Salisbury, after thinking a moment or two, "they can do nothing without you. Go you must. I see no help for it. And go you ought, too, there can be no doubt of that."

"And go I will," added Mr. Lyons, with bloodless face, and lips livid with emotion, "if"—

"It would not interfere with your election for the Borough?" anticipated Mr. Salisbury. "Well, I

heard just now that our present Whig member meant
to contest it to the utmost; and you know his party
is pretty strong? Besides which, if ministers can
tide it over this session anyhow, it's not likely they
will give up office till they must. You might be
there and back in six months if you liked."

"True," said Mr. Lyons, with his usual calmness.
"And now, then, hear me. I will go, if—as I was
about to say—Lady Ada will go out with me."

"When Lady Ada is your wife, you mean, and
Mr. Percy Thornhill your son in law?"

"I do."

"The very thing I came to speak to you about.
Sir Compton sent for me yesterday. Poor man! we
must spare him all the worry we can. He is mend-
ing; and you are well again; so it rests with Miss
Lyons now. Percy has taken what she said to him
a good deal to heart, and asks to have that wound
healed. In short, what's to hinder your obtaining
her immediate consent to be Lady Thornhill some
day? You could do it this very day. What influence like a father's? Then less than a week would
suffice for what I have to do to make you all fashion-
ably independent of each other—and happy. And,
yes—you are right—Ada Lyons would be an immense card with them at Trinidad!"

It brought a momentary flush to Mr. Lyons's
brow; his eyes sparkled; and linking his arm in

his solicitor's, he sauntered up High Street and down it. Till having heard all Mr. Salisbury had to say about " how much good a change of air and scene would do him ; and what a pity it was that he went to the Infirmary to be continually annoyed as he was about that silly Abel's monomaniacal non-sense "—

"Farewell," smiled Mr. Lyons, as they shook hands at his door. " I will immediately speak to Rachel. And there will be a ship of mine going out early next month—by when"—

" Yes, yes, it may be all sealed, signed, and delivered—the deed done which can't be undone," smiled Jonathan Salisbury, with great unction; "and which, if it is to be done, ought to be done, for the best of all reasons, with as little delay as may be."

Bravely armed with which, Mr. Lyons summoned his housekeeper to him for a few preparatory words before going up-stairs to his daughter.

CHAPTER XIII.

FAITH LINCOLN, like every other woman, however handsome and interesting, owed something to dress. And Faith perfectly well knew what best became her, which is more than every handsome woman can say. On the special day, some eventful incidents of which remain to be recorded before the close of the story, Faith dressed herself with unusual care. What prompted her to do so was best known to herself. Most women, with the weight Faith had at heart, would have presented to the man who was the cause of it a far different appearance to what she did that day. But Faith was no copyist. She selected the *toilette* that she not only looked best in in the eyes of him she loved, but also in her own. It was due to herself to rise rather than fall in her own estimation. He might see by her face what her heart could not conceal from him, and guess the source of her settled woe; but she would lose nothing in his opinion, if she gained nothing; she would act up to herself, to the standard she had never sunk below since she entered his house." Faith knew the man she served. What gave her the power over him she had? Her respect for herself, her firm purpose, her fixed principle, her faithfulness to him, her candour and consistency, her patience, her forebearance, her determination, under all circumstances, to insure his esteem, however little he seemed to appreciate it.

In dress, as in all else, Mr. Lyons was a connoisseur. In female dress especially. And though he appeared to take no notice of what any of them wore with whom he came in contact at home, no eyes saw quicker than his did when he was pleased, and when he was not, cynically indifferent, as he seemed, to such vanities. Had Faith worn the dress, on the day we are speaking of, most in harmony with her feelings, not a word would have escaped Angelo Lyons's lips; but he would have thought none the less; which was the reason, perhaps, why Faith took such care to so present herself to him when he summoned her, that he should see " rather an improvement in the old face and form, than the reverse; if, after a glance in his glass, he felt inclined to congratulate himself on his once alone-eye and heart for Faith Lincoln."

' "You expected me home sooner," Mr. Lyons said to her, with an approving gaze at her rich plain-made black silk dress, and antique cameo-brooch, his presents, and which so well became her figure. "Don't deny it. I sadly want a little comfort. Sit down."

She took the chair facing him; and his eyes again measured her from head to foot.

It called the blood into her cheeks.

"Ah!" he said, with, for him, almost a tone of tenderness, "you wear better than I do, Faith. How is that?"

"It ought not to be, ought it?" she answered, as cheerfully as she could pronounce it.

"Why not?"

"What! weak as I am, and strong as you are? It should be the reverse."

"But, seemingly, it is not. At all events, I have enough to perplex me just now. Read that"—and he handed her Mr. Mungo's letter.

"Terrible!" said Faith, as she doubled it up and placed it on the table. "Then Mr. Lambert's influence is at an end. Well, if no blood be shed."

"What's to be done?" asked Mr. Lyons, as if appealing to one from whom he looked for consolation as well as counsel.

"You must go to them," said Faith, with flushed cheeks, as though a sudden pleasurable thought had

struck her; "go at once.   Your presence alone can
put a stop to it.   There is no help for it.   Well, if
you can get there before worse befalls."

"So Mr. Salisbury also seems to think.   Hem—
yes—I must go, I suppose—must."

"Without delay," added Faith, eagerly.

Mr. Lyons left the contemplation of his nails, on
which he was intent, and looked fixedly at her.
But she governed herself admirably.   She read his
thoughts.   And he knew that she did; which was
why he kept his eyes on her, as though "wondering
whether she loved him sufficiently to generously
break her heart for him, if needs must?"

"There is no alternative," added Faith, firmly.
"'Your little finger,' as Mr. Mungo says, 'would
suffice, if there it were.'   It must be so, to save them."

"So it seems."

"In which case"—and Faith struggled hard to
say it calmly—"of course you would wish, before
you left, to see Miss Lyons Mrs. Percy Thornhill, if
it could be done."

He stared at her.

"And Ada Chilvers Ada Lyons, too?   Would
you not?"

"How, if my answer scarcely convey what my
heart could wish?"

"Would you not?" repeated Faith, with heaving
breast.

" Yes ; for reasons we have often alluded to before, and need not repeat now."

She saw his confusion, spite of his assumed assurance, and bore it, without the visible tremor of a nerve, though her heart was bursting.

" Faith, you cannot misunderstand me ?" he said, in a tone so melancholy that it was a moment or two before she would trust herself to answer him.

" I do not," she replied.

" You see my meaning ?"

" Perfectly."

" That my duty to my child—my duty, as her father and only parent—demands from me this— this"—

"Self-sacrifice !" anticipated Faith, as the blood of her race mounted to her neck and face, till her brilliant black eyes burned like balls of fire.—" Self-sacrifice !" she repeated, almost mirthfully. " How very noble of you ! how disinterested ! how exceedingly grateful I ought to be !"

His brow darkened.

" Nay," she smiled, " we must clearly comprehend each other now. Why not ? Else, how should we stand in each other's eyes ? I quite see it all. Your duty to your child ? Yes, yes ! you are right. It demands that she should have—with wealth like hers—a titled husband and a titled stepmother ? Good !"

18—2

" Go on."

" I have no more to say."

" Faith !" but it sounded hollow in his throat—
" why misconstrue me ?"

" I do not. As God is my judge, I would tear
my heart from my breast rather than wrong you
with a breath. Have I ever done so ? do I now ?"

" You wrong me, deeply wrong me"—and he
drew his chair close to hers and grasped her hand—
" and not only me, but yourself, too, if you think I
am, at heart, false to my plighted troth to you—to—
to"—

" Hush ! hush !" she cried, disengaging herself
from his circling arm ; " if you would not that I
should"—but if *despise* were the word that trembled on her lips, it could find no utterance. Faith
was but mortal loving woman, weak, fond, faithful,
devoted, foolish woman ; she could heroically bear
up against his coldest looks, but in those fond eyes
now fixed on her, in those tender tones in which he
now addressed her, blissful memories of the past
came crowding—oh, so blissful ! so thrilling ! so
agonizing !—that feeling the mastery over herself
slipping from her :—

" Yes, yes, what is to be, let it be," she sobbed
convulsively. " Heaven's will be done !" and
blinded by the tears that would no longer be suppressed, she rose and left the room.

Mr. Basil Horne, of Barbadoes, used to call his brother slave-owner of Trinidad and Tobago 'a man of steel.' But there is no metal, however hard or well-wrought, but has its vulnerable point; and for some minutes after Faith's abrupt escape from him, Angelo Lyons was conscious of such weakness somewhere in that iron nature of his, that had his lawyer, Mr. Salisbury, walked in and said to him 'Go and make that poor, fond, faithful heart happy, which loves you more than any other heart on earth,' in all probability he would have done it. But what had Jonathan Salisbury just laid it down, as law, that he must do?—" marry his daughter with all possible speed to the next heir to the Buck baronetcy, and himself simultaneously to the titled widow of a Lord. Then would he be free to take the highest places among his fellow men, and vanquish all his foes."

Calling which to mind, as he stood looking up at a lovely portrait, in oils, of Rachel, over the mantle-piece:—

" Yes," mentally mused Angelo Lyons, " what is to be will be—that is clear and incontrovertible. We but fulfil our destinies, whatever happens. The potter fashions the vessel to his fancy; it had no hand in its own construction; and may it say ' why hast thou formed me thus ?' Why are men fools ?

" ' Is it that things terrestrial can't content?
     Deep in rich pastures, will thy flocks complain ?
     Not so ; but to their masters is denied
     To share their sweet serene.'

As the beasts themselves do, so does man ; but less
wisely.   Man is worse than the beasts ; for they are
happy—and what is he ?"

Not finding any satisfactory solution, seemingly,
to which query :—

"Sweet girl !" he went on, as if addressing the
portrait, "and you, too, have your destiny to fulfil.
How, then, sillily say 'you would rather work for
your bread with Alan Lambert, than be Percy
Thornhill's bride if it would make you a princess?
Is it not already written whose bride you shall be ?
Sweet child ! how like her mother she is ! And,
yet, not like her, if it be, as Lady Ada says, that she
is 'too much her father's child to let even *his* will
bend her against her own.' We shall see. What's
o'clock ? Yes,—her sleep will have refreshed her.
Time it was done. Poor Faith !"—and he walked
slowly up stairs, with the help of the banisters, till
he came to his daughter's room,—when, as if suddenly recollecting something—on hearing strange
sounds from below—he hurriedly crossed the gallery to his own chamber, and locked himself in.

But he could scarcely have done so three minutes
when he rang his bell for the page.

"Send the housekeeper to me," he said to Felix —"quick!"

Which bringing Faith to him before he had agitatedly measured the room from his bookcase to the door half-a-dozen times:—

"I have been looking for something I wanted in a private drawer of my secretary," he said to her, with white lips, "and cannot find it—cannot find it," he repeated, with a piercing scrutiny that evidently meant, "who has dared to rob me?"

"If you allude," she said, with calmness, but with visible discomposure, "to the snuff-box the housemaid found under your pillow one morning when making your bed, it is easily explained."

He had stood breathless while listening to her; but seemed relieved by what he heard; and fetching a deep breath, leant against the wall.

"Well, and where is it?" he asked, agitatedly.

"If I did wrong," replied Faith, "in not sooner mentioning it to you, I am alone to blame for that —not Frances."

"Where—where is it?" he repeated, with a suppressed wrath that made her tremble.

"At Mr. Nathan's—to be mended."

"What!" he cried, with a spring towards her, and fixing his straining eyes on her, as he savagely grasped her arm—"you dared, did you, to— to—"

"Foolishly risk the chance of your displeasure to screen another? Yes."

"What do you mean? Speak!" he said, sternly, and with tightened clutch of her.

"I will, if you will let me."

He sank into a chair.

"In making your bed, Frances unwittingly threw the box on the floor; but I did not observe, when she gave it me, that two of the precious stones—a large pearl and turquoise—were missing; nor could they be found, after the room was swept, though we searched everywhere. The girl was frightened; and, as you were ill, and did not ask for it, I took the box to Mr. Nathan's, where I thought you might have bought it, for two other stones of the same quality, if he had them. He promised to supply them in a week; but not being able to procure a sufficiently good turquoise of the colour wanted, there the box is now, I believe—to prove how deceitful I was, and to what crooked ways will bring one, seemingly, when the straight are so safe and easy."

"Ring the bell," said Mr. Lyons, faintly; and drawing his chair round to the table, he instantly despatched a few lines to Mr. Nathan by the page, with an order to Felix to bring him back the answer. Then he looked earnestly again at Faith, as if in two minds whether to resent the liberty she had taken, or make it the pretext for one of those tender scenes between them, which, though they never shook her one iota from her 'rock of rocks' in which she trusted, were never without a charm for him, perhaps for the very reason it most pained him to confess to.

But Faith gave him no encouragement by word or look; when, bidding her see if Rachel were awake and well enough to admit him, he walked to the window that commanded a clear view over the Broadway to the top of Market Street; then to the gallery-landing, where the painted window was that always reminded Rachel so much of poor Aunt Joyce and Anne Balfour; then to where he could see Felix coming back from Mr. Nathan's. But Felix was in no hurry when once he got among the shops and shop-girls. So, hearing from Faith that "Miss Rachel was much better, and up writing," Mr. Lyons went straightway to her; with a face, full though it was of many cares, with no lack of fatherly love in it for his child, though, to prove it, it doomed her to destruction.

"Oh, my dear father!" exclaimed Rachel, after returning his kisses, "what dreadful news from Trinidad, Faith tells me."

He put Mr. Mungo's letter in her hand, and, while she read it, stood at the window over-looking the garden, as it was called, at the rear of his house, and the 'short-cut' thoroughfare that led down to the water. There were the masts of his rich ships rocking to and fro with the swelling tide momentarily lifting their nodding heads higher and higher, as if to greet him. It was a proud sight. And though Rachel's ejaculations of grief, and dread, and hope, combined, grew louder and louder as her dimmed eyes read over and over Mr. Mungo's concluding words—"Please Heaven, nothing too terrible to think of happen to forestall us,"—Angelo Lyons was seemingly so absorbed in his own thoughts, that she was close to him, and with her arms round his neck, before he remembered where he was, or what he was doing. Then being recalled to recollection by those beautiful, uplifted eyes of his child's, filled with tears, as she laid her head on his shoulder—too much choked with the fulness of her heart to trust her voice—he led her to a sofa, and sitting down by her side, gazed on her with a love that perhaps he had never felt for her till that moment, dearly as he thought he loved her above every other object on earth.

"Oh, my dearest father!" she sobbed, "I have such a pain at my heart!"

He folded his arms round her; he drew her to his breast; nor cared to break the deep silence that ensued—broken only by her sobs,—till pressing his lips to her burning cheek :—

"Courage! courage!" he said. "I am not without hope. My presence there would put all right again. I shall go to them. Mr. Salisbury advises it; so does Faith; and so will you, I am sure."

It touched the chord her father wanted. From burning red her face became deadly pale, as for a little while she sat with marble fixity looking at him, as if to be sure she understood his meaning before opening her lips.

"It is time," he said affectionately, but in a tone Rachel too well knew the purport of, "that I should clearly tell you my wishes as to your union in marriage with Percy Thornhill. I would have delayed it till you were quite well again; but matters press; time is short, (if I must go to Trinidad); and it is best we settled it now."

Rachel listened.

"I can have but one motive in wishing to marry you to Mr. Percy Thornhill—your welfare and happiness. He is heedless and profuse, like his father, but has a good heart, and will grow wiser with years, and the experience taught him by trouble. Whether or no, I shall take care to secure you from any risk on that score. Your separate provision will be commensurate with my love for you, and your rights, as my daughter. Your position will be splendid. And to make it more so, Lady Ada Chilvers has consented to be my wife, and your second mother. Nothing is wanted, therefore, but your consent to my plans, which will put an end to the anxious state of things up at Buck Park; and to the impossibility there would be of my going out to Trinidad, if you did not give it. But there is no *if* in the case—you *will*."

"Be Percy Thornhill's wife?" said Rachel, as well as her trembling lips could give it utterance.

"Yes—and Lady Rachel Thornhill some day, I hope," smiled her father, with his peculiar look when he finally meant what he said—"the proud mistress of Buck Park, and Greystone House, and the dear 'Old Home' at Trinidad into the bargain, if you are wise."

"Be any other than the wife of the man I have given my heart to, and solemnly vowed I would never forsake while he was true and steadfast to me?" cried Rachel, with head erect, and glowing eyes, beneath whose lightning flash even Angelo Lyons's quailed—"be false to my pledged word? my plighted troth?—Never—before God, never—I will die first!"

"Hem," muttered her father, with a constrained calmness that had in it more fury than his utmost rage—"that is your determination, is it?"

"Oh, my dearest father! why look at me in that way? You never looked at me so before. I would willingly suffer death, rather than disobey you in dight that I am bound to consider your will and wishes before my own. But I cannot give my hand in marriage to any man to whom I could not give my heart. Father—my dearest father—don't turn away from me—hear me—pray, pray—do, do hear me !"

" For what ?" he asked, with his hand on the door—" for the sake of that smooth-faced, penniless youngster you have thought proper to prefer to your daughterly love and duty to your parent ? No, no ! by the blood in both our veins, I will not hear you. Hear you for *him*—for an ungrateful alien, who, in return for my kindness, abused my hospitality, courted my daughter under the guise of her drawing-master, betrayed my confidence, and, for ought that has yet been proved to the contrary, meanly"—

" Hush ! hush ! my dearest father. It is a foul, base, treacherous falsehood ! Else"—and his piercing eyes dropped under his child's, as piercing as his own—" else, let justice be done—let him be proved guilty—and then, as surely as God hears me ! I will—I will—I will—be Percy Thornhill's."

" Guilty or not," answered her father, with the froth on his lips—" you will be Mrs. Percy Thornhill before my next ship leaves, or take the consequences."

Rachel gazed at him with a vacant stare, as

though doubting the evidence of her senses. Could
it possibly be her father who thus unnaturally looked
at and addressed her in a tone and language that
curdled her blood. Oh, yes! it was her father.
But ere she could run to him—to stop him, to fall
at his feet, to clasp his knees, to implore him, by
the memory of her beloved mother, to stay and
lovingly listen to her, as he had ever done—hurried
feet crossed the gallery,—" Sir, sir, I want you—
quick, quick!" gasped Faith, catching him by the
arm and dragging rather than leading him to his
own room.

" What do you mean?" he asked, trembling in
her grasp, as a culprit might with the constable's
clutch on him.

" The parlour is full of men—Norton let them in—
they would go into your room—hark! they are in
the hall—and Mr. Lambert is with them—yes, yes,
Norton says so—and a great mulatto-man—and
the Mayor, and Doctor Bruce—hark!—my God!
they are coming up"—

" See, see," said Mr. Lyons, with perfect calmness. " Impossible! You must be mistaken.
Some Borough business, maybe ; or about the general
election, perhaps, if there is to be a dissolution."

And it was cunningly done. For before Faith
could return to say that Doctor Bruce was on the
stairs, Mr. Lyons had seized a loaded pistol from

his bed-head and concealed it in his breast. Then he walked on to the landing to meet the Doctor, as though his visit were a professional one to his daughter, and not to himself. But there was that in the Doctor's face and manner which told of haste, and alarm, and little inclination just then for further speech of any kind than would suffice for the prompt discharge of the "very painful task he had undertaken, at the request of the Mayor, who was waiting below to see him." So leading the way to his own room, Mr. Lyons closed the door, and awaited an explanation of the "very painful task" that had brought the Doctor up to him with such mysterious looks.

Whereupon the Doctor acquainted him without circumlocution, that " in consequence of the grave charges made against him by Abel White, the 'black,' then in the Asylum for Idiots, but who strongly persisted in his assertions that he, Angelo Lyons, was ' the man who came out of Greystone House on the night of the murder of Joyce and Ann Balfour,' —a warrant had been issued for his apprehension, that these charges of Abel's, and other matters afloat, might be met and cleared up, as the town was in a tumult about it."

" Other matters afloat!" smiled Mr. Lyons, with perfect self-possession, though ghastly pale, as it was natural enough that any man would be under similar circumstances. "What do you mean, Doctor Bruce?"

"If you will have the kindness to come with me," replied the Doctor, "the Mayor is in the parlour, and will answer you better than I can."

"By all means"—and if Angelo Lyons turned even a shade more ghastly, if possible, than he was up-stairs, when not only his worship, the Mayor, bowed him in, but also no less a personage in Shiphampton than Mr. John Strong, the town constable, together with a police sergeant beside him—again we say, the complexion is nothing to go by in such cases. It being quite physiologically consistent that the purest innocence should, under suspicion, blush or shudder more than the foulest guilt; wherefore, as evidence, one way or the other, it is not worth a pin's point. Added to which, not only had Mr. Lyons to encounter the by no means pleasant faces of the two constables, thus unceremoniously confronting him, unbidden; but, more startling than all, there were also the two last faces in the world he expected to be brought *vis-a-vis* with that day, viz., no other than Mr. Alan Lambert's; and, stranger still, that of his old freed mulatto slave Hercules', his head carpenter's at Trinidad.

But Mr. Lyons could command himself under all emergencies; and though with enough on the present occasion to try his temper, he did so in perfection.

The Mayor bowed; and Mr. Lyons bowed; they all bowed; but, with the exception of young Lambert who involuntarily extended his hand when he saw his patron, but blushingly drew it back on Mr. Lyons merely smiling at him, the greeting of the company was confined to bows. Which over:—

"May I beg to know," asked Mr. Lyons, with his grasp on the chair-back, as he rose to his full height and addressed the Mayor in a tone so placid and sweet that even the town constable winked— "what has entitled me to the honour of this unlooked-for visit?"

"Our duty here to-day is a most painful one," replied the Mayor, "as I believe Doctor Bruce has intimated."

"Whatever it may legally be, pray do it," returned Mr. Lyons.

"You are aware that we hold a warrant for your apprehension, to answer the charges made against you by the 'black,' Abel White, relative to the murder of Mrs. Joyce Balfour, and Ann Balfour, her niece, late of The Broadway, Shiphampton, in this county, on the night mentioned in the depositions?"

"I am," said Mr. Lyons, with the curl of the

lip peculiar to him when he scorned to express what he felt. " Is that all, pray ?"

" All for which we are warranted in thus reluctantly intruding ourselves on you to-day," returned the Mayor, with solemnity. " But I grieve to say there are other charges—for investigation in a civil court—of most serious import to the executors of the late Mr. Tristram Balfour, of Greystone House, as well as yourself, involving an accusation of unlawful possession of the property you are now enjoying, in virtue of your claim as heir at law, under Tristram Balfour's will. But with this we need not concern ourselves now."

" May I ask," inquired Mr. Lyons, with perfect composure, " who purposes to dispossess me ? Mr. Abel White ?"

" No, this young man here," answered Hercules, stepping forward and pointing to Alan Lambert, whose cheeks were scarcely less pale than his patron's.

" Oh, indeed !" smiled Mr. Lyons, with a look at the young ' under clerk' that made John Strong bite his lip. " That is funny ! Alan Lambert heir at law to Tristram Balfour—failing Leonard Balfour, or his issue lawfully begotten ? What next ?"

" Leonard Balfour, of Antigua, _had_ issue," said Hercules ; " and here he is."

" Ha !" cried Mr. Lyons, almost gleefully— " Alan Lambert the son of Leonard Balfour !"

"Not Alan Lambert any more, if you please, master," grinned Hercules, till he shewed his great glittering white teeth from ear to ear; "but Leonard Balfour—so christened after his father."

Mr. Strong gave a start! and squeezing his hat into all manner of shapes between his knees, had some difficulty to control himself as became the dignity of the town constable.

"Indeed!" smiled Mr. Lyons, good-humouredly; "and risen from the deep after all these long years?"

"Aye, aye! master," grinned Hercules—"there he is sure enough, you see."

"How?"

"This way, master—your housekeeper, Mrs. Faith Lincoln, nursed Mrs. Ann Balfour's baby that was stolen out of her lap, at Pau, while she was asleep under the trees?"

Mr. Lyons nodded assent.

"Well, then, master—I stole him from her. Why, don't matter now. But I did—and put a mark on him under another there was on his left breast—a ✕-like, next two moles; and there they are now. Maybe Mrs. Faith knows of the moles?"

"That we shall see," said the Mayor.

"But that's not all, master," went on Hercules. "On your kinswoman Ruth Lyons's death-bed, she gave Judith Hercules, my sister, who sat by her

when she died, a written paper, written with her
own hand, that puts it all clear. Then I went
back to Trinidad, when Judith sent it me, to see
about it; and now the paper's—somewhere else.
God-A'mighty did it! I had led a wild life. But
that's over. He brought me to where I saw with
my eyes what I say—and what's true. Else, how
would I have been here now? Or"—pointing to
Alan—"him either?"

The officer in attendance on Mr. Strong looked
at his watch.

"May I ring for the housekeeper?" asked the
Doctor.

Mr. Lyons nodded.

Faith, on hearing the summons, was with Miss
Lyons, who had fainted when told of Mr. Lambert's
presence down stairs, and who were with him.

"Go," said Rachel. "I am better now. The
Mayor must have come on some Borough business.
Oh, Faith! what is the reason of this gnawing pain
in my heart?"

Faith kissed her; and saying she would be "back
directly," hurried away. When impelled by an
irresistible anxiety to ascertain "what business so
many persons could simultaneously have with her
father," Rachel crossed the gallery—listened—and
thinking she heard voices in dispute, went down to
the parlour. She plainly heard the Mayor's voice

—then Faith's—then Alan Lambert's—then a strange, gruff one she did not know—then the soft, sweet tones of her father's, as he always spoke when he was | sad or weary,—and caring for nothing but the gratification of the ruling impulse, she threw open the door and entered the room. Alan Lambert made a joyful spring towards her—with his chest bared as it was for Faith's identification of the mole on the left breast, and a face corpse-like. But Rachel, after a terrified glance at the officers, could see none other than her father, whose smile showed how glad he was she was there; and rushing into his arms, she clung to him, kissed him, threw her arms round his neck, hung on him, while he strained her to his bosom, and again and again pressed his lips to her cheek; when, at an impatient movement of the constables—

"Come here, Faith," said Mr. Lyons.

Faith hastened to him from where she was in earnest conversation with Mr. Lambert, as well as her beating heart would let her, and grasping his offered hand, he drew her to him:—"Hear me!" he whispered, with his cold lips to her cheek—"cling to her—never desert her—be to her a mother—her second mother—yes, you—*you!*"—and before the Doctor could reach him, to seize his arm, the pistol-muzzle was in his mouth—a wild, sardonic, half-laugh, half-cry of agony indescribable rang through the house, and the next moment—with those who alone loved him, in life, still clinging to him, in death—Angelo Lyons went to his dread account.

Terrible scenes like the one of which a slight sketch has just been given, may be better conceived than depicted. Chambers of horrors are not for healthy minds; though, by reason of the sins and wickedness of mankind, they occasionally find an unenviable place where but the moment before all was, seemingly, sinless, and pure, and bright, and good, and not even an evil thought had existence.

Angelo Lyons had cheated the hangman. But was the Almighty will any less done for that? Was the Law of Laws one whit less vindicated by the fall of the suicide by his own hand, than if he had been formally tried and convicted; handed over to the sheriffs to have his neck broken *secundum artem*; brought out on the scaffold for a spectacle to a brutal mob; set writhing in ghastly agonies to amuse them; and then tumbled into his quick-lime grave? And for what? To save the state the expense of bringing him—if there is truth in what Christianity teaches—to atonement, if possible, through what opportunity alone was yet left him for that salvation which the Saviour himself has said shall be extended to *all* alike, who repent, 'though their sins be as red as scarlet and more in number than the hairs of their head.' Either there is a solemn charge conveyed in that promise, or of what value is it? It charges the sinner, however great his crimes, to atone, through contrition and repentance, for what he has done, if he would be saved. But what a farce to preach *that* to him, as his only hope; and then, when it would take more than a whole long life-time for the chaplain himself to obtain the fitting 'garment' in which to appear before his Judge, to send the naked, uncleansed soul to its account, *amply provided* with as much as it could be crammed with during the few weeks' preparation given it, for appearance-sake. The whole thing is a solemn farce. It is a wicked and fearful farce, too, if there be truth in law Divine.

To tell the best of us that we can only be saved, eternally, by sincere and continuous amendment and repentance, and to huddle the necessary conditions for the blackest culprit's salvation into an official six weeks, when go to his doom he must, whether it damn him or not—may well startle the thinking Christian !

Angelo Lyons had defrauded the law of its *rights*, and terrible was the popular indignation. Could it have brought him to life again, to have had the gratification of tearing him limb from limb, or yelling at him on the gibbet, its wrathful breast would have been somewhat solaced. But the sinner had escaped them, had slipped out of their hands into his God's—and they were furious. The mob had been 'shamefully cheated,' and would have its revenge. Who was the Mayor of Ship-hampton, or the Borough Council, or the Bench of Magistrates, or the High Sheriff, or the Lord Lieutenant, or even The Secretary of State himself, that the fine old Borough of Shiphampton should tolerate the sight of one stone upon another of a house that not a butcher-boy passed in the Broad-way but turned white as a sheet when he looked up at it, and with bated breath talked of what had been done there?

So, the smothered vengeance found vent. And though the law, by main force, saved the empty carcase from demolition, how looked Greystone House again, when once the people had said *we will*, and not even the mighty John Strong, the town-constable, could raise up an arm in its cause?

To Alan Lambert's eyes—its now rightful lord and master's—it presented a spectacle too dreadful for contemplation. He heard of the work of venge-ance going on with brow of agony, but without a murmur. He was told that the mob " would not be appeased till they walked over its ruins," and he buried his face in his hands, as though to shut out the terrible sight which he had neither the wish nor the power to prevent. And when they said to him that " nothing but the bare-walls were standing of

what only a month before was a princely palace,"
he heaved a deep sigh of relief, and muttered words
to himself with clasped hands and looks on High,
from which came peace, or his heart would not have .
bounded and his tearful eyes brightened as they did
with happier thoughts.

"Yes, yes—I will erect *that* in its place," he
mentally exclaimed, "which, with God's blessing,
shall cleanse it, and be a memorial how, out of what
human ignorance calls evil, He is acknowledged,
He is vindicated, He is glorified ; whose law is in all
things, and just and perfect above all, even though
it please Him to confound the worldly wisdom of
the wise by the folly of fools."

"Poor Rachel !" It was in every mouth. None
but loved Rachel Lyons. Not a house in Shiphampton, rich or poor, but echoed the same heartfelt "poor Rachel !" The town rang with it.

"What will become of her ?" people asked.

"She shall share my home," said Lady Ada ;
"and lie in my bosom ; and I will be a mother to
her."

And, truly, Ada Chilvers was not one to idly talk.
Rachel was carried to The Priory, with life in her ;
or her breath would not have sullied the mirror they
more than once put to her lips, after untwining her
arms from round her father's neck, to see if she
were dead ?

Oh, no ! the avenging Arm that had struck down the parent, was able to save and sustain the child. Rachel lived. And when after many days of almost hopeless watching at her bed-side, Doctor Bruce's efforts prevailed, and they were obliged to tell her, in answer to her inquiries, of the fate of her princely home—

"It is well," she said, with her hand in Alan's. "Because it is *His* doing, not their's. Else, O my God! how could I bear it ?"

But on none did the fearful news of Angelo Lyons's fall come more crushingly than on the troubled family at Buck Park. In a few weeks they were to be " so free from all anxieties, so proud, so happy," as Clara told Percy in her letters ; and now " what would he say to her next ?" Sir Compton was paralysed ; Lady Thornhill was struck aghast ; Clara sat speechless—the last plank had failed them—there was not a straw more to trust to—ruin stared them in the face—Buck was lost to them— they were " homeless—aliens—refugees"—and— " Oh, how different it might have been with them if they had taken more care."

Far otherwise came the tragic tidings to old Molly and Hester, on *The Green*, living out their few remaining years to the ceaseless tune of " poor dear Mistress and Mrs. Ann !" and whether it would " ever please the Great Giver to avenge them ?"

They smiled and wept by turns. They listened to the stories brought them, at once, with joy and grief. When Rachel Lyons's goodness was the theme, their tears fell fast; but at the mention of her father, there was an almost savage glee in their looks when told where the wealth had all gone that had dyed his hands in blood. Till, with her arms across her breast, Molly would recall to mind every little treasured incident of Mr. Lambert's sojourn with them, as the poor thread-bare artist, and toiling under-clerk; when, do what she or Hester would to try and please him, he would persist in "eating up the cold-meat to the last morsel, rather than go in debt or give them trouble." Now—who and what was he? And at the thought of it, Molly turned pale; and fell sick; and from thinking of it too much, was carried to her bed, as if in a trance; and so lay, thanking the All-Seeing, with muttering lips, for all His mercies. Till one calm evening, when Alan's hand was in hers, she fell asleep, talking of his poor dear mother, and blessing him. And when Alan came next day to see her again, and tell her "how happy he meant to make her and Hester for the rest of their days;" and how much he "loved Rachel, and should ever love her, notwithstanding what had happened;" and how he intended to do his utmost to "dissuade her from being a Sister of Charity, and some day to become his wife,"—Hester met him at the garden-gate, bathed in tears—Molly had "gone to her rest, full of joy."

And not only had Molly cause for thanksgiving; so also had Mr. Alan—or, rather, as we ought now to call him, Leonard Balfour. For as Lady Ada had had full power given her by the late mortgagee of Buck Park, &c., to make over the title-deeds thereunto appertaining to her nephew Percy, or, if she preferred it, to throw them in the fire—of course, now they had devolved to him, Leonard Balfour, to the entire satisfaction of all men, Leonard had a perfect right to do as he pleased with his own. So into the flames went the parchments, and all belonging to them, as far as Sir Compton Thornhill's interests therein were concerned. And when Lady Ada took the news of it to the Hall—just as it happened in her own drawing-room, with Mr. Salisbury and the Vicar and Mr. Nestor Blythe to witness it, as also the Deed of Release simultaneously sealed, signed and delivered, according to law, which would realize Clara's utmost ambition, and, if Percy would be prudent, make him some day as fine an old English gentleman as his father was,—more need not be said than that the Squire had "taken a new lease," he told them all; and, next day, was being rolled round the Park in his wheel-chair, to see "how his young oaks were growing:"—which, as the Doctor truly observed, "was a sight—now they were his once more—likely to put him on his legs again far sooner than all his tonics. "But he won't be quite the thing, and so I tell you," gravely added the Doctor to Lady Thornhill, "till after the 'Derby.' It is not in human nature to be content at Buck, any more than elsewhere, while there's anything more to be had."

Clearly, the Squire was fairly entitled to feel sanguine about *Flower-of-the-Flock*. He stood well at Tattersall's; but so had many horses before him which had sadly disappointed their friends. The Squire was immensely proud of his oaks and his horses and hounds; but his good name was very dear to him, too; and though he felt extremely comfortable with his 'clean-bill' in his drawer, as regarded 'dear old Buck,' he would not have been a Buck-Thornhill if he had owed the payment of his just debts to any means but his own. So he got shockingly fidgetty as the 'Derby' drew near; so much so, that the Doctor's carriage was seen more than once at the door, as the eventful day approached; and Lady Thornhill had almost forgotten about the *Release*; and Clara and Percy felt quite a load on their spirits, and wandered about the Park with anything but the faces they ought to have had, while acknowledging " what a demoniacal monster that awful old Crassus must have been !" and " what a splendid fellow was the penniless

Alan Lambert"—though "not fit to hold a candle to a Thornhill," as they used to think him.

The 'Derby' was run. The Squire lay on his back, with his eyes fixed on a life-like portrait of *Flower-of-the-Flock* over the mantel-piece, with Tom Titt in the saddle, waiting for the carrier pigeon from Percy. There was a strange commotion among them in the court-yard; then in the servants-hall; then in the hall; then on the stairs—Lady Thornhill tried to be up first; but Clara was the younger, and had she not been obliged to stop a moment to support her mother, whose heart beat so that she could not stir a step further, the Doctor and Mr. Blythe and Leonard would not have had the first burst of the Squire's wild cry of joy, when— "Hurrah! hurrah!" cried the Doctor, literally leaping over the chair in his way, to get the first shake of the fist—"true as that's a bed-post, I have won my six bottles of champagne of Mr. Blythe"— and "Dear! dear! yes," giggled Nestor, "it seems I have lost them; for *Flower-of-the-Flock* was first horse—positively so—dear! dear! dear!"

Reader, you can well imagine the rest. Words would be utterly valueless to convey any idea of a joy which you must be a Compton Thornhill, and similarly circumstanced as the Squire of Buck was, to understand and appreciate. Suffice it to say, the Squire not by this the *great deed* of his life something over Fifty Thousand Pounds. It was a nice help to him. Nor need it be added, how, like a fine old English gentleman as he was, at heart, he paid his debts with it to the last farthing; made it 'all right,' as Percy expressed it, with Leonard Balfour; took a solemn oath that he would "never risk another guinea again on the turf;" and then settling down among his old hounds and horses and oaks, &c., &c., bade fair to keep Buck Park up in capital style still; though, as the Doctor said, he had had "a touch of experience that would luckily stick to him for the rest of his days."

"But," remarked Mr. Blythe, when, on Percy's triumphant return from Epsom, they had talked over the race till something was said about the new Hospital that was being built on the ruins of Greystone House, at Mr. Balfour's expense, "do you not see, my dear friends, how the merest accident, as it is called, is a means, in the hands of the Almighty, to bring to light the hidden things of darkness, in His own good time? Till when, who or what is blind man that he should say 'God sleeps,' because His ways are inscrutable? For instance—Mr. Alan Lambert, as we will call him, having a severe head-ache when in the mango-grove at Old Mill House, thought a swim in the river would cure it; instead of which it threw him into a deep sleep, while dressing, but for which the mulatto,

Hercules, might never have identified him by the
cross on his breast, made with his own hands when
he stole him from his nurse at Pau. Then, again,
but for the remorse of mind that prematurely laid
Ruth Lyons—under whose directions Hercules
acted, for some ulterior dark ends of her own, in
conjunction with those of her kinsman's—on her
death-bed, he Hercules would never have learnt
what had befallen the stolen boy after they were
wrecked at sea, and miraculously saved by being
picked up by fishermen, as you know, bound to
opposite ports.   That paper of Ruth Lyons's,
wrung from an accusing conscience on her death-
bed, led to the identity of the stolen babe and the
man-grown, Leonard Balfour. They were one and
the same, as has been fully proved."

"For which Heaven be praised!" said the Doctor;
"seeing that, already, Julius Bruce, M.D., holds
the honourable appointment of Head Physician in
Ordinary to the new Infant Hospital."

"But signal instances, my dear friends, as these
are of Divine interposition," went on Mr. Blythe,
warming with his subject, "how manifestly beyond
man's conception were the conclusive events that put
at rest the 'mad jabberings' of that poor fellow,
Abel, as we used to call them, about his lost knife;
and also brought to light *that*, but for which, how

have substantiated it for certain by whose hands Joyce and Ann Balfour came by their deaths?"

"Infamous! horrible!" exclaimed Percy. "He must have been a fiend in man's form."

"While talking to his jabbering brother negro in the Infirmary, Hercules drew the knife from his pocket—that, with other things, he had picked up out of the *debris* of the burnt-down house at Trinidad, to cut some cake with it for Abel; and I, for one," agitatedly added the curate, "would have given all I have in my pocket, and a great deal more, to have witnessed the poor 'jabberer's' extacy at the sight of his bosom friend—the friend whose suspicious desertion of him, in his need, had branded him as a murderer, and turned his poor, weak brain. It must have been a touching and instructive sight to all present; one of those sights which tell us, through the best sympathies of our natures, how there is an inextinguishable spirit in innocency that outlives every hardship and ill-treatment—dear me! yes, yes! even the loss, almost, of reason itself."

"Which is verified in Abel," rejoined the Doctor, "who is now as sane on every point but his passionate, love for his 'angel saviour,' as he calls 'Missie Rachel'—to whom he says he will give his darling knife, 'if she will come and be with him for ever—as you and I are.'"

"But most signally conclusive of all," continued

Mr. Blythe, with a shudder, " was the mere 'accident' by which is now brought home to the murderer
the crushing certainty of his guilt. He put the box
under his pillow, after his midnight fight with the
cat that crawled on to his chest while he was asleep,
as a charm against further molestation. It seems
incredible that a man of Angelo Lyons's powers of
mind should have been a prey to such superstition;
but so it was. Perhaps he imbibed it from the
blood of his race. The box contained an *Ear* of each
of his victims, the having which in his possession,
would, he believed, be a sufficient safeguard, in case
of danger, against any vengeful acts of their ghosts.
He forgot he had placed the box under his pillow;
it was thrown on the floor by a servant while making
his bed, by which two of the precious-stones it was
set round with were lost; to have which replaced,
the houskeeper took the box to Mr. Nathan, who,
not having the stones required, entrusted it to
another dealer in jewels, who, on touching a secret
spring, discovered what he took to be two pieces of
' dried skin and cartilage, kept for curiosity;' but one
of which, having ' a white hair or two, visible through
the microscope, sticking to it, and the other some
auburn ones,' proved to be two human ears—the
damning evidence of what inhuman deed done, and
by whom, who need be told?"

" Let us think of something else," said the Doctor, at sight of Percy Thornhill's pale face, listening with horror to the Curate's words, and the grateful beatings of his own heart in conjunction.

"All I desire to prove," added kind-hearted Nestor, "is how the wicked plan, and plot, and make perfect, as they blindly suppose; regardless of how the Recording Angel has taken note of every thought and act in that Book which, though sealed from man's eyes, lies ever open before Him whose vengeance, like His love, though it come late, is sure, and will indubitably avenge the wronged, and, in His own good time, bring the counsels of the wicked to confusion."

"Poor Rachel!" they all said; but were there none who said, "poor Faith?"

If not, Faith mourned not as one who had no comforter. She had the consolatory support of an unaccusing conscience; and, humbly bowing to her burthen, bore it meekly. She might have lived without labour, for she had enough for idleness, as far as money went; but Faith knew better than to pamper a mind too apt to prey upon itself. So, after a year's residence with Rachel Lyons at The Priory, she became chief matron of the Balfour Hospital; and, in the diligent discharge of her duties therein, gave the best proof of how the mind, under the severest trials and struggles, may rise superior to them; if, of whatever else it is deprived, it never loses its self-respect.

Lady Ada more than ever realized the tranquil joys of her elegant cottage-life, devoted as it was to the substantial delights of, as far as in her lay, making those around and dependent on her as happy as she herself was. Her life was one of usefulness, as well as of ease and elegance; and, so, as she grew older, she "grew handsomer," her neighbours said; who, looking at her through her active kindness and benevolence, had "no fault to find with her" but that she was "too good."

Leonard Balfour—"come to his rights"—as our friends at *The Jackdaw* expressed it, was a rich man; how rich he scarcely knew himself. He was more, for he was a man of unblemished character; as was triumphantly proved—touching that infamous missing-money affair in Master Enoch the younger's office, for some crafty ends of his own—by the cunning young fox's bolting away from the town, as soon as he heard of Mr. Lambert's return. While the tide was with him, Enoch, junior, sailed on easily and merrily enough; but, when it turned, he was a craven; and packing up what he could lay hands on, had but one regret, as he left 'the works' far behind him, viz., that he had "not been revenged, as he wanted, on Master Alan, for that night he passed in the 'lock-up,' without his supper, and which trust him! he never meant to forget to the day of his death."

But immensely rich as Leonard was now—

"I shall deem myself very poor," he said to Lady Ada, his grand confidant, "till I can prevail on Rachel to set the world at nought, and redeem her plighted vow to me—to be the best of all my treasures. What is the world to us if we love each other? Rachel has done no evil. What recompence can the world make me for her loss?"

It filled Ada Chilvers's eyes with tears; for well she knew the pain the only true answer she could make to it would give him.

"Yes, her plighted vow!" repeated Leonard, fervently; "which I am sure Heaven smiles on, and will bless, or would the thought of it fill me with such joyful visions as it does? Oh, yes! Rachel will—she must—she shall be my wife!—or of what value will all my other possessions be to me?"

To which what could Lady Ada reply? For, true to her purpose—that inflexible purpose which, seemed, by the many yearning conversations she had about it at The Priory when she could get Lady Ada to listen to her, to be foreshadowed so early in her young mind—Rachel accompanied Lady Thornhill, and Clara, and her *fiancé*, the young heir to the Chilvers' peerage, on a three mouths tour abroad. Shortly after her return from which, she

presented herself to Leonard and Lady Ada in the
sombre garb of a Sister of Charity. And when
Leonard saw the uselessness of tears and entreaties
to shake her purpose, and his heart was full of
woe : —

"Be of good cheer, Alan!" she said—emphasizing
the name she loved best to call him by—"I am
going to do Heaven's bidding. God has brought
me to this, of his great goodness and mercy, that I
may learn wherein my little strength lies, and His
great riches. Oh, dearest Alan! can I ever want for
aught in His service?" And then—with the farewell
embrace—"Shall we not always think of each other
in our prayers?" she added, with quivering lips.
"As you were, so you are still, and ever will be to
me—dearest of all! But what Heaven has
ordained—that—oh, yes—that, Alan, is best of all
for us both."

But, nevertheless, Leonard is not without hope ;
which Lady Ada tells him "there can be no harm
in his indulging, within reason ; seeing with what
sweet visions of joy it fills him whenever he dreams
she is his."

A word more, and I have done :—

Light-hearted, merry, joyous Jane Rosse had
every sublunary wish fulfilled when she gave her
hand, at the altar, to the Reverend Mr. Nestor
Blythe, on his appointment by his Bishop to the

perpetual curacy of Buck. Jane never tires of talking of that, "the happiest day in her life," as she calls it, when she was "the unquestionable means of helping dearest Nestor 'off the hooks,' however he may now be too happy to own it. Such blushes," she declares, "become him exceedingly, and immensely raise him in her esteem." And as for Nestor himself—"Dear! dear!" he says to his bachelor-friends, with those jubilant little squeaks which delight them so much; "do you wish to know what I call a pattern of a wife, mother, and mistress, to make a man hug himself when he compares his actual with his possible state? Then, dear! dear! come and see me and my wife at the Parsonage; and, as soon as you can, go by all means and do likewise—yes, yes."

THE END.

BILLING, PRINTER, GUILDFORD.

MESSRS. SAUNDERS, OTLEY & CO.'S
NEW PUBLICATIONS.

DEDICATED TO THE RIGHT REV. THE LORD BISHOP
OF OXFORD.

The UNIVERSITIES' MISSION to EAST
CENTRAL AFRICA, from its commencement to its withdrawal
from the Zambesi. By the Rev. HENRY ROWLEY, one of
the two Survivors of Bishop Mackenzie's Clerical Staff. 1 large
vol. 8vo. with Portraits, Maps, and numerous Illustrations.

[Just ready.

THE REV. S. C. MALAN.

An OUTLINE of the JEWISH CHURCH,
from a Christian Point of View. By the Rev. S. C. MALAN,
M.A., Vicar of Broadwindsor, 8vo.   *[In the Press.*

LIEUT.-GENERAL SIR T. B. ELLIS, K.C.B.

MEMOIRS and SERVICES of the late
Lieut.-General Sir T. B. ELLIS, K.C.B. &c., Royal Marines.
From his own Memoranda. Edited by LADY ELLIS. 1 vol.
8vo.   *[Just ready.*

NEW NOVEL, BY THE AUTHOR OF "THE UTTERMOST
FARTHING."

VICTORY DEANE. By CECIL GRIFFITH,
Author of "The Uttermost Farthing," 3 vols. post 8vo.

[In the Press.

NEW NOVEL.

A WIFE and NOT a WIFE. 'By CYRUS

REDDING. 3 vols. post 8vo.   [*In the Press.*

NEW STORY.

META'S LETTERS: a Tale. By Mrs.

E. J. ENSELL. 1 vol. post 8vo.   [*In the Press.*

A TAHITIAN NOVEL.

HENA; or, Life in Tahiti. By Mrs.

ALFRED HORT. 2 vols. post 8vo.   [*Just ready.*

LONDON PAUPERISM.

The FEMALE CASUAL and her LODGING;

with a Complete Scheme for the Regulation of Workhouse
Infirmaries. By J. H. STALLARD, M.B. Lond., &c., Author
of "London Pauperism," &c. Post 8vo.   [*Just ready.*

NEW NOVEL.

PHILO; a Romance of Life in the First

Century. 3 vols. post 8vo.   [*In the Press.*

NEW VOLUME OF POEMS.

The QUADRILATERAL. 1 vol. fcap. 8vo.

5s. bevelled boards.   [*Ready.*

"There is much melodious writing and many graceful thoughts.
.........Decidedly above the average, and there is quite enough in it
to make us hope we may hear more hereafter of the three active
partners in 'The Quadrilateral.'"—*Union Review.*

"'The Quadrilateral,' with its quaint but telling title, and its
triad of as yet unknown authors, deserves, and we are sure will
receive, a warm welcome from all thoughtful and appreciative lovers
of poetry."—*Churchman.*

"The poems are in good taste, and always graceful and pleasing."
—*John Bull.*

NEW WORK ON POLAND BY MR. SUTHERLAND
EDWARDS.

The PRIVATE HISTORY of a POLISH

INSURRECTION, from Official and Unofficial Sources. By H.
SUTHERLAND EDWARDS, late Special Correspondent of the
Times in Poland, and Author of "The Three Louisas," &c., 2
vols. With an Introduction and Appendices. 21s.

[*Ready.*]

NEW NOVEL.

The ROMANCE of MARY CONSTANT.

Written by HERSELF. 1 vol. post 8vo. 10s. 6d. bevelled
boards. [*Ready.*]

" Hélas! hélas! que les choses passent et les souvenirs demeurent."

THE LATE REV. J. M. NEALE, D.D.

ESSAYS on LITURGIOLOGY and CHURCH

HISTORY. By the Rev. JOHN MASON NEALE, D.D.,
Warder of Sackville College. With an Appendix on Liturgical
Quotations from the Isapostolic Fathers. By the Rev. GERARD
MOULTRIE, M.A. 1 vol. 8vo. 18s. [*Ready.*]

DR. M. J. CHAPMAN.

The GREEK PASTORAL POETS:

THEOCRITUS—BION—MOSCHUS. Translated and Edited
by Dr. M. J. CHAPMAN, Trinity College, Cambridge. Third
Edition, revised. 1 vol. post 8vo. 10s. 6d. bevelled edges.

[*Ready.*]

DR. M. J. CHAPMAN.

HEBREW IDYLLS and DRAMAS. By

Dr. M. J. CHAPMAN, Trinity College, Cambridge. Originally
published in *Frazer's Magazine*. 1 vol. post 8vo. 10s. 6d.
bevelled edges. [*Ready.*]

MRS. ALFRED GATTY.

The HISTORY of a BIT of BREAD.

Being Letters to a Child on the life of Man and of Animals. By
JEAN MACÉ. Translated from the French and Edited by
Mrs. ALFRED GATTY, Author of "Parables from Nature,"
&c. Part I. Man. Fcap. 8vo. 5s. cloth. Also Part II. Animals,
(Completing the Work.) Fcap. 8vo. 4s. 6d. cloth.   [*Ready.*

UNIFORM WITH "THE HISTORY OF A BIT OF BREAD."

The LITTLE KINGDOM; or, The Servants

of the Stomach. A New Series of Letters, addressed to a Child.
upon the Life of Man and of Animals. By JEAN MACÉ
2 vols. fcap. 8vo.   [*In the Press.*

NEW POEM.

The MAIDEN of the ICEBERG; A Tale

in Verse. By S. G. 1 vol. post 4to. with nine page Illustrations.
                                          [*In the Press.*

MILITARY ADVENTURE.

The SOLDIER of THREE QUEENS. A

Narrative of Person Adventure. By CAPTAIN HENDERSON.
2 vols. post 8vo. 21s.   [*Ready.*

NEW VOLUME OF STORIES.

DISENCHANTED, and other Tales. By

HARRIET POWER, Author of "Beatrice Langton," &c. 1
vol. post 8vo.   [*In the Press.*

LONDON :
SAUNDERS, OTLEY AND CO., 66, BROOK STREET, W.

www.ingramcontent.com/pod-product-compliance
Lightning Source LLC
Chambersburg PA
CBHW020951030726
47496CB00005B/1462